THE BODY IN

The theater door opened, accompanied by an eruption of chatter. A handful of cast members entered the theater and proceeded through the house.

"Lola, we've got to do something." I stepped backward into the Act Two area, my foot grazing a large, immovable object. I looked down.

Even in the dim light I could see it was a body lying in front of the first row of folding chairs. With a knife sticking out of its chest. Dressed in a camo jacket and trapper hat.

Lola had bolted onstage and was standing behind me.

"Don't move," I rasped, my heart in my throat.

"Dodie, you sound awfully funny—"

"Call 911."

My hand wobbled as I pointed downward...

Books by Suzanne Trauth

SHOW TIME

TIME OUT

RUNNING OUT OF TIME

Published by Kensington Publishing Corporation

Running Out of Time

Suzanne Trauth

LYRICAL UNDERGROUND
Kensington Publishing Corp.
www.kensingtonbooks.com

LYRICAL UNDERGROUND BOOKS are published by

Kensington Publishing Corp.
119 West 40th Street
New York, NY 10018

All Kensington titles, imprints, and distributed lines are available at special quantity discounts for bulk purchases for sales promotion, premiums, fund-raising, educational, or institutional use.

Special book excerpts or customized printings can also be created to fit specific needs. For details, write or phone the office of the Kensington Sales Manager: Kensington Publishing Corp., 119 West 40th Street, New York, NY 10018. Attn. Sales Department. Phone: 1-800-221-2647.

Lyrical Underground and Lyrical Underground logo Reg. US Pat. & TM Off.

First Electronic Edition: October 2017
eISBN-13: 978-1-60183-723-3
eISBN-10: 1-60183-723-2

First Print Edition: October 2017
ISBN-13: 978-1-60183-724-0
ISBN-10: 1-60183-724-0

Printed in the United States of America

For my sisters and mom...always cheering me on.

1

Winter in Etonville, New Jersey was not for the faint of heart. The temperature had hovered at fifteen degrees all morning. I backed my Chevy Metro out of the driveway and inched my way down Ames, turning in a wide arc onto Fairfield Street. The streets were empty. Smart folks had stayed home this Sunday morning. I shifted my right foot from the accelerator to the brakes and back again, wary of the layer of ice that glistened on the roadway. Living down the Jersey Shore had not completely prepared me for the ordeals of cold weather months: substantial snow, ice, cold, wind, sleet, more snow, freezing rain—

A horn honked and I jammed on the brakes. My Metro did a one-eighty, skidding into the intersection of Fairfield and Main. I came to rest three feet from the front bumper of a late-model silver Lincoln Continental. I was panting audibly as an occupant of the other car's passenger seat alighted. A middle-aged man in a camel-colored coat with a bronzed face, slicked-back dark hair, and sunglasses.

"Are you okay?" he shouted at me.

I nodded dumbly and studied my shaking hands on the steering wheel. Foolishly, I'd ignored the yellow light and hadn't seen his car heading south on Main. It was my fault, though he was probably driving over the speed limit.

I wound down the window. "I'm so sorry. Didn't see you..." Puffs of cold breath shot out of my mouth.

"No worries. All's well." He kicked one leather-clad shoe against the bottom of the doorframe to remove snowy muck. "Take it easy." He climbed into his Lincoln with a Massachusetts license plate—it was a game of mine, noticing and remembering plates: a white background with red letters and numbers, *Massachusetts* printed at the top, *Spirit of America* at the bottom—and said something to the driver.

"Yes. Yes, I will," I said quickly and watched them back up, maneuver around my Metro, and continue down Main Street. I completed my turn onto Main and eased down the road. Twenty-five miles an hour.

"Achoo!" A sneeze burst out of my stuffy nose and scratchy throat. For the fifth time in the last two hours, I told myself I should have been home installed on my sofa wrapped in a warm blanket, hot buttered rum in one hand, the latest thriller by my favorite author in the other. Or binge-watching a series on Netflix. Instead, I was watching a baking class create early American cakes in the Windjammer restaurant kitchen while listening to the wind howl as it rustled down Main.

Betty from Betty's Boutique, Etonville's version of Victoria's Secret, popped out of the Windjammer's pantry. "Bless you!" She brushed a shock of brown, shoulder-length curls off her face with one floury palm. "Dodie, I can't find the nutmeg."

"Try the spice shelf. Second from the top," I said, blowing my nose and eyeing the recipe for Swamp Yankee applesauce cake. Georgette, of Georgette's Bakery, had volunteered to take her "students" through their pastry paces before the opening of the next Etonville Little Theatre production. We'd been baking for three Sundays now and today was the final session.

"That's one teaspoon of salt?" asked one-half of the Banger sisters duo, two elderly siblings who kept their ancient digits on the pulse of the town. Gossip was their game.

"No, it's a tablespoon," Georgette said patiently. "And remember we are multiplying everything by twelve. We want to end up with a dozen cakes." She jabbed at a copy of the recipe—her stubby, thick fingers were born to knead dough.

The sisters bobbed their gray heads and began to measure.

"Mildred, be sure the baking soda is dissolved in warm water before you add it to the batter," Georgette said to Etonville's choir director and turned to me. "It might have been easier to buy the concession goodies," she muttered.

"Maybe, but I needed something that fit the American Revolution." For the past two years the Windjammer had provided food that matched the period of the ELT plays: themed dinners, a food festival, and now stocking the concession stand. "These early American desserts are perfect. Apple pie, pumpkin bread, hot cider punch, mulled wine. It's going to be great." I smiled my big fake grin, the one I trotted out on occasions when I knew I was in over my head, because it was too late to call things off.

The Windjammer freezer was jammed with the apple pies and Georgette had offered to store the pumpkin bread and applesauce cake in her bakery. The punch and mulled wine were left for later this week.

"I hope it's all edible." Georgette returned to the group of bakers and cautioned them. "Let's beat that batter until it's well mixed."

I heard the tinkle of the welcome bells above the restaurant entrance. Probably an out-of-towner who didn't know that the restaurant was closed on Sundays and the only culinary activity afoot was a baking class on steroids. I crossed my fingers that the ELT audiences would be hungry before the show and during intermission.

I pushed open the swinging doors that led into the dining room and was greeted by a blast of cold air. Lola Tripper, current artistic director of the Etonville Little Theatre, forced the front door shut and leaned against the jamb.

"It's feels like zero out there!" She stamped her knee-high boots on the doormat, leaving bits of frozen slush to settle into its bristly fibers.

"With the wind chill, yeah."

Lola flipped the fur-lined hood of her high-end winter coat. "I ignore that wind chill stuff. It's either freezing or it isn't."

"Right." I took her coat, some Icelandic clothing brand. "Looks warm."

"Canadian goose down. Windproof and waterproof." Lola fluffed her blond mane.

Definitely not wallet-proof. I sneezed.

"You poor thing. What are you taking for it?" she asked.

"The usual. Aspirin, vitamin C, a shot of whiskey." That last was my great-aunt Maureen's remedy for whatever ailed you. She usually came down with "something" once a week. "What's happening next door?" The ELT was about ready to open its version of *Our Town*.

"We're actually ready for tech rehearsal. With only a few items to catch up on. Chrystal has to let out the waistcoats for some of the men. And her crew is still altering aprons and breeches. Good thing we have the ruffled shirts and the men's stockings from *Romeo and Juliet*." Lola grimaced. "I told Walter we needed to stay on budget for this show."

"So…that's why he insisted on a rotating stage?"

Lola grunted. "He had a vision. You know Walter and his visions."

I certainly did. "You're the director. Walter's only the playwright."

Walter Zeitzman was the on-again-off-again director of most ELT productions. But when the board balked at the budget for a big musical, Walter offered his adaptation of *Our Town*—called *Eton Town*—as a replacement, shifting the script to colonial America to celebrate the founding of Etonville, shortly after the American Revolution. I got Walter's vision; I just wasn't sure his playwriting skills were up to the challenge.

Lola twisted one strand of hair in a recognizable nervous gesture. "The turntable sounded like a good idea. One side for Act One, the other for Act Two. Passage of time. Life moving round and round…you know."

I'd been to rehearsal. It was more like life grinding to a halt every few seconds. "I hope he gets it running more smoothly before opening night."

"That's where he is now. With the cast off today, he and JC are working on the turntable to make sure it's spinning properly." She crossed her fingers.

I crossed mine back. "Come on. Let's see what bakery mayhem the good folks of Etonville are creating. Georgette is so good natured." The smell of something burning leaked into the dining room. I bolted, Lola close on my heels.

I burst into the kitchen just as Georgette withdrew four cakes from the oven and slammed the door shut, stifling a cloud of smoke by locking it away in the oven. On the center island the remaining pans of Swamp Yankee applesauce cake batter were lined up like victims about to face a firing squad.

Georgette cut open one of the four baked cakes: charred on the outside, gooey on the inside. A thin film of sweat covered her forehead. "Not to worry. A minor mishap." She paused and eyed her baking staff, who were staring open mouthed at the burnt cakes. "We need to remember to set the temperature at 350." Her bakers nodded.

"We should have done the regular *Our Town*," grumped Mildred's husband Vernon, who played the Narrator in Walter's adaptation. Until now he had pretty much kept his mouth shut, either because he had nothing to add or because he was missing both his hearing aids and the gist of the afternoon's conversation. "Walter should have let well enough alone. He's not a playwright."

"I like the costumes in our version," said a Banger sister.

"The tricorn hats and the men's breeches," giggled the other.

Walter had kept many of the original play's elements—the narrator, two families, a love story, everyday life in Etonville, and a visit to the town graveyard. Even the theme was preserved: appreciating life and living in the moment.

"I don't know, I kind of like the early American feel. The founding of Etonville, lovers separated by the war," said Sally Oldfield.

She was a quiet, pretty, twenty-one-year-old transplant from New England. I'd known her since mid-January when she appeared, unannounced, on my doorstep, wondering if I had any advice on places to live. I gave her some recommendations, made a few phone calls, and within twenty-four hours she had rented a room in a boarding house in Etonville and found a part-time job as a car wash cashier in Bernridge, Etonville's next-door neighbor. My younger brother, Andy, who'd moved from San Diego to Boston in November, had apparently given her my contact information.

Sally had seemed lonely and disclosed that she'd done some acting in high school so I suggested she audition for the ELT production. Now a Townsperson and member of the *Eton Town* choir, Sally eagerly agreed to join the baking class.

"Well, I still think Walter went too far this time." Vernon put on his galoshes and made ready to leave the Windjammer.

"Vernon, you're doing a lovely job as Narrator," Georgette said.

"Say what?" Vernon asked.

Definitely no hearing aids. Mildred and Vernon bundled up and left arm-in-arm, Vernon still grousing.

Sally offered to help with the cleanup.

"Thanks. You've been a really good addition to the class," I said. "You don't complain, you can read a recipe, and you know how to multiply and divide."

Sally grinned. "It's been fun. I've enjoyed meeting everyone. It's given me something to do."

"If you want to stay busy, I could use help with the hot drinks—"

Lola stuffed her cell phone in a pocket. "Dodie, sorry to run off and leave you, but Walter and JC are into it over the turntable—"

"Go. We're fine here," I said.

"I hope that contraption doesn't go any faster than five miles an hour," said one of the Banger sisters and wrapped a muffler around her neck.

More like minus five miles an hour. "I don't think you need to worry," I said.

The other sister studied me over the rim of her glasses. "I was dizzy from the spinning and nearly fell off the stage one night."

Dizzy yes, turntable no.

My cell chirped. It was a text from Bill. Aka Etonville Chief of Police Thompson. We'd gotten to know each other during the past year when I'd assisted in the investigation of a couple of homicides. Okay, so I "investigated" on the sly and jeopardized our budding relationship. But Bill was still grateful for my detection skills and I still got all jittery when I saw that sandy-colored brush cut and former-NFL-running-back build. We'd been dating for the last couple of months. Which included a New York Giants football game, Thanksgiving dinner with Lola and her daughter, home from college, a couple of movies, Christmas Eve dinner at the Windjammer, and an aborted attempt to go sledding in the town park. At the last minute, Bill had had an emergency.

Lola swaddled herself in her Canadian goose down coat and prepared to brave the cold. "Want to stop by my house later for a bite to eat? I shouldn't be more than an hour at the theater."

I waggled my cell. "Bill…"

Lola beamed. "Ooh la la! Things are really heating up there!"

Not sure, but I might have blushed. "We're still keeping it low-key." His text was an apology for cancelling our dinner date last night. Valentine's Day! I didn't have the heart or energy to explain to Lola that I wasn't sure if things were heating up or cooling down.

Lola smiled knowingly. "Call me later. I want details."

I sneezed.

"And take care of that cold."

This time of year, days ended by five o'clock. I watched Lola step into the dark, freezing night. "Good luck next door." Lola was going to need more than luck to get the stage rotating.

I sprayed the kitchen counters with a cleaner, removing all traces of the Swamp Yankee applesauce cake. "Need a ride?" I asked Sally, who was stacking mixing bowls in the pantry.

"I left my car at the boarding house. I like to walk," she said.

"It's starting to flurry. Pretty windy too," I said.

"I'm used to it." I looked up from my wiping. Her pale complexion gave her a waif-like appearance. Not for the first time I noticed how extraordinary her eyes were: one brown and one hazel. Heterochromia iridium. I'd googled the condition the first time I'd met Sally.

"I'm from Boston," Sally said.

"Right."

"Weather like this? Normal for winter. It has to be zero before Bostonians think it's really cold."

"You never told me what brought you to New Jersey."

She hesitated. "I wanted a change in scenery."

"Sorry to be nosy. In Etonville everyone ends up knowing everyone else's business," I said.

"So I gathered." She laughed amiably.

I realized I knew virtually nothing about Sally's past except for the connection to my brother. He was a therapist, and I wondered if their relationship was that of doctor and patient. "Stay away from Snippets hair salon if you want to avoid town gossip. I call it rumor central."

Sally took off her apron. "I'll be able to help with the hot cider and mulled wine."

"Great! Because the rest of the baking class will be busy getting skittish for opening night."

Sally and I finished up the kitchen. She slipped into a parka and tugged on her snow boots; I donned my own down jacket and turned out the lights.

The sun had set. It was already dark and the streetlamps were shining. "See you later," Sally said and turned to go. Then she froze and caught her breath, staring across the street.

Barbie's Craft Shoppe, one of the only businesses on Main Street open on Sunday, was closing up, lights were being flicked off and Barbie was hanging the Closed sign. On the sidewalk outside the store, two kids rolled snowballs and got set to throw them until their mother intervened and escorted them off. Nothing unusual as far as I could see.

"Are you all right?" I asked.

"I...uh..." she stuttered.

I glanced back to see what had disturbed her. To the left of the shop, a man stood under the street light. Big, burly, filling out a camouflage coat, he wore a trapper hat with the ear flaps flipped up. A full beard sprouted out of a face that stared back at Sally.

"Do you know him?"

Then he opened his mouth as if about to shout something at us. Before he could say a word, an Etonville police cruiser, lights flashing, came to an abrupt stop in front of Barbie's Craft Shoppe. Officer Ralph Ostrowski, an agreeable, semi-capable Etonville cop, who was usually assigned crowd control, jumped out. They talked briefly, then Ralph escorted him into the back seat of his squad car. They drove off, but not before the man twisted in his seat and pressed his face against the window, still gazing intently at Sally.

She stuffed her hands in her pockets and backed up, looking around and checking our side of the street. Then she pulled the hood of her coat over her head. "I have to go," she mumbled and ran off.

"Sally?" I watched her leave. Despite the fact that I was warm inside my down jacket and scarf, I shivered. The tiny hairs on the back of my neck stood upright. My radar system giving me a warning: Something wasn't right.

Falling snow had sprinkled a light layer of powdery white stuff on all surfaces. I stuck out my tongue to catch the moisture. Reminded me of afternoons I shared with my little brother, Andy, on those rare occasions when it snowed down the shore. I cranked the engine of my red Metro, ninety thousand miles and counting, flipped on the windshield wipers to clear a patch of window, and set off down Main Street. Slowly. Carefully.

My cell binged again. I pulled over to the shoulder and checked the text. It was Henry, owner/chef of the Windjammer reminding me that I had to do a freezer inventory first thing in the morning. He intended to add a few new cold-weather items to the menu, like roasted parsnip soup and a pasta-and-veggies dish.

I eased back onto the roadway. Between the ice and wind chill—which could last anywhere from three months to five months in New Jersey—I was ready to flee to Florida where my parents resided. I could have moved there two years ago after Hurricane Sandy hit my Jersey Shore community and destroyed the restaurant where I worked, as well as my rented home. But I opted to go north across the Driscoll Bridge and ended up in Etonville, a stone's throw from New York City, managing the Windjammer restaurant, soothing Henry's feathers on a daily basis, riding shotgun on the staff, and providing support for Lola's theater ventures. After all, she was my BFF and the leading diva of the ELT. And Bill was in Etonville...

By the time I pulled into my driveway in the south end of town, a fresh coating of white covered tree branches, my small patch of front yard, and the walkway leading to my door. I stamped the snow off my boots, flung my jacket over a kitchen chair, and debated. Should I call Bill and listen to him apologize? He'd had a work conflict last night...I got it. But it was the third time in the last few weeks that he'd had to bow out of a dinner date. I sneezed, plucked a Kleenex from a box on the kitchen table, and blew my nose. When my high school boyfriend dumped me for my best friend two weeks before the prom, my great-aunt Maureen said: *Dorothy dear, life is messy but love is messier.* As usual she'd nailed it. Tonight I had to be content with the mystery novel and the hot buttered rum. I'd leave the mess for tomorrow.

2

I stuck my nose out from under my down comforter. The air was chilled and I peeked at my alarm: seven thirty a.m. Sun just risen. I had hours before I needed to be on duty at the Windjammer and snuggling under the covers for another thirty minutes felt good. My nasal passages were still slightly stuffed, but my throat was clear. I closed my eyes. The last bits of a dream played around the edges of my mind...something about the American Revolution. I was tramping through several feet of snow while eating burnt applesauce cake. Lola, Georgette, and Mildred stood on a rotating platform laughing at me. And someone else? Was it Sally? I closed my eyes and the image that popped up was not the wayward turntable but the heavily built outdoorsman who spooked Sally on Main Street last night. What was that about?

A draft of cold air hit the house, startling me fully awake and rattling the window panes. I needed my landlord to re-caulk the glass. My bungalow wasn't as large as my house down the shore, but its five, cheerfully painted rooms suited my lifestyle. Small enough to be cleaned on the fly; large enough to entertain a few friends, like Lola and my other my BFF, Carol Palmieri. Owner of Snippets Salon.

I created my mental to-do list. Besides doing the inventory at the Windjammer this morning I had to order the supplies for the hot cider punch and—for those needing a touch of alcohol to make it through Walter's reinvention of *Our Town*—the mulled wine. Which reminded me I needed to work out the staff schedule for the weekend. Benny, the Windjammer bartender and assistant manager, would be sharing closing duties with me on the nights of the show, while waitstaff Gillian and Carmen covered the dining room. Carmen's husband, Enrico, was Henry's sous-chef, and rarely stepped foot outside the kitchen.

A beeping demanded my attention. My cell was sitting across the room on my dresser where I'd dropped it last night before tumbling into bed. Checking out the text meant I had to surrender the warmth of my cocoon. But curiosity got the better of me and I threw the cover aside and plopped my feet on the icy floor. I needed another throw rug in here. I whipped on my terry cloth robe and shoved my feet into my New York Giants slippers—a Christmas gift from Bill. The text was from him suggesting we have a do-over dinner this week: *call me.*

I would, but first, a hot shower, coffee, vitamin C, and aspirin: marching orders for my cold. I turned up the heat and stepped into the shower, the water pinging off my body and warming my skin. I shampooed my hair, letting the sudsy residue run down my face and shoulders. I toweled off and slipped on a sweat suit. I shivered and had a dream flashback. Snow and ice and…Massachusetts! I was trekking in Massachusetts during the American Revolution. Made no sense but it did remind me of Sally's saying New Jersey's freezing temperatures would be nothing more than a nip in the air compared to Boston. She was a nice addition to the Etonville Little Theatre—sane! My cell beeped once more. *Bill was eager to talk this morning...* But it was Lola asking if I was up. I tapped on her name in my contacts.

"Hey," I said.

"How's the cold? Did you take some Echinacea? Carol swears by—"

"I know. She dropped some off Saturday." I was a little iffy on an herb cure. Especially after last fall's run-in with a Chinese herbalist and a prescription of tree bark, wet leaves, and clods of dirt for back pain which I didn't have anyway. But that's another story. "I think I'm getting better." I sneezed.

"Good. Look, I hate to ask you, I know how busy you are with the restaurant and concessions. If you have a break, could you come to tech rehearsal for a while tonight? I need to know if this show is working. I'm having second thoughts," she said.

"Lola, it's a little late for second thoughts."

I could hear Lola's hesitation. "I need an honest opinion."

It was a little late for an honest opinion too. But I couldn't refuse; I'd cover dinner and then slip out for an hour. Benny could keep an eye on the dining room. "I'll see what I can do."

"Thanks, Dodie. I really appreciate this one."

I called Bill's cell but no answer. I would have to wait for his second round of apologies. By ten o'clock I was well fortified by two cups of coffee, whole wheat toast, and the *New York Times*. I wrapped myself in layers to win the battle with the cold. The air was crisp, the temperature hovering around thirty, and the snow underfoot crunched as I scraped an inch off the windshield. I shivered inside my Chevy Metro. My sturdy little car was sluggish on winter mornings and the heat trickled out of the vent at its own slow pace.

I eased out of my driveway, my tires leaving parallel tracks lined with mini mounds of snow. I was hoping for a rise in temperature to melt the fresh blanket of white as well as the residual ice packed underneath. The salt trucks had been out in force already and most of Main Street was clear. I slipped into a space in front of the Windjammer and noticed the parking meters had paper bags covering their faces. An Etonville signal that parking was free due to the weather.

Inside the Windjammer, I put on the coffee and turned up the heat.

"Brrr. I love wintertime," Benny said, rubbing his hands together, his knit hat pulled low over his forehead.

"Wise guy. You're here early," I said.

"Not early. Just not late. Which is early for me, I guess."

"Right."

Benny hung up his scarf and coat, placing them on a hook next to mine, and popped behind the bar. "How was the baking class yesterday?" He sniffed the air. "Is that *eau de* burnt cake I smell?"

"Only the first batch." I laughed. "Poor Georgette. She had her hands full."

"I was going to come by. But I had to babysit."

Benny's wife had gotten a new job at a toy store in the Bernridge Mall, in the next town over. It was a good deal for the family: She got a twenty-percent discount on products and Benny's six-year-old daughter was thrilled with the results.

"People were out shopping in that weather yesterday?"

Benny shrugged. "Kids and toys."

"How's the princess doing?" I asked.

"Another earache. I'm taking her to the doctor later, okay? I'll be back for dinner."

"Sure."

"You sound better," he said as he scrubbed down the bar and cleaned the soda taps. "Good enough to have celebrated Valentine's Day." He grinned and winked.

Benny had closed for me Saturday night and still assumed I'd had my romantic dinner with Bill. "Uh-huh."

I made for the kitchen, snatching the clipboard off the wall. I was still getting used to the fact that as police chief, Bill was on duty 24-7. Which meant last-second cancellations and reshuffled plans. Why was I so hesitant to admit that I'd spent Valentine's Day alone nursing my cold and my ego? I attacked the freezer with a vengeance, noting what meats and seafood needed to be restocked this week.

"Dodie!" Henry boomed at the entrance to the storeroom.

I jumped, caught gathering wool. I'd been so lost in thought I hadn't heard him come in. "Henry, you want to give me a heart attack?"

Henry ran a mittened hand over his bald head and eyed me warily. "Who burnt what in my kitchen?"

"A few cakes. No big deal."

"There is cake batter on the oven," he said, peeved.

Henry was fussy about his domain. "I'll check the vegetable bins. You're good to go for the broccoli cheddar soup for lunch." I slammed the freezer shut. Henry's soups were legendary in Etonville and often ran out during the lunch service.

"I'm glad no more baking on Sundays," he harrumphed and stomped off, his damp boots leaving a puddle by the storeroom entrance.

There was no doubting Henry's skill in the kitchen. It was his personality that sometimes needed a transplant. He was still cautious about my theme food ideas for the Etonville Little Theatre as a marketing tool. It started with dinners that reflected the subject matter of the plays—seafood for *Dames At Sea*, Italian fare for *Romeo and Juliet*, beef bourguignon for the French farce.

But last fall I upped the ante with the 1940s food festival for *Arsenic and Old Lace*, and when the director died during the event, poison was suspected and the Windjammer suffered a setback. Henry was still smarting from the loss of customers, even though business came roaring back when the Windjammer was exonerated. And now here I was, taking over his territory on Sundays and messing up his immaculate equipment. For what? ELT concessions. Even I had to admit that the theme food idea might be growing old. Maybe the concept had outlived its usefulness. After all, both the theater and the restaurant were thriving and who needed the publicity? Thanks to the Windjammer's website, we were creating an online presence. Maybe it was time to come up with another gimmick to promote—

Benny appeared in the pantry. "Gillian called in sick, and Enrico and Carmen had a fender bender on the way here. They're going to be late."

"Better tell Henry we'll be short-staffed for lunch. I'll call Enrico's cousin." One of our part-time waiters.

"Okay. I'll set up the dining room," Benny said.

"Maybe everyone will stay home," I added hopefully.

"In your dreams." Benny hurried off to warn Henry.

It felt as if much of Etonville opted not to stay home today and descended on the Windjammer for lunch. I'd done the prep for Henry's soup and his special burgers while he chopped and sautéed onions and garlic for his pot of chili. Fish tacos were scratched from the menu and grilled three-cheese sandwiches substituted. I ran from the kitchen to the dining room, Benny ran from the bar to tables, and Enrico's cousin bussed dishes double-time. By one thirty the broccoli cheddar soup was gone, the crowd had thinned; Enrico and Carmen had finally shown up; the dining room was well in hand and I felt comfortable collapsing in the back booth near the kitchen that served as my "office." I pulled my hair into a ponytail and leaned my head against the back of the booth. I couldn't help it: my eyes closed.

"Any food left?"

I lurched upright. I could sense rather than see the corner of his lip tick upward. A quirk I was used to by now. Bill was swathed in his official bomber jacket and winter cap. A muffler was wrapped around his head, partially concealing his mouth. "Hey."

"Hey yourself. Can I join you?"

"Have a seat." I tried to play it cool. But there was no way I could avoid my pulse rising in the presence of his ruddy face. I nonchalantly flipped off the scrunchie that held my hair in place.

Benny set a cup of coffee in front of me and handed Bill a menu. "Hi, Chief."

"Benny."

"How's it going out there?" Benny asked.

"Let's see... I had three minor collisions, two dead batteries, and the Banger sisters got locked out of their car." He removed his cap and monitored me over the edge of his menu. "Winter in the northeast." His cheeks were redder than usual and his spiky hair was matted to the surface of his head.

"The soup's gone," I said apologetically.

"That's okay. I'll have the chili."

"Good choice. It's extra hot today." Benny grinned and ambled off.

"Maybe the Banger sisters shouldn't be driving in this weather," I said.

"You want to be the one to tell them?" he groused. "So... sorry again about—"

"Saturday night. Yeah. Me too."

He unzipped his jacket and threw it onto the bench of the booth. "Look, Dodie, it comes with the territory. Job conflicts."

"Seems like a lot of job conflicts lately," I said, pretending to study an inventory sheet.

Benny set a bowl of chili and crackers in front of Bill. "Take it easy. I think Henry said it's three-alarm."

"Good. Just what I need." Bill picked up his spoon, and Benny gave me the eyeball before backing off.

"I'd like to make it up to you. How about dinner Thursday night? Maybe Benny can cover? Something fun."

I'd have to work out the concessions at the ELT, but once we got through the opening Wednesday, the front-of-house crew should be comfortable with the cakes, pies, and mulled wine. "Sure. It won't involve seat warmers, will it?" In December Bill had suggested we do "something fun." Our date consisted of sitting in the freezing rain for three hours watching the New York Giants battle the Washington Redskins. It took all night to thaw out.

Bill relaxed against the seat and grinned. "I have something special in mind." He seemed pleased with himself.

"Okay...how special? Dressy?" I stopped. "Not La Famiglia special? Because the last time we ate there, Henry sulked for two days. It was like me eating with the enemy." La Famiglia was the Windjammer's primary competition and nemesis. Mainly due to its receiving four stars from the *Etonville Standard* compared to the Windjammer's three. Of course, it was only the local rag, but still...

Bill held up his hand. "It's not La Famiglia. In fact it's not even in town." He smiled sphynx-like.

"You're being very mysterious."

"Pick you up at six thirty." He dug back into the chili. "Kind of dressy." His lip curved again.

Usually I took a break at three o'clock for an hour or so and did some paperwork, ran errands, or, lately, held Lola's hand. *Eton Town* was taking its toll on her. But today I stayed in and worked from my back booth. I made a list: cider, cinnamon sticks, orange and pineapple juices, honey, cloves, nutmeg, anise seed. And of course red wine. That should do it for the concession drinks. I scribbled in the margin of the order form. "Kind of dressy..." Bill had said. What exactly did that mean? I had my little black dress...and my Jimmy Choo knockoffs. Both of which Bill had seen before. That particular night, a nor'easter was threatening Etonville, the

Windjammer had lost electricity, the ELT had to cancel its tech rehearsal, and two criminals were at large. But that was last October...

Still, it was a killer outfit.

My cell pinged. It was Snippet's ID. "Hi, Carol."

"Uh...hey. It's me. Pauli."

My eighteen-year-old Internet-and-all-things-computer guru. And Carol's son. "Pauli! What's up?"

He cleared his throat. "Like, I did the website updates. You know with the photos from the baking class."

"You did? You're the best. Really on top of things, kiddo," I said.

I could almost hear him blush. "Yeah. Well...like, no big deal."

"I'll log on and check it out."

"Okay. Gotta bounce." A note of pride crept into his voice. "Like, I'm taking this photography class...and so I'm like the uh...official photographer for the ELT production."

"Wonderful. Talented guy," I said.

"Yeah. I'm watching the rehearsal tonight."

"I'm stopping in too. I'll see you there."

"Sweet."

He clicked off and I smiled to myself. Pauli was coming into his own. It was nice that his activities were all legal now. At least I hoped so...

3

"Hey, O'Dell." Penny Ossining had been the ELT stage manager for twenty-five years. She fancied herself the linchpin of the volunteer theater troupe when she wasn't busy at the Etonville post office. Not much got by her, or so she said.

I looked up from my cell phone. I was checking out the Windjammer website with Pauli's new updates. He'd added interior shots of the restaurant that highlighted the nautical-themed décor, based on a nineteenth-century whaling vessel, complete with central beams, floor planking, and figurehead of a woman's bust above the entrance. Penny stood, arms akimbo, in the left aisle of the Etonville Little Theatre, fairly oblivious to the chaos around her. As stage manager, it was her job to keep things moving and in control. *Good luck with that.* "Hi, Penny. Are we about to start?" I checked my watch. It was eight p.m. I'd been sitting in the house for half an hour. "Things are running late."

Penny gave me one of her world-weary expressions. "O'Dell, we're now on tech time. In the theater, there's—"

"Theater time versus real time. I know." I'd already been schooled in that particular bit of theatrical practice.

"Tech time is different."

"You mean eight o'clock in real time is actually seven o'clock in tech time?" I asked innocently.

Penny tapped her pencil against her clipboard and hooted. "O'Dell, you crack me up. Anyway we already did a cue-to-cue. Walter likes to do a stop-and-go after the dry tech."

Cue-to-cue? Dry tech? Theater jargon was still like a new language to me.

"Penny!" Walter called from the stage. "It's time to start!" He slapped his tricorn hat on his white wig.

Penny tooted her whistle and the entire theater winced. "Move your butts for the opening of Act One," she yelled. The actors trickled onstage from the house, from the backstage green room, and from the lobby where a handful were drinking coffee and chatting. "No drinking while in costume," she bellowed again. Though the full dress rehearsal was tomorrow night, most actors wore bits and pieces: skirts, hats, shoes, coats.

Lola sat in the last row of the theater with the lighting designer and JC from JC's Hardware, the ELT's set designer. He and Walter usually tangled on every production, and Walter ended up reminding him that the theater was intended to create the illusion of reality. Fake walls, not the real thing. Two sets of tables and chairs occupied the infamous turntable.

While Lola was dealing with light cues, Walter took the opportunity to do a vocal workout. Most of the cast were used to his exercises and warm-ups and moved into a circle to begin the night. Rolling their heads, as well as their eyes, shaking their bodies, releasing sounds up and down the scale, and garbling the tongue twisters designed to improve their articulation. "Rubber baby buggy bumpers." Ten times quickly. The veteran actors took it semi-seriously; the newer ones looked self-conscious, sticking out their tongues, blowing through their lips, and stretching their mouths.

"All right. Knock it off," Penny said to two young guys who were poking each other and then made notes on her clipboard.

"Open and close your mouths. Tongues up, down, side to side!" Walter demonstrated. "She sells seashells by the seashore!"

The actors repeated the phrase. I could see *myself* down the shore, walking on the beach, picking up shells and stones, digging my toes in the sand—

"Dodie, thanks for coming," Lola whispered at my back. "We'll be underway soon. Having some issues with the lighting on the turntable."

"No problem."

Lola shook her blond head. "This is the last time I'm directing."

"Hey," Pauli said, backpack slung over his shoulder.

"Hi. Is your Mom here?" Lola asked.

He jerked his thumb over his shoulder as Carol entered the house. Since she ran Snippets hair salon, Carol was the ELT's hair and wig specialist and had the job of convincing Vernon and a few other men that their thinning heads wouldn't work with the tricorn hats. Walter, of course, reveled in the eighteenth-century headgear. She stopped to talk with Chrystal, the costume designer.

"I've got to get back to work." Lola waved to Carol and strode away with purpose.

"So you're photographing *Eton Town*. Nice," I said.

"Uh, like, tonight I'm watching so I know what it's about." He paused. "You know what it's about?"

"Well, it's the story of the founding of a New Jersey town, and its citizens, and the American Revolution."

Pauli nodded wisely. "Got it. Like a history lesson."

"Kind of. With some singing and dancing and a turntable." Besides the church hymn, there was also a colonial square dance that ended the Act One wedding scene. Walter loved his choreography.

Pauli ambled down the aisle and plopped into a seat, then peered into his digital camera to practice framing shots. I watched the vocal warm-ups; this was the largest cast I'd seen on an ELT stage. Edna, the Etonville Police Department dispatcher, and Abby, manager of the Valley View Shooting Range, had graduated from zany elderly sisters to genial, friendly neighbors. Their animosity during *Arsenic and Old Lace* was replaced with a theatrical détente. Besides, Lola had informed them that either they kiss and make up or they had to take a hike. The Banger sisters and some ELT newcomers were doing their best to follow Walter's instructions; but bored after ten minutes or so, they gave up and sat on the folding chairs that served as the graveyard in Act Two. I saw a few others I knew—the cute actress who played Juliet last spring, texting, Mildred's husband Vernon, jiggling his hearing aids, and the obnoxious guy who played Romeo, whom we still called Romeo, flirting with a teenage crew member. I also saw Sally, standing at the back of the stage, facing out, performing Walter's exercises conscientiously. Maybe later I could ask her again about the man on the street. Did Ralph arrest him?

"I brought you some tea," Carol said in a stage whisper and unscrewed the cap of a thermos, bending her curly head over her task.

"That's so thoughtful, but I'm really feeling much better." I sneezed. *Geez.* I hadn't sneezed for hours.

She handed me a takeaway cup. "Drink this."

I sniffed it. "What's in it?"

"Peppermint and cloves. Good for a sore throat."

"I don't have a sore throat anymore and—"

"You'll be one hundred percent by morning."

I was already about 90 percent; I wasn't sure the herb tea would get me the last ten. I sipped the steaming liquid anyway. I was surprised. "Not bad."

Carol smiled. "I swear by it. I make Pauli drink it every day."

He was sitting five rows in front of us, camera resting on his chest. "Nice that he's the ELT photographer."

"Isn't it? Of course, I can't keep up with all of his projects. The computer classes, digital forensics, now photography…well, at least it keeps him out of trouble." She laughed and sprinted down the aisle.

If she only knew. Eleven months ago he was my email-hacker-in-chief.

By eight thirty, Lola had the lighting cues ironed out, the warm-ups were complete, and Penny had announced "take ten" and "break's over" and the tech finally began. Lights shifted and the Narrator described the ending of the Revolutionary War, the founding of Etonville, and two families going about everyday life in town. Actors moved onto the stage, the turntable jolted and slowly began to revolve, powered by stage hands who would be dressed as townspeople. Vernon was orating, extra loud, and the two mothers—Edna and Abby—came into view busily miming cooking breakfast. The turntable jolted, trembled, and stopped. Abby latched on to the edge of a kitchen table to steady herself.

"Hold," Penny shrieked.

Everything stopped. JC jumped onstage to adjust the rotation mechanism, and the actors dropped character. He wiggled something, tapped something else with a hammer, and gave a thumbs-up to Walter.

"Go!" Penny shouted.

So this was stop-and-go… The technical rehearsal continued until the turntable halted again, or a light cue came in late, or Lola wasn't satisfied with the focus of an instrument.

Tedious, to say the least. I was missing the impact of the story with the constant interruptions, but I saw enough to realize that Walter wasn't a half-bad playwright. The problem was the other half. Actors' energy flagged toward the end of Act One, still going after an hour and a half, and even the tricorn hats had wilted.

During one of Penny's "holds" I slipped to the back of the house and squatted down next to Lola. "Going okay, yes? I mean for a tech rehearsal."

Lola was frazzled, her hair a tangle where she'd been twisting strands. "You think? This is making *Arsenic and Old Lace* look like a picnic in the park."

That was saying a lot, considering that show had had a leaky roof that rained on the scenery and a leading lady who couldn't act. "Sorry to desert you but I've got to pop next door and help Benny close up."

Lola nodded miserably. "Talk to you tomorrow. If I live that long."

I patted her arm and slinked out of the house, wrapped up in my down jacket to cope with the night air. I inhaled, staring into a clear sky dotted with bits of stars. It would be a fine day tomorrow. As I tramped through the slushy snow still covering parts of the sidewalk, I marveled at how invested I had become with the Etonville Little Theatre. I took its successes personally and felt bad when things went off-kilter. As they had with *Eton Town.* They would have done better to stick with the original version and left the history of the town founding to the library. Too late for second guesses now…

By three o'clock Tuesday things had quieted down in the dining room; I took my break by heading next door with a hot plate for tomorrow night's concessions. I loaded a double burner, to keep the mulled wine and cider punch warm, on a hand truck—refusing Benny's offer of help—and pushed my equipment to the ELT, avoiding patches of melting ice on the sidewalk.

Lola, her blond hair pulled into a topknot, in faded jeans and a paint-stained sweatshirt, emerged from the business office carrying a tablecloth and some red, white, and blue bunting to decorate the concession table.

"Everything ready for tonight?" I asked.

"Walter wants to do a run-through of the wedding square dance and Vernon says he needs to run his monologue for the second act opening. But other than that, we're all set," Lola said.

"I'll bring over the punch bowl and cups later tonight." We got the hot plate in place, the table ready for the desserts that only needed to be thawed.

"And I'll remind Chrystal about the costume pieces for the concession crew," I said.

Lola returned to the office, and I was envisioning myself in a colonial skirt, apron, and mob cap when the lobby door opened and Sally bustled in, arms full of paper plates and napkins.

"Hi, Dodie. I offered to pick these up for Lola." She deposited her stash on the concession table.

"Nice of you." I smiled. "I saw you during the warm-up last night. I think you're all good sports."

"Walter's right. We need the warm-up to get our articulators working," she said seriously.

Defending Walter. Not something many ELT folks were doing these days. *Hmmm.*

I thrust my arms into my jacket sleeves and we walked out the door, pushing the hand truck. "Sally, you seemed awfully upset the other night. About that man on the street," I said carefully.

"Not really. I mean, I thought it was someone I knew. But I guess I was mistaken." She waved and moved off.

* * *

Sally slipped my mind during the hours that followed. The Windjammer was packed with Etonville's citizens who preferred Henry's recent experiments to eating in. Tonight we featured his grilled pork tenderloin with an avocado and sour cream side sauce. He'd added a pineapple-and-onion topping for good measure. Henry was taking a few more chances with his entrées, obviously still feeling the competition with La Famiglia.

When the dining room was this full, I liked to meander from table to table and check in with patrons.

"Dodie, tell Henry that we love the pork," said Mildred. She and Vernon had popped in for an early dinner before their ELT call.

"Will do," I said. "You need to fortify yourselves for the big night ahead." I refilled their coffee cups.

"Hunh," Vernon grunted. "Long night you mean. I still don't understand why Walter didn't cut something. Like that silly dance. Who does a square dance at a wedding?"

Mildred poked her husband. "Vernon, it was the 1700s. They did a lot of things differently then."

"Yeah? Well, I'll bet they knew enough to cut a play when it topped three hours."

I'll bet they did too. I moved on to the Banger sisters. They'd had their hair permed for the show; their ringlets were identical to the men's powdered wigs.

"Dodie, we're so excited. It's our first time treading the boards, don't you know," said one sister.

"We're eating light," said the other.

I looked down at their half-empty plates, at the remnants of the tomato, corn, and lentil salad.

"Good idea. Acting on a full stomach might not be the best idea. The salad's pretty filling."

"We're also trying to keep our weight down," said the first sister.

"Really? You two look fine to me," I said.

"We're going to try out for the musical," said the second sister. "We want to compete with some of the younger actors."

"Do you sing? I mean like musical-theater sing?" I asked, lightly skeptical.

"We're going to take lessons." They smiled in unison.

I guessed hope—as well as delusion—did spring eternal.

The pork tenderloin was a big hit and soothed Henry's always fragile culinary ego. The last of the stragglers were finishing their dinners; the rest of the evening would be primarily bar service. For certain the ELT crowd, who often stopped in for a late drink after a show or rehearsal, would be abstaining. By the time the turntable made its last rotation, the Windjammer would be near to closing. Not that some of them couldn't use a drink to drown their theatrical troubles.

My cell beeped. Lola wanted to know what time I was coming by. I slid into my back booth with a cup of vegetable soup left over from lunch and a plate of the tomato-and-lentil salad. Benny brought me a seltzer.

"Okay by you if I visit next door about ten? I want to drop off the punch bowl for the concession stand," I said.

He nodded. "I have a babysitter 'til eleven. Peggy's doing inventory tonight at the toy store."

"I'll close up." I dipped a spoon in the soup.

At ten I dressed in my winter gear, loaded the punch bowl and cups on my hand truck, and stepped outside the restaurant. The sky was cloudy, the moon covered in a foggy layer—more snow was expected tomorrow. I exhaled and a thread of cold air streamed away from my mouth as I hurried next door. In the dimly lit lobby, I deposited my boxes in a corner near the concession stand. All was quiet.

I checked my watch and decided to sneak a peek at the end of Act Two; since the dress rehearsal started at seven, *Eton Town* should be gasping its last: the funeral over, the choir having sung, the turntable about to take its final bow.

I opened the door softly and slipped into a seat in the back row of the theater. Onstage the graveyard was filled with Etonville dead sitting in folding chairs, hands crossed, humming a hymn. The little blond who had played Juliet last spring—now the young wife of Thomas Eton, the Revolutionary War hero—threw herself on the ground and wailed about life passing in a flash, as she called "good-bye" to everyone and everything: her husband, her children, her house, her garden, her dishes, her wedding dress…etc. etc. We got the picture. Edna, as her deceased mother, waxed philosophical proclaiming that the living don't appreciate life. It takes death to give one perspective. Which was fine as long as you weren't the one who'd died.

The turntable started to chug to life, then it stopped and it appeared as if all onstage held their breaths. With a mighty heave by the stage crew, the platform creaked and moved again, the Banger sisters hanging on for dear life. Vernon walked into a spotlight and reminded the audience that tomorrow was another day in the life of Eton Town. He wished us all a good night. The stage went dark.

After a second of silence, the costume crew, the light board operator, Lola, and myself applauded enthusiastically as the lights came up on a swarm of actors buzzing about the performance, their costumes, and the turntable. Vernon and Romeo fist-bumped. I gave Lola a thumbs-up as she sped down the aisle to arrange actors onstage for the curtain call.

"Am I glad this night is over," whispered Chrystal before she plunked down in a seat next to me.

"Lots of costumes," I said.

"If I never see another tricorn hat, it will be too soon for me. And Walter's talking about continuing the theme next fall with *1776*. I told him I'd quit."

I stifled a laugh.

Chrystal dashed to the stage to save her wardrobe as the actors ran to the dressing rooms to change.

* * *

"Only a few more minutes," Lola said to the antsy assembly.

She flicked a page to check notes. "Chrystal? Costumes?"

Chrystal hauled herself to her feet and took notes on everything from boots that were the wrong size to wigs that popped off when the men removed their hats. The cast gathered their things while Lola encouraged them to get some sleep, the irony not lost on the exhausted actors.

"Sally?" Chrystal called out.

A few actors paused and looked around.

"She had the wrong apron in Act One. Where is she?" Chrystal asked.

There was a shrug here and there, a couple of "I don't knows" and a frustrated exhalation from the costumer. I hadn't seen her since the end of the play.

"Chrystal," I said, "I don't think she was in the curtain call."

"You know, come to think of it, I didn't see her there either," Chrystal said.

"Maybe she left early. Was she sick or something?"

"Sick of this show," Vernon groused at my back.

"Oh, Vernon, bring it down a notch. You have the biggest role and the most lines. You should be happy." Mildred thumped his back and gave him a shove toward the exit.

I stifled a chuckle. "I guess Mildred's taking no prisoners tonight."

"Everyone's kind of fed up with the play," Chrystal confided.

"That's nothing new at the ELT, from what I've seen during the last two years."

"This time it's a little different." She lowered her voice. "People are afraid the town won't come to see it. Once everyone finds out how long it is. And how it's…you know…"

I hesitated. What was the right word? "Kind of mind-numbing?"

Chrystal tittered and trundled off. "If you see Sally, tell her I'm gunning for her. No one's supposed to leave without checking with me or Penny first."

Penny! I scanned the house that was fast emptying out. Lola, onstage, was twisting a length of hair and listening to Walter pontificate about a piece of stage business. He flopped on the ground to demonstrate his point. Behind them, Penny tapped her leg with the clipboard and pushed her glasses up her nose. I waited until Walter was flat on the ground, practically licking the floor, while Lola watched with her "Oh brother" expression, to walk to the front of the house and signal Penny.

She walked importantly to the lip of the stage. "What's up, O'Dell?"

"Penny, have you seen Sally?" I asked.

"Sally Oldfield? Third chair, second row of the graveyard?"

"Yes."

"O'Dell, final dress is over. It's after midnight. Where do you think she is?"

Was this a quiz? "Home, right?" I said.

"Duh!" Penny loved to stump me.

"Okay but she wasn't here for the curtain call and Chrystal was looking for her. No one seemed to know where she went. Did she check in with you—?"

Penny smirked. "She was in the curtain call. Everybody's in the curtain call."

"I didn't see her."

"O'Dell, actors are not allowed to miss the curtain call. She had to be here."

"But Chrystal didn't see her either," I said.

Penny's eyes narrowed as she checked her clipboard. A note of alarm crept into her voice. "Actors gotta tell me if they leave early," she blustered.

"I know," I said sympathetically. Obviously Penny had no idea where Sally Oldfield had gone. I couldn't help thinking about Sally staring across Main Street at a strange man. And despite saying she thought he was someone else, Sally looked like she'd seen a ghost.

4

Opening night. I spent the morning prepping the Windjammer for the weekend crowd and reserved the late afternoon for setting up the mulled wine and hot apple cider. I figured I could work at the theater uninterrupted: JC had finished final touch-ups on the scenery this morning and Lola had an early afternoon appointment at Snippets to get her roots dyed before the curtain rose on *Eton Town*.

I'd already combined the ingredients at the restaurant and allowed the mixture to boil for a few minutes. At four thirty I enlisted Enrico to help me haul the gallons of hot drinks to the theater—to simmer on the hotplate—along with twelve apple pies. The cast would be showing up in the next hour or so, and I wanted to have everything set before the organized chaos of actors and crew and Walter disturbed my serenity.

I gave the mulled wine one last quick stir before I went to the women's dressing room backstage. Reluctantly, I had agreed to don the same early American costume as the cast, one more way to tie the theme food to the play, Lola had said. Chrystal had laid out a black skirt, white bodice, and mob cap with a full crown and a ruffled edge. My great-aunt Maureen wore something like the cap to bed whenever she had a cold. I never knew why.

I caught a glimpse of myself in the dressing room mirror, my wavy, auburn hair tucked up inside the mob cap. I had to admit, it wasn't the most attractive get-up I'd ever worn. But I was taking one for the team.

I walked into the hallway outside the dressing room and cut through the green room. Soon the lounge would be filled with the noise of actors getting into costume and makeup, rehearsing the hymns, and running through the wedding square dance. But now the backstage was deathly silent. I walked onstage and inhaled the sharp aroma of paint and sawdust and a hint of mold. Work lights cast a dim wash of illumination over the scenery, already set up with the Act One side of the turntable facing the house. On the opposite side of the platform, the crew had set up the seats for the graveyard scene. I gazed at the set, wondering what Walter and the rest of the cast would do if the rotating stage stopped rotating. They might have to—

A gasp.

I whirled to my right. "Hello?" Chills ran down my spine.

There was no answer. I made a tiny move forward and listened. I could have sworn I heard someone panting. Must be the draftiness of the theater, air currents flowing into and out of the space.

Scram, I told myself. *No sense creating scary scenarios.* I'd had several run-ins with the theater, chased and chasing. And nearly getting killed. I should have learned my lesson and stayed away when the theater was empty. But the fall skirmish with two murderers seemed like a lifetime ago.

I hurried to the staircase that led from the lip of the stage to the front of the house and had one foot on the first step when I heard it again: sharp intakes of breath, as though someone were crying. I spun around. "Who's there?"

A shadow moved behind me and my blood ran cold.

"Dodie," a voice whispered.

I squinted into the semi-dark. "Sally? Is that you?" Relief flooded my body, my heart moving out of my mouth, its rhythm slowing down. "You scared me. Where have you been? I know you missed the curtain call last night even though Penny swore that…"

She slid out from the shadow of the front drape. And then *I* gasped. Her face was blotchy and tear-stained. She stared at her hands as if she didn't recognize them. One palm was covered with dark streaks, the other hidden in a closed fist. My pulse quickened. "Sally? What's wrong?"

She looked up, her eyes darted wildly. As I ran toward her across the stage, my shoe caught in the hem of my skirt and I tripped, falling forward. I reached down to break my tumble and when I looked up again, she had disappeared. I yelled after her, "Sally, wait!" But she'd had a good head start. I hiked up my skirt and ran down the stairs into the house after her.

Walter appeared from the green room. "What are *you* doing here?" he asked coldly.

He hadn't gotten over my digging into a murder last spring that revealed his playing fast and loose with the box office till. If it wasn't for Lola running the show now, I'd be banned from the ELT. "I was setting up the concession stand," I said with as much dignity as I could muster.

"In here?" Walter asked sarcastically.

I dropped my skirt. "Never mind about me. Sally just ran out of here."
Walter looked puzzled. "Sally?"

"Oldfield. One of your actors?" What had Penny said? "Third chair, second row of the graveyard."

"Oh. Her," he said dismissively.

Walter should think of Sally with a little more respect. She was one of the few cast members who didn't mock him behind his back. He removed his overcoat.

"Something's wrong. She wasn't in the curtain call last night and just now she was really in a state, it looked like her hands were—"

"What do you mean she wasn't in the curtain call? All actors are in the curtain call. No one is excused," Walter said.

It was Penny all over again. "I'm telling you she wasn't and she—

"Dodie? Walter? What's going on?" Lola flipped on the house lights as Walter examined the placement of the furniture for Act One.

"Sally Oldfield was here a few minutes ago. She'd been crying and then she ran out of here," I said.

"Why would she do that? Her call is in five minutes," Walter said.

I'd had it with Walter's snarky attitude. I stomped onstage. "I hate to break the news, but Sally Oldfield is not going on tonight. She's not even going to be in the theater. She's on her way to who-knows-where." I was practically roaring.

"Dodie?" Lola, confused and worried, ran down the aisle. "What's this about Sally?"

"Something is wrong." I whirled around, grabbing for the dividing wall on the turntable that separated Acts One and Two.

Walter waved his hand. "I need to get into makeup." He headed for the dressing room.

The theater door opened, accompanied by an eruption of chatter. A handful of cast members entered the theater and proceeded through the house.

"Lola, we've got to do something." I stepped backward into the Act Two area, my foot grazing a large, immovable object. I looked down. *Even in the dim light I could see it was a body lying in front of the first row of folding chairs. With a knife sticking out of its chest. Dressed in a camo jacket and trapper hat.* Lola had bolted onstage and was standing behind me.

"Don't move," I rasped, my heart in my throat.

"Dodie, you sound awfully funny—"

"Call 911." My hand wobbled as I pointed downward.

Lola looked where I was staring. "Oh my God! Oh no! Who is it...? How did—"

"Now!" I screamed.

* * *

I sat in the last row of seats, taking deep breaths to keep my growing dread at arm's length. *Not again.* Another ELT production and another murder. I watched the crime scene unit busily scouring the stage for evidence, upending the furniture, searching the nooks and crannies of the turntable. It rotated easily enough with the CSI techs pushing and pulling. My mind kept replaying the moment when Sally appeared from the shadows, panicked, saying my name as if it were a plea for help. There was no mistaking the fact that the deceased was the same man she and I had seen standing in front of the Craft Shoppe Sunday night. What was their connection? One thing was for certain: Whomever he was, Sally was as shocked to see him in Etonville as she was horrified to view her hands an hour ago. Though I knew what the dark stains were then, my mind refused to process the information. But now there was no mistake: Her hands, at least one, was covered in blood.

Off to the side, Bill spoke softly to Officer Suki Shung, his second-in-command and a solid professional. I should know. Last fall we'd both been tied up and stuffed under the theater seats by a couple of jewel thieves. Bill made his way up the aisle. "Third time's a charm," he said grimly.

Did he think this murder was somehow linked to the ELT? "He didn't have any connection to the theater." My chest still pounded, my palms were sweaty.

Bill leaned in to me, scanning my face. "How do you know?"

"He wasn't an ELT member." Did Bill realize Ralph had picked the victim up Sunday night?

Bill fished a writing pad out of his pocket. "I gather you had a confrontation with one of the actors before the victim was discovered."

The skirmish was with Walter not Sally. "I had come out of the dressing room in my costume," I said rapidly.

Bill scrutinized my appearance—hair a mess from the mob cap, sneakers that clashed historically with my colonial skirt and blouse, the apron hanging off my shoulder. "Then what?" he asked.

"I heard a noise—" I shivered spontaneously.

His eyes narrowed. "What kind of noise?"

"Like a...gasp."

"You heard a gasp?" he asked.

"Right. Like someone breathing. Heavily."

"Breathing."

I sat up straighter, freaking out. "Are you going to repeat everything I say?"

"Just trying to get the facts," he said patiently. "And then what happened after you heard the breathing?"

I exhaled. "Then I heard what sounded like someone crying and Sally, she's one of the cast members, walked out of the shadows from the back of the turntable." I stopped myself. Is that what she'd done? Come from the Act Two side of the platform? Where the dead man now lay? I hadn't thought that through before this moment.

Bill was studying me. "What?"

"What what?"

"I know that look. What did you realize?" His eyes narrowed.

"Sally came from the area where the guy is lying."

"What did she do or say? How did she look?"

I closed my eyes and saw her. Terrified. "She said 'Dodie.' She was in tears. Her face was all smudged. Then she ran off. I called her and tried to follow but got tangled up in my skirt."

Bill scribbled on his pad, then turned and surveyed the theater. "No one else was here at the time?"

"Right. I was alone. Until Walter showed up. *That* was the confrontation."

"Oh?"

"I told him about Sally and he blew me off. You know ever since Jerome's death and that box office business—which he blames on me somehow—he and I haven't really seen eye-to-eye," I rambled on.

"Really." Bill couldn't have cared less about my contretemps with the ELT director-who-would-be-playwright. "Let's get back to Sally. The stuff on her hands. Was it blood?"

"The light was dim and she was in a shadow, but yeah, I think it was probably blood."

Was this the time to tell him about Sunday night? "One other thing, after our baking session on Sunday, Sally and I left the Windjammer and across the street—"

Walter burst into the house, with Lola on his heels. "Chief Thompson," he called out, "We need to know how to proceed."

I wanted to say "proceed this," but Lola looked so agitated I held my tongue.

"Walter, we have a very fluid situation here. The CSI team is still collecting evidence and the theater is a crime scene," Bill said.

No kidding. *Our Town* had been murdered long before the strange man died on the set.

"It's nearly seven. What do we say to the actors? The audience will start to show up any minute," he said.

Bill stuffed his hands in his pockets. "I'm sorry to tell you, but there's not going to be any performance tonight. I know that's a disappointment, but the theater is off-limits indefinitely."

Walter flushed an intense shade of scarlet: rage at fate, no doubt. Then he turned his icy stare on me. "It had something to do with Sally Oldfield, didn't it? I knew she would be trouble. An out-of-towner."

"Walter, please, Sally was a very sweet young woman," Lola said.

"She was a complete stranger," Walter said.

"Not to me. Sally was lovely. Responsible," I said. And willing to play your silly warm-up games, I wanted to add, without laughing behind your back.

"You all talk about her as if she has passed as well." Bill looked at Lola, then Walter, and, finally, me.

Silence.

"I'll need contact information on her and anything else you can tell me. Like when she arrived in Etonville and anything about her personal life."

"Of course, Penny can help you. Walter, let's break the news to the cast. We'll post some people in the lobby to intercept the audience," Lola said, weary.

"Good idea," Bill smiled sympathetically.

"Dodie, what do you want to do about the desserts and drinks?" Lola asked.

The colonial food! I'd been so angsty, I hadn't given any thought to the concession stand. I jumped to my feet. "I'll take care of it."

The minute they were out the door, Bill touched my arm. "Still on for tomorrow night?" he asked quietly.

Our redo-Valentine's-Day dinner. My insides fluttered. "I'm in if you are."

5

Georgette, who'd come to see the show, helped Carol distribute Swamp Yankee applesauce cake and pumpkin bread to a morose and frustrated cast and crew. Under the circumstances, they deserved a little free food to keep their spirits up. Not to mention the mulled wine. It disappeared like hotcakes. Lola had explained the situation and that they were free to go, but they were an ensemble, after all, and hanging around the theater was something they just did. Maybe they were hoping that Bill might walk through the lobby doors and announce a stay of execution for the production: There hadn't been a murder after all and the show would go on. That was a fantasy. Besides, Penny was stationed by the entrance to the theater and had been announcing the cancellation, clipboard in hand. Word would no doubt go viral through Etonville, setting the gossip machine working overtime.

"Dodie, did you see the dead man?" one of the Banger sisters asked.

"I'm afraid so."

"Tell me," the other one lowered her voice. "Did it have something to do with the turntable?" They looked at me eagerly.

"I'm pretty sure the turntable was not responsible for his death."

"Because we think it's a deathtrap. Dangerous." They nodded their heads in unison.

"Excuse me," I said. Never mind sipping mulled wine from a paper cup, I wanted to dunk my entire head in the punch bowl.

Lola detached herself from Walter, who was sitting in the theater office, scribbling on his script of *Eton Town* as if he was getting ready to rehearse. He looked as lost as the actors, who huddled in small clusters, whispering.

"This is a nightmare," Lola said.

"How's Walter taking it?" I asked, brushing crumbs from the pumpkin bread off my early American blouse. I was on my third slice, eating to remain calm.

"I think he's in denial."

"That's the first stage. Wait until he gets to stages two, three, and four. And forget about acceptance," I said.

"I don't understand. What was that man doing in the theater anyway?"

I pulled her aside. "I think Sally knew him."

"Our Sally?" A light bulb went off. "Do you think that's why she was in the theater? I wondered about that. Her call wasn't until five thirty. But if she knew him, why was she running away?" A second bulb. "Unless… Oh no… Do you think she had something to do with his death?"

"I don't know. But she must have been with him. Her palm was all bloody."

Her eyes widening, Lola clapped one hand over her mouth as if to keep her shock from escaping.

Penny sauntered over, the only member of the ELT taking the catastrophe in stride. She consulted her clipboard. "Got to most of the audience. Good thing we only had half a house tonight."

Which was a mixed blessing. Most things were where Penny was concerned.

She checked her watch. "Woulda been show time." Then she pushed her glasses up a notch. "We got to keep an eye on Walter. He might schiz out. You know he can be a little manic, kind of tri-polar."

Penny had managed to mashup three psychological disorders and still not get Walter right. "It's bi-polar. And I don't think he's either manic or schizoid." Personally, I'd have gone with narcissistic.

"Whatever. He could be…you know." She put her hands on her hips.

"What? Suicidal? Over this show?" If the night wasn't so tragic, I might have laughed.

Lola closed down the discussion. "Penny, Chief Thompson wants Sally Oldfield's contact information. And he might want to speak with cast members. Can you take care of it?"

I could see Penny mentally calculating her role in this disaster. "I'm on it. What do you want me to tell the actors about tomorrow night?"

"The truth. The show's cancelled for this weekend. The chief said no one is to go onstage until further notice," Lola said.

Penny tapped her clipboard and cackled. Tact and discretion were not in her wheelhouse. "Well, that's show—"

Lola lost it. "If you say 'that's show biz,' I'm going to scream. And then I'm going to fire you."

Penny gulped, looked aghast at Lola, and considered the threat. She slowly backtracked, turned on her heel, and toddled across the lobby.

"Getting to you?" I asked softly.

"I need a drink. And not mulled wine."

"Me too. I'll clear up the food, you clear out the lobby, and let's get out of here. I'll tell Carol."

"What if the chief…?" she asked.

"I'll check with him. He can find you if he needs you. Or he can consult with Walter."

We both leaned sideways to get a better look inside the theater office. Walter was doing a face-plant on the sofa, a pillow over his head, with Penny bent over him, talking in his ear. Not for the first time it occurred to me that they deserved each other.

"Maybe he is tri-polar," I said solemnly.

Lola and I traded looks, both of us borderline hysterical from the evening's events. I anticipated the prospect of storing pies and cakes in the Windjammer refrigerator for who-knew-how long and having to listen to Henry's complaining about it. Lola had to face the prospect of no audience and its effect on the ELT budget. The turntable might turn out to be a boondoggle after all.

* * *

I called Enrico and had him haul what was left of the concession cakes back to the Windjammer. Bill was still observing the CSI unit onstage when I told him that Lola and I were moving next door. He nodded and said he'd be in touch, whatever that meant. I was back in the lobby when I realized I'd left my clothes in the dressing room. I groaned. I would have to spend the rest of the evening dressed like a refugee from Betsy Ross's sewing circle. In sneakers. Without the mob cap. I ran a brush through my wild waves, chucked the apron behind the concession stand, and donned my down jacket.

A fine mist was descending on us as we slogged through the cold and damp, past a waiting ambulance, to the Windjammer. The brisk air was like a shot of adrenaline. We discarded outerwear on the coat tree inside the restaurant, and Lola and Carol deposited themselves at the bar.

Benny scanned my costume.

"Don't say it, I know. Betsy Ross," I said.

"I was going to say Dolly Madison. Without the—"

"Sneakers. Yeah."

Dinner had wound down but the bar area was packed. Talk about refugees: The ELT's loss was the Windjammer's gain. Gillian was helping out behind the bar and Enrico's wife Carmen was picking up the last few tables.

"Set us up, Benny," Lola said.

"Tough night. Sorry about the play," he said as he poured red wine for all three of us.

I never drank on the job, but technically Benny was closing tonight and I was in the restaurant in a purely advisory capacity. Like advising Benny when to refill our glasses. "That's the first homeless guy in Etonville in a long time," he said.

"Homeless?"

"That's what I heard. A homeless guy wandered into the theater and got himself killed," Benny said.

Now who was spreading that piece of information? "I don't think they confirmed that he was homeless."

"What else would he be doing in the ELT?" Carol took a drink of her wine. "Strange that he chose opening night to come in. Of course, with the weather we've been having, I'm not surprised someone wanted out of the cold. But too bad he had to die on the set. Now if it had happened in the lobby…"

I eyeballed Lola over the rim of my glass: Mum's the word on Sally. She responded with a faint nod.

"How did Henry take the news that we'd be housing what's left of the concession desserts?" I asked Benny, to change the subject.

"You know Henry. Grumble. Groan. Then it blows over."

"I hope we can put the show up next weekend," Lola said and twirled her wine glass. "We *need* an audience. And we had the *Star-Ledger* reviewer coming Saturday!"

It was quite the coup. After years of sweet-talking and downright begging, the Etonville Little Theatre had finally gotten the attention of north Jersey's primary newspaper. With the caveat that the reviewer be able to see *Eton Town* before he went on vacation.

"I suppose it depends on how long it takes the Etonville PD to solve the murder," I said.

"Once they identify the guy, we should be good to go. I mean, he had no connection to the theater," Carol said.

"He was murdered in the theater. There was a knife sticking out of his chest!" Lola said, a trifle too dramatically.

Carol paused, glass halfway to her mouth. "What?"

I swallowed a mouthful of wine, choking lightly. That bit of data was not known to the theater at large. Only Walter, Lola, and I knew the details of the man's death. Bill wanted to keep a lid on things for a few hours until he could identify the deceased. As if.

"That's privileged information, Carol. You can't repeat it," I said in a hurry.

Carol's salt-and-pepper curly head bobbed. "Sure," she said, her voice a little shaky.

Lola mouthed "sorry" and I shrugged. It was only a matter of time—hours rather than days—before the whole story ricocheted around Etonville like the eight ball on a pool table. One, Sally's distress, how she ran off with blood spattered on her hand, two, how the dead man had the knife protruding from his body, three, how—

"Another murder at the theater," Carol said, sotto voce.

We sat in glum silence for a moment.

Lola stirred. "I'm going home. Dead on my feet. Oh, bad choice of words." She stood up. "Call me?"

"Sure," I said.

They left and I finished the last dregs of my wine. I was done in, weighed down by the night's events. I couldn't begin to think what would happen next with the investigation, the show, Sally... My usually overactive imagination was on furlough. "'Night, Benny."

He dipped glasses in soapy water and rinsed them in the bar sink. "Something about that guy next door. Do you think the chief has any evidence?"

I had no clue. But now that *Eton Town* was indefinitely on hold, I was available to work evening closings and give Benny some time off this weekend. "No idea. I can cover for you this weekend." I knew he also worked shifts at UPS.

Benny gave me a thumbs-up. "Appreciate it. But take your day off tomorrow. You look like you could use it."

The icy drizzle had ended by the time I'd hit the street and walked down the block to my red Metro. I was numb and didn't even mind the drop in temperature in the last two hours. I turned the engine over along with ideas on Sally's whereabouts. I drove slowly through the slick streets; the mist had frozen into a thin layer of ice, coating trees and sidewalks and roadways. I pulled into my driveway as my cell binged. I desperately hoped it wasn't anyone with a problem. I'd had my fill of crises for one night. I checked the screen. I couldn't identify the number but the message was loud and clear: *Need to talk. S.*

I stuffed the cell in my bag and walked into the house. I stripped off my colonial clothing, pulled on my favorite sweats, and flopped down on the bed. I stared at my cell, a part of me hoping the message had somehow disappeared. No such luck. I contemplated my options. If I texted back, I might be abetting a possible murderer. If I pretended I hadn't seen the message, I might be leaving an innocent acquaintance stranded. I closed my eyes and saw her face—the terror, the tear-stained cheeks. I made a decision. Acquaintance trumped murderer. Besides, in my heart of hearts I knew the Sally Oldfield in the cast of *Eton Town* could not have killed anyone. At least not on purpose. Maybe in self-defense?

I tentatively tapped out a message: *Where are u? What's going on?* Then I added: *Did u know that man?* Of course she did. Maybe if we talked, I could convince her to visit the Etonville Police Department. After all, at the moment she could only be considered a person of interest. Until I told Bill that she'd seen the man days ago. Though my body had conceded defeat to the sheets, my mind got a reprieve and started whirring. I closed my eyes to think and was dozing in minutes.

* * *

I woke early—strange dreams of a spinning turntable that no one could stop—but intended to take it easy today. Time for me to contemplate my potential outfits for dinner tonight. I had a couple of dresses and a cream-colored silk suit with a V-neck jacket and slim slacks. It had been a Christmas gift from my parents and hugged me in all the right places. Given the predicted temperature tonight, low twenties, I opted for the suit. It was sophisticated and sexy; neither of which I was feeling at the moment. I squinted into the bathroom mirror. I was past the sore throat, sneezing, and stuffy nose, but my eyes were rimmed in red.

* * *

I'd spent the day checking for Sally's return text, pampering myself with a bubble bath, and snatching an afternoon nap. By the time Bill picked me up, I was relaxed and excited about the evening.

"So...you're okay going out with the murder hanging over your head?" I asked as he backed out of my driveway.

"Been doing a lot of grunt work today and Suki is following up. We're trying to ID the man," he said.

"Still not telling me where we're going?" I asked, teasing.

Bill smiled and ran a hand over his blond brush cut. His aftershave—a minty, woodsy aroma that I was used to—wafted across the front seat as he turned away. "Sorry, it's a—"

"—secret. I know." I smiled back. We passed a young woman bundled up against the cold, head tucked into her scarf. I inhaled abruptly.

"Something wrong?" Bill asked.

Could it have been Sally? "No. All good." Why hadn't she texted me back?

He glanced at me sharply, then veered onto Route 3 East, diving into traffic, crossing lanes to avoid the back-up of cars. I had assumed we were eating at a restaurant in Creston, four miles away from Etonville. A city of twenty thousand with a range of shops and services and socioeconomic areas, from high end to low income. It had a variety of eating establishments, several of which could be described as "special." But Creston lay in the opposite direction off Route 53.

"Mmm...so not Creston," I said. "How about a hint?"

"Nope. Curiosity killed the cat."

Bill maneuvered his car this way and that, navigating the stop-and-go of New Jersey congestion until I realized where we were headed. "That was the last exit in Jersey."

We threaded our way into the Lincoln Tunnel, evening commuters bumper-to-bumper. New York City. He turned sideways, the light from the streets casting shadows on his chiseled profile. "Yep. Something special."

6

By the time we'd negotiated Seventh Avenue traffic, found a parking lot, and walked a block, I knew exactly where we were going: Rondelay, in the heart of Greenwich Village, one of the most romantic eating establishments in the city. I'd offhandedly mentioned that it was my favorite New York restaurant. I guess Bill had been listening.

As he took my coat, Bill's eyes slid up and down my suit. "Nice outfit. Attractive," he murmured.

OMG. Had he really called me "attractive"? This evening *was* going to be special. I eyed his pinstriped black suit, the tapered waist accentuating his broad shoulders. He'd managed to stay in great shape even after a career in the NFL. "Thanks. Not so bad yourself."

Bill was a bit of a wine connoisseur, especially reds, and I had confidence in his judgment. We sipped a California cabernet at a candlelit table by floor-to-ceiling windows, the fireplace emitting a cozy warmth complemented by the rustic feel of the brick walls. The light from the chandeliers was reflected in the windows that overlooked snow-covered shrubs in a private garden. In a corner, a tuxedo-clad man played a baby grand piano. The ambience was intimate and inviting.

"Guess I hit one out of the ballpark with this place," he said, sipping his wine. "I see why you like it. A nice place to have a belated Valentine's Day dinner."

I lifted my glass. "To Valentine's Day."

"I'm sorry about that. Duty called and—"

I raised a hand to stop him. "No need to explain. I understand."

Bill cocked an eyebrow. "Really?"

"I'm surprised you felt you could take tonight off."

"I'm delegating to Suki more."

Really? "Any leads on Sally's whereabouts?" I asked cautiously. I still hadn't heard back from her.

His eyes narrowed. "Dodie, let's have a nice dinner and forget about shop talk, okay?"

We had decided on the three-course prix fixe menu and the waiter brought our appetizers—oyster chowder for me, crispy octopus for him. I inhaled the fragrant steam off my bowl. "This smells amazing." We dove in.

"You know the other reason I brought you here?" he asked.

"Besides it being my favorite restaurant?"

"Yeah. And romantic," he said matter-of-factly.

My spoon halfway to my mouth, I paused. "Why?"

"Its history." Bill cut into a piece of octopus.

I knew it had been a carriage house in the 1700s. "Early American, right?"

"Built before the American Revolution. So...this restaurant, the ELT production..." He waited for me to respond.

"Both colonial America," I said and took another spoonful of the chowder.

Bill laughed. "Yeah. You and everyone else in Etonville have their heads buried in the eighteenth century lately."

"It's a big undertaking for the theater. Large cast, powdered wigs, a grumpy turntable..."

He nodded. "I receive updates from Edna daily. Hard to keep her mind on dispatch."

"Well, she's saying what a lot of folks are thinking. I guess Walter just got a vision that he had to run with. There's a stubborn streak there," I said.

"Stubbornness. Must be the drinking water in Etonville," he said wryly. "Anyway, things have been pretty quiet around town until yesterday. The only crises were the Banger sisters forgetting to pay their bill at Coffee Heaven and Mrs. Parker's cat caught up a tree. But now..."

Coffee Heaven was an old-fashioned breakfast diner with a few modern coffee items on the menu. Caramel macchiato was my obsession.

"Right." I had a sudden brainstorm. "I didn't have a chance to tell you yesterday and I know you don't want to talk shop, but Sunday night I had just come out of the Windjammer and it was already dark but across the street Barbie's Craft Shoppe was—"

"What?"

Our entrées appeared—beef Wellington with root vegetables and beets in a cabernet reduction for me, and a rack of lamb with parsnip potato gratin and onion rings for Bill.

"I guess you know Ralph picked up the dead man on Main Street Sunday night?"

Bill stopped pouring wine.

"I knew it was him because the jacket and hat were the same," I said.

"You're telling me the victim was on the streets of Etonville days before he was found murdered?" Bill asked.

"Some coincidence, right?" No need to mention that Sally was with me. Yet.

Bill exhaled heavily. "The Craft Shoppe called in a complaint about a vagrant and Ralph responded. He told me the guy seemed nice, wandering down the street, and he paused to look in the shop window."

That's not all he paused to do.

"Ralph brought him in to the station?"

Bill shook his head. "He dropped him off at the library parking lot. The guy said he was meeting someone there."

The library?

We ate and drank, and I could feel myself melting—relaxed and satisfied—even though Bill now seemed a little preoccupied. "Well, this makes up for last Saturday night," I said.

He blinked. "You're still holding a grudge?"

I laughed. "Of course not."

I was too full for dessert, but a third course came with our dinners so we settled on crème brûlée and chocolate mousse. It had been a perfect night so far. Now, if Bill invited me back to his place for a nightcap—

"Do you?" he asked.

I had gotten lost in my fantasy. "Sorry?"

"Want to find someplace for an after-dinner drink?" He placed his credit card on the check.

"Sure."

We put on our coats, Bill held the door, and I slipped out into the night. It felt like the temperature had dropped a few degrees and I shivered involuntarily.

Bill took my arm. "Let's walk to the corner. There's got to be a spot down Seventh Avenue."

He shifted places with me, moving to the outside of the sidewalk as a couple bounced down the walk, laughing and nudging each other. They were probably high on something besides love. We shuffled aside to let them pass and Bill stepped off the curb. When he attempted to get back on the sidewalk, his foot caught the edge of a wrought iron tree guard throwing him off balance. He grasped a branch as his other foot hit a patch of black ice, whisking his legs out from under him, sending him onto the pavement with a thud and smashing his right foot into the tree guard.

I lunged for his arm, but the whole thing happened so quickly that he was on the ground before I could help. "Bill!" I stooped down.

The couple disappeared around a corner. Totally oblivious.

"Are you all right?" I asked, suddenly in disaster-mode. I knew it would be impossible for me to try to lift him.

He brushed me off. "I'm fine. Just bruised my backside a little."

And his ego.

Bill moved into a kneeling position, then he struggled to stand, putting weight on his right leg. "Ow," he said through gritted teeth.

"Did you bruise your foot too?" I asked.

"I think I might have sprained my ankle."

I helped get him to an upright position.

"Sorry about the drink," he said.

"I'll take a raincheck," I said as we hobbled down the street. I wanted to take a taxi to the parking lot, but Bill, being stoic, insisted he could walk. I didn't argue, but by the time we got to the lot, he was flinching badly with every step.

"I don't think I can drive," he said apologetically.

I sobered up immediately. "I can handle your car." Normally I would have been thrilled to test drive his BMW. I inspected the instrument panel: It was like facing an airplane cockpit.

I drove slowly, so as not to send Bill into vehicular panic, and crawled up Eighth Avenue, through the Lincoln Tunnel, and onto Route 3. At the turnoff to Etonville, I broached the subject carefully. "Maybe we should go to St. Anthony's." It was the area hospital in Creston and I was intimately familiar with the emergency room having spent the wee hours of a morning there last fall. I'd been conked on the noggin while doing investigative surveillance. But that's another story.

"I'll wrap it up when I get home. I had a handful of ankle sprains when I was in the NFL. I'll be fine." He adjusted his position and cringed. I wasn't so sure.

"Bill, I think I need to make an executive decision here. Remember when you forced me to go to the hospital to get checked out last fall?"

"That was different. You might have had a concussion."

"And you might have more than a sprain," I said gently.

He put a face on. Before he could protest further, I exited Route 3, cut through the north end of Etonville, and hopped on State Route 53. By the time we pulled up to the emergency entrance of St. Anthony's Hospital, his face was contorted with pain.

I parked the car and settled myself in the waiting room. The television was turned to late-night entertainment: Stephen Colbert interviewing an actress I'd never seen before. Was it after eleven thirty already? The night had been perfect—the food, the wine, the almost-after-dinner-drink that could have led to who-knows-what... I checked texts. A reminder from Henry to order shrimp for the weekend, a shout-out from Pauli to see how I liked the website updates, and three SOSs from Lola wondering what she was going to do about the show. I texted Henry that I might be late opening up in the morning.

Only five minutes had passed since I'd sat down in the waiting room. I closed my eyes.

A door opened. Bill appeared in a wheelchair, his right foot and ankle in a cast, accompanied by a male nurse in wrinkled scrubs who seemed even more worn out than me.

"Okay, Mr. Thompson. Don't forget your prescriptions." The young man set the brakes on the chair. "Are you alone?"

Bill looked to be beside himself. He stuffed the prescriptions in a pocket, flipped up a footrest, and stood up, nearly losing his balance. "No."

"Whoa there. Take it easy." He resettled Bill in the chair.

I got up.

The nurse shifted his attention to me. "Are you Mr. Thompson's wife?"

"No," Bill and I said simultaneously.

The nurse squinted at us. "He needs to take it easy the next few days."

I ran to get the car and drove up to the emergency entrance again.

"Stay off that foot," the young man said as we pulled away.

Bill was so still I assumed he'd fallen asleep.

"You were right. Fractured talus. A clean break but I'm going to have this thing on..." he tapped his cast, "...four to five weeks."

"Any pain?" I asked softly.

"Just in my neck," he said. Then snorted.

It was the beginning of a laugh. "Sense of humor still intact, I see."

"How about that nightcap at my place?" he asked.

"Terrific." Of course, it would not be as interesting as I had envisioned...

With the aid of crutches, he managed to get to the guest bedroom on the first floor of his center hall colonial. He texted Suki, alerting her to the situation. Good thing he was delegating. I removed the shoe off his good foot, and he shrugged out of his suit jacket and shirt and insisted he could take it from there. He was in the middle of thanking me and apologizing at the same time—forget the nightcap—when his eyes closed and he passed out. Turns out the pain meds were a little bit more potent than Bill had counted on.

It was two a.m. I scrounged up a blanket and pillow out of his linen closet and collapsed on his sofa. It was a disappointing end to a wonderful evening for both of us. Of course, I was the only one conscious enough to realize that. Soft snoring drifted out of the guest room since I'd left the door open in case he needed something. I probably wouldn't have any trouble falling asleep...

My cell binged at eight a.m. from my purse where I'd left it last night, or rather this morning. It was a text from Lola, wondering if I was awake. I rose and tiptoed to the door of the guest room. Bill had shifted positions in the night but was still dozing. I tapped Lola's number and listened to the phone ring several times before she picked up.

"Dodie! Finally. I expected you to call me when you got home last night. I was up 'til all hours. Worrying, of course. Did I wake you?"

I mumbled, "Not really."

"Why are you whispering? Did you lose your voice? Carol's herb tea—"

"I didn't lose my voice. I don't want to wake Bill."

I could hear her smile. "Aha... So that's why I didn't get a call back."

"It's not what you think. He broke a bone in his ankle last night, and we didn't get out of the emergency room until almost two and then he passed out from the pain meds and I ended up on the sofa—"

"He broke his ankle? How?"

"Dodie?" Bill stood in the doorway of the guest room, his trousers rumpled, his brush cut tousled, and pale blond stubble shadowing his face.

"Gotta go, Lola."

"Call later!" she begged as I clicked off.

After a civil but heated discussion, I helped Bill up the staircase, clunking step after step with the crutches, to the second floor where he insisted he could bathe and dress himself. He maintained, again, that he'd played through worse injuries on the gridiron. I reminded him, again, that he was supposed to stay off the leg.

I sat at his kitchen counter with a cup of coffee and waited for him to reappear, mentally ticking off my errands this morning.

"Got any more of that?" Bill hobbled his way to the counter.

He'd been right...he was able to clean up pretty well, shave off yesterday's stubble and get himself into a clean uniform. Despite the hour of the day, his freshly scrubbed look and muscular torso were able to raise my heart rate. But work? "You're not intending to report for duty, are you? I don't think that's what they had in mind when they said 'take it easy.'"

Bill dismissed my point with a wave of his hand and sipped from the mug I filled. "I have a murder to solve." He strapped on a shoulder holster.

"Okay. Let's go. I'll leave your car—"

"No need. Ralph will be here soon to pick me up and he'll drop you off." Bill set his mug down. "Thanks for last night. I mean it. I really appreciate your help."

He sounded so touched I could feel some heat creeping up my neck. "It was no big deal. You'd have done the same for me, right?"

He adjusted his crutches and clomped over to pick up his jacket.

"Right?" I asked again.

He turned to me, his eyes twinkling. "You even have to ask?"

My heart was aflutter.

7

I'd never been on an Etonville Police Department ride-along. Surprising, considering my participation in recent homicide investigations. I snuggled into my wool coat—not as warm as my down jacket—but dressier. It had been fifteen hours since I'd donned my sexy, silk pantsuit and I was feeling rumpled, grimy, and worn out.

Ralph had arrived at Bill's, lights flashing, siren blaring. Bill nipped the "emergency" thing in the bud so now Ralph drove slowly while the walkie-talkie in the front seat squawked and Bill spoke with Suki. Ralph was due a personal conversation with the chief as well, regarding the supposed vagrant who was now lying dead in the morgue.

The day was sunny, the temperature hitting mid-thirties, promising the possibility of melting snow. Ralph stopped for a red light, and I watched a German Shepard harnessed to a sled pull a little boy through a front yard. They hit a snow embankment, toppled over, and the kid jumped up and hugged the dog. To be that resilient…and energetic. I yawned.

"…and call the mayor's office. Ask them about salting roads in the north end of town. We got complaints this weekend." Bill paused and listened as Suki talked. "Copy that. 10-4."

"Chief, would you like me to stop at Coffee Heaven?" Ralph asked hopefully.

Bill cut his eyes in Ralph's direction. "Coffee can wait. Let's get Dodie home."

Ralph swung right on Fairfield and left on Ames and pulled into my driveway. I hopped out and waited as Bill lowered his window. I could see he hesitated saying anything with Ralph all eagle eyes and ears two feet away. "So…uh…thanks. I'll…uh…"

"Yep. Copy that," I quipped. I picked my way cautiously through the sloppy ice and snow that covered my walkway.

As the cruiser backed out of my driveway, I let myself into the house, unzipped my boots, stripped off the pant suit, and flung myself into the shower. The steam and hot water streamed off my shoulders and back, soothing every muscle while flushing away the night's grunge. I would have killed for a quick nap, but the day was moving fast and I wanted to get to the Windjammer to manage the lunch crowd. I blew my hair dry, noticing that I was due for a trim at Snippets—my bangs were into my eyes. My Irish knit sweater and skinny black jeans would have to do today; my schedule called for functional.

With the streets mostly cleared of snow and ice, the population of Etonville was out in droves, cars creeping along, braking when someone made an unexpected left turn, beeping at each other. Etonville was impatient and feeling its oats. I popped into Lacy's Market to pick up some cayenne pepper for Henry's soup today.

I was perusing the shelves when I heard a grouchy, reproachful voice behind me. "So the chief broke his leg last night."

The accuser was Mrs. Everly who worked frozen foods. Our paths had crossed briefly last year when her tenant, my good friend Jerome, was murdered and I needed to do a little snooping around her upstairs. "Hello." I tried to smile. "Not his leg, his ankle."

"Huhn. He still can't walk on it." She waited for me to prove her wrong.

I guessed I was to blame. I nodded and scooted off. The rumor mill in Etonville had already begun to grind and it looked like I was going to be today's grist. I had enough time to buy a caramel macchiato from Coffee Heaven before reporting to the Windjammer.

The diner was bursting at its seams. At the carry-out line, folks on their way to work jostled regulars who usually sat at the counter. There were three topics of conversation: the crime wave in Etonville, Bill's broken ankle, and the crime wave in Etonville. As I joined the carry-out line, I heard:

"…he died from inhaling paint fumes. The set was still wet, you know."

It sounded like a Banger sisters' theory.

"Really? I heard he was robbing the box office."

Again, not true.

"…three murders in one year."

Sadly true.

"Hi, Dodie," waitress Jocelyn said.

"Wow, lot of traffic in here today."

"The Donut Hole down on the highway closed. The pipes froze overnight and flooded the place. We're getting their business. Everybody wants to talk about that man on the ELT stage. Did you see him?" she asked and leaned over the cash register, eager for any tidbit of information.

"Well, I did. Kind of. I mean, he was hidden by the turntable divider." All of which was also true.

Jocelyn tsked. "Edna told me that turntable was nothing but trouble."

While I waited at the counter for my takeout container, I scanned the front page of the *Etonville Standard*. The headline for a follow-up story cleverly blared: STRANGER DIES IN *ETON TOWN*. They'd included a quote from the Medical Examiner: "...victim stabbed in aorta and bled out..." Below the fold was a brief mention of Bill's misadventures in New York.

Jocelyn prepped my drink, peering at me over the espresso machine. "So I hear the chief got pushed into the street. You gotta be careful in the city."

I looked up. "What? No! He stepped off the sidewalk and—"

"The last time I was in New York someone pushed me. The street was real crowded because of a parade and they'd closed the block off," she said.

"Well, no one touched him except me." Jocelyn smiled. I realized how that sounded. "What I mean is—"

"Next time you two need to go to some place safer." She handed me a full cup and a lid.

I gave up, took my drink, and smiled my thanks.

"Got to run." Jocelyn waved and moved on to the rest of her impatient crowd.

* * *

Benny was already wiping down the bar and restocking the red wine when I let myself into the Windjammer. "Hey, it's Nurse Nancy," he cackled.

"Not you too! Etonville must be over-the-top this morning."

"Well, you did rescue its chief of police. Or else you stomped on his foot and broke it," he said slyly. "Depending on who you talk to."

"So there's two sets of rumors swirling." I hung up my coat. "Henry here?"

Benny pointed in the direction of the kitchen. "He's agonizing over his pizza special for today."

I had convinced Henry a month ago that a nice wintertime lunch special would be piping hot pizza. And to seal the deal, we'd serve several different varieties during our pizza week: stuffed pizza with mozzarella, tomato, and basil; taco pizza with refried beans, salsa, and seasoned beef; and veggie pizza with tons of olives, roasted red peppers, and arugula.

In theory it was a great idea. In practice the palates of Etonville needed more diversity during the week. So Henry was offering his homemade soups as an alternative. Today's specials were vegetarian pizza and cream of mushroom soup.

Since pizza week was my idea, I'd probably never hear the end of it.

The dining room was humming by noon as the town crowded into the Windjammer, more eager for gossip than the pizza and soup. Bill was on everyone's mind.

Edna, picking up lunch for the police department, waited by the cash register for her takeout order. "We had an 11-24 down on the highway this morning."

As dispatcher for the department, Edna knew her police codes backwards and forwards and loved to trot them out for us civilians. "Yeah?" I said and rang up her food.

"Abandoned vehicle in a snowbank."

"Guess it's that time of the year."

"The chief wanted to take it, but with his ankle, Ralph's going to have to step up." She gave me a look. "No pun intended."

"I'm sure he's up to the job."

"Dodie, been meaning to ask you. When you were in New York, why was the chief chasing that couple on the street anyway?"

I wanted to scream, but then everybody in the restaurant would gawk at me even more meaningfully than they were now. "Here's your order, Edna. Have a good day." My face was beginning to ache from holding my tongue.

"10-4," she said.

I saw the Banger sisters wave to me from their table in the corner. I groaned inwardly, gave them a "just a minute" signal, and sent Gillian to wait on the two dotty siblings. Then I escaped to the kitchen.

* * *

"Dodie! What a night you must have had and sleeping at Bill's—" Lola glanced around at a few occupied tables in the restaurant and caught herself. "The emergency room must have been exhausting." She lowered her voice. "Sorry about that. I know how everyone talks in this town."

"Hey, you look done in too," I said.

Lola sighed. "I was in bed last night when Walter called in the middle of an anxiety attack."

"He's really shook up over the show. I get that—"

"Not just the show. The whole ELT. He said he's resigning as director and washing his hands of the whole thing. I tried to talk him down off the ledge, but he was adamant. He's sending a resignation letter to the board," Lola said.

That's all the theater needed right now. Walter wasn't my favorite person, but he had kept the theater running for many years and usually his arrogance was offset by his neediness. But when you added frenzy to the mix, he was a recipe for disaster. "Maybe he needs to have the day to chill and rethink things."

"So how are you holding up?" Lola asked as she nibbled on a slice of pizza.

"I'm fine. But tired of fending off Etonville's ridiculous belief that I am somehow responsible for Bill stepping off the curb and breaking his ankle."

"How was the dinner before the accident?" Lola asked softly.

"To die for. Rondelay—"

"Oooh, I love that place," Lola said.

"The ambience, the food, the wine. Everything was going so well. And then his ankle."

"At least you spent the night together," she teased.

"With him snoring in the guest room and me on the sofa."

The two of us started to giggle. Benny deposited two cups of coffee on the table and leaned over the back of the booth. "Is it true the chief's hiring some more help until his foot heals?"

"Who said that?" Lola asked.

Benny shrugged. "Word has it that with this murder, Officer Shung will take over the department and the chief has someone else to help head up the investigation."

I hadn't heard any of this. "Ralph? I doubt that."

Benny chuckled. "Game on for the Etonville PD."

I promised Lola I'd let her know if I heard anything that might result in the theater re-opening. Then I texted Bill to see how he was coping, with his ankle and the scuttlebutt, but got no response.

8

A howling wind and a steady tap-tap-tap on my bedroom window forced my eyes open at seven a.m. Freezing rain outside. I burrowed farther into the blanket, debating how badly I wanted my morning coffee, the end of a dream still haunting me. A young girl clawing her way up the sheer face of a rock cliff, then waving furiously at me, as she leaned back against nothing and floated to the ground. It was disturbing. All the more so because I realized the girl was Sally.

Sally! I hopped out of bed and seized my cell. Finally, a reply to my text: *Meet me?* I hesitated for only a fraction of a second before I repeated: *Where are u?* She answered with an address in Creston and I agreed to be there at three thirty this afternoon; I would still be back in time to release Benny before the dinner rush. Then she responded: *Don't tell police yet PLEASE.*

As I showered and dressed, I revisited the wisdom of my decision to meet Sally and to keep our meeting secret for the time being. After today's meet-up, whether she liked it or not, I had to let Bill know about her reaction to seeing the man Sunday. We had a history, Bill and I, of jockeying positions regarding my participation in previous murder investigations. He was a *tad* sensitive about my tendency to, as he said, play lone wolf and leave him out of things. I just assumed I was being proactive.

By the time I had my second cup of coffee in hand, my cell rang. I checked the caller ID. "Hey. How's the ankle this morning?"

"A pain in the neck," Bill grumped.

"Sorry."

I could hear the smile coming, the mouth ticking upward. "But the dinner was worth it."

"Yes! I can still taste the oyster chowder and foie gras."

"So I'm off the hook for missing Valentine's Day," he said.

"Absolutely." I laughed.

His tone shifted. "I'd like to talk with you this morning."

His voice was low, intense. I imagined a warm, intimate moment between us. I forgave him every missed date these last months and even—

"Because I have some news." He was all business.

"Well…okay."

"I'm getting some assistance with the investigation since I'm, well, sort of moving slowly."

Sort of? "That sounds like a good idea."

"Yeah. I'm not thrilled, but I don't have the mobility to get out and about."

I had a vision of another Ralph on board: donut breaks, crowd control, rescuing Mrs. Parker's cat, Missy, from wherever. Anything else was probably punching above Ralph's weight class.

"And I'd like you to talk with him. Tell him what you told me about Sally Oldfield, maybe fill him in on the theater," Bill said.

Maybe the officer was an old guy nearing retirement, like one of those TV detectives who got burnt out from thirty years on the force—

"We'll meet at the theater. How's nine? I have Lola opening up."

"I'll be there."

* * *

Lola was waiting for me in the lobby of the theater, nervously fingering her keys as if they were a set of worry beads.

"Dodie?" Bill stuck his head into the lobby. "Archibald is here. Let's join him onstage."

Archibald…definitely old school. Bill held the door for me as I squeezed Lola's hand and gave her an encouraging smile. We made our way down the aisle, Bill plodding, crutch, step, crutch, step, while I stayed a pace behind.

"Retell your whole story, okay?"

"Sure. So where is Columbo?" I joked.

"Who?" Bill was focused on his crutches.

"You know, that police lieutenant on television? My dad loved him, watched all the reruns. Columbo always wore the same rumpled rain coat and smoked a cigar and—"

"Archibald is not a police lieutenant."

We'd reached the stage and Bill started his ascent up the stairs.

"What is he? A detective?" I asked.

"Private investigator," he said.

The stage was brightly lit, yellow crime scene tape encircling the entire turntable. A white outline marked the spot where the body was found. I stepped closer to the platform to study the location of the murder.

"Hello." The voice was unfamiliar but velvety smooth.

I whirled around. *Whoa.* He was no Colombo. Tall and slender, with a day's worth of black stubble, hair that skimmed his collar, penetrating brown eyes. He wore a leather jacket and scuffed cowboy boots. "Dodie O'Dell." I took his offered hand. It was cool and surprisingly soft.

"Archibald. Means truly brave." He looked me up and down. "Hmm…I'd guess Irish on both sides."

"Good guess. And you?"

"The Archibald is from my maternal Scottish grandfather. The Alvarez from my old man. And yeah I paid for my name with some pretty gruesome playground brawls." His eyes crinkled in a warm grin.

Yowza. I grinned back. Charming.

Bill cleared his throat. "Archibald would like to review your statement."

Archibald stuffed his hands in his back pockets, his eyes ending up on me again. "So why don't you tell me what you saw."

"Okay. Well, I was in the women's dressing room changing my clothes—"

"Are you in the play?" he asked politely.

"No, no. I was running the intermission concessions and we all planned to dress in the period since we were serving colonial—"

"Dodie…" Bill steered me back on course.

"Right. So I came out here and stopped when I heard a noise."

Archibald listened to my story, prompting me when he needed more information or interrupting me with an apology when he had a question. I led him through the incident—Sally's gasping, then her sudden appearance, her fixation on her hands before she ran off, and, finally, my finding the man with a knife stuck in his chest. "That's about it."

Bill stood silently resting on his crutches.

Archibald nodded a few times, walked around the crime scene. "Was it a sold-out house?"

"Excuse me?" I asked.

"Were there any seats available?" he asked.

"Actually, they'd only sold half the house." What did ticket sales have to do with the murder?

"Too bad. So much effort goes into getting a show on its feet."

"True." I looked over at Bill whose expression was blank, no opinion one way or the other.

"Did you know Sally Oldfield well?" Archibald asked.

Did I? "Not really. I met her when she came to town last month. I suggested she audition for *Eton Town* since she'd done some acting in high school."

Archibald squatted down and viewed the location where the dead man was found. Then he abruptly stood up. "I think that's it here. We'll be in touch if we need to speak with you again," he said to me.

"Dodie, can you stop by the station at three? Suki will have your statement ready for a signature," Bill said.

He knew I usually took my break then. I hesitated. I'd agreed to meet Sally at three thirty in Creston and meeting Bill would be cutting it close.

"Something the matter?" he asked.

"Uh, no. I'll be there."

I said good-bye to Archibald, who seemed engrossed in the turntable, but still courteous and friendly, and made my way to the theater office. Lola was concentrating on an Excel spreadsheet on her laptop and didn't hear me walk in. I watched her brow pucker as she scrutinized the screen. "Can I help?" Business management had been my college major and I had mastered the principles of finance and accounting before I had turned my hand to the restaurant game.

Lola looked up. "I'm trying to see what kind of hole this show blew in the theater budget. If we can't open it, we might have to cancel the spring musical."

"It's that bad?"

"Yes. No income from *Eton Town* might mean no more theater until we do our summer fundraiser."

That is desperate. "I wish there was something I could do. Besides supply the intermission desserts."

Lola swiveled in her office chair and stared at me.

"What?" I asked.

"Dodie, you know I think the world of Bill and everything he's done for Etonville," Lola said.

"Well, sure. I think the whole town appreciates him. He has his own place on the ego wall in the Municipal Building. There's the *Etonville Standard* article on his solving Jerome's murder and the photo display of his youth football team."

"And having another detective—" she continued.

"Private investigator—"

"—on the case will certainly help the situation now that Bill is incapacitated," Lola added hurriedly.

"Archibald Alvarez," I said mock seriously. "Quite the sexy guy, looks like a real bad boy but has the voice of a Latin lover. If I wasn't already spoken for...at least I think I'm spoken for—"

"Dodie. You have to do something!" Lola slammed the lid of her laptop.

"Like what?"

"You need to find out who killed that man so we can open our show and get an audience and make some money and save the theater. And you have to do it before the reviewer from the *Star-Ledger* leaves on his vacation," she said urgently.

"What? Pump the brakes. I'm not a cop or detective. I'm only—"

"Who discovered Jerome's killer?"

"Well, it was a joint effort—"

"And who discovered how Antonio died?"

Lola was giving me far too much credit. Wasn't she?

"Dodie, you know what I mean. You see things that everybody else misses. And you don't let go. You're like a puppy with a bone."

Not sure I liked that image.

"Lola, I want to see the theater saved," I said gently. "But there are now two guys on the case, three if you count Suki."

She moaned. "I don't know what we're going to do."

* * *

I blew out cold air, watching my breath form puffs of carbon dioxide. Poor Lola. The theater's future was a heavy weight for her to lift alone. Walter should have been sharing the load, but his ego was having a pity party and Lola had no intention of attending. I knew that I'd been instrumental in solving the two previous murders, but I'd more or less fallen into the investigations, trying to honor a friend, trying to save the Windjammer. Lola was suggesting I "fall" into the investigation one more time—to save the theater. What could I do that Bill couldn't? Or Archibald, for that matter.

I schlepped to the Windjammer, unlocked the door, and put on the coffee. I could hear activity in the kitchen. Henry already working on stock for his homemade chicken noodle soup. Better to let him work out his usual morning crotchetiness alone. In my back booth, I opened my laptop and eyed my own spreadsheet: the weekend's staffing schedule. I made a few adjustments, now that the show wasn't running and I wouldn't have to be present for intermission duty, wrote a few notes to myself on an inventory sheet, and doodled in the margins of the paper.

I couldn't get Lola's plea for my help out of mind. She'd been flattering when she suggested that my detection skills were responsible for solving the recent murders in Etonville. But was it more than flattery? Was she right to think I could do more than the Etonville Police Department? There were so many unanswered questions...who was the dead man, why was he in the theater, what was his relationship to Sally, and most importantly, what role did Sally play in his death?

Already my little hairs were frolicking. And what about Archibald Alvarez? What was his story? Why had Bill called in a private investigator? Had he worked with him before?

I closed the spreadsheet and typed the PI's name into my search engine. Surprisingly, there were several pages of Archibald Alvarezes from around the country. I skimmed the first page and saw a link for a Patrolman Archibald Alvarez who had been part of an undercover drug detail in Trenton. The story featured an interview with the cop about his clandestine work for the state police. He was no longer working in that capacity, the article indicated. I scanned a few other links that referred to his time with law enforcement in Texas and Pennsylvania. But the entry that caught my eye appeared on page three. The link read "Hottest Male Models of 2002." I clicked on the site and a series of photos popped up. *Yikes!*

"Hi."

I flinched. I'd been so engrossed in beautiful bodies I'd missed Benny's entrance into the restaurant. I shut my laptop.

"Surfing unsavory sites?" he asked.

"Yeah, right," I said and forced a laugh. I could feel heat crawl up my face.

Benny wrapped himself in an apron. "Shame about that *Star-Ledger* reviewer. Everybody says this was a once-in-a-lifetime for the ELT."

"I suppose so," I said absentmindedly.

"What?"

"I was thinking maybe there's a way the show can go on," I said.

"How?" he asked.

"I don't know. Maybe another theater?"

"Like at the high school?" he said.

Etonville High had a cafetorium—combo cafeteria and auditorium. It housed guest speaker events, graduation, and dances, as well as noonday food fights. "Not the best venue."

Benny rinsed a few glasses left in the bar sink from last evening. "There's always the theater in Creston."

"The Players? Walter has had a feud with them for the last year. He'd never stoop to begging for space from them. Anyway, I think they have a dance concert this weekend. I saw it advertised in the *Etonville Standard*."

"That means the only solution is finding out whodunit, wrapping it up, and getting Etonville back on the boards." Benny dried his hands on a towel, then flipped it over one shoulder.

I stared at him. Out of the mouths of bartenders...

9

Lunch was a steady barrage of patrons chewing over the murder and the latest Etonville gossip as well as Henry's BLT-with-roasted-tomatoes-and-avocado special. I had convinced him to perk up the menu and maybe move half a star closer to his nemesis La Famiglia. The jury was still out.

"Henry is getting a little ahead of himself," pouted a Banger sister. "I like the regular BLT."

"Me too. I like my tomatoes cold and hard, not hot and soft," said the other, crossing her fleshy arms.

I could have commented, but the Windjammer was rated PG. "Henry likes to try new recipes. Give a little zing to his specials," I said.

The sisters exchanged looks. "We get enough zing at the theater. At least we did until it shut down," said the first one.

"Yeah, so unfortunate," I said.

"I'll tell you what's unfortunate. Having that man killed by the turntable. I warned Walter but no one listens to us." The other sister nodded.

For good reason. "It wasn't the turntable. It was a knife." I smiled through gritted teeth. "Enjoy your lunch." I was getting accustomed to the quirky ways of Etonville, but every town crisis tended to release its inner-daffy.

"Look who the cat dragged in," Benny muttered from a table behind me as he set down a tray of drinks.

I nudged waitress Gillian to get off Instagram and checked the entrance. It was Walter looking morose and bedraggled, a muffler wound around his neck, his cheeks above his brown-gray beard cherry red. He stomped his feet. Was he removing ice from his boots or having a temper tantrum? Customers eyed him surreptitiously, no one wanting to stare too long, everyone a little uncomfortable witnessing Walter in his miserable state. I crossed the distance between us.

"Walter. Let's get you a seat." Despite my general uneasiness with the former artistic director, I was the Windjammer's manager and had to suck it up. I took his elbow and steered him to a booth. "It's been a while since we've seen you in here." Truth be told, I couldn't remember the last time Walter Zeitzman had darkened the doorway of the Windjammer.

He twisted his head and glared at me. "Coffee Heaven was full and La Famiglia is closed for lunch today."

"Right. So...I'll get a server."

"You don't like me, do you?" he asked.

He caught me off guard. It wasn't a question, more an assertion of fact. "Well...I...uh..."

"You think I've mismanaged the theater."

I couldn't agree more. "Not exactly." I tried to sidestep his allegation and held out a menu. "Today's special is a tasty BLT with—"

"You and everyone else around Etonville will be sorry when they don't have Walter to kick around anymore." He plucked the menu from my hand.

Not what did that mean? Could Penny have been right about his tri-polar manic-depression?

I lowered my voice. "Look, we all know you and Lola are under a ton of pressure with the show not opening and the theater's future up in the air. But I'm sure everything will—"

"—not work out," he grumped and studied the menu insert.

I debated, then decided no guts no glory. "Walter, can I give you a piece of advice?" Before he could answer and refuse, I dove into the breach between us. "If you were a little bit..." Nicer? Less of a jackass? "...more sensitive to people, maybe they wouldn't want to 'kick you around.'"

"Is that right? That's rich coming from you," he said.

"And that means?" I asked.

"You've been a pain in the ELT butt since you came to town. Sticking your nose in theater business, pretending you know something about police procedures...offering 'advice' where it is neither wanted nor helpful!"

Metaphorical steam billowed out of my nostrils and my voice might have inched up a few degrees. "Lola appreciates my advice." Ears pricked up all around us, Benny's eyes growing larger at the bar. "And as for sticking my nose—"

Saved by a booming crash from the kitchen. Heads swiveled from me to the swinging door into Henry's inner sanctum. I turned on my heel and walked—when I wanted to run—to the kitchen, smiling reassuringly at customers on the way.

"What's going on in here?" I asked, looking first at Henry, then at Enrico. Both were frozen, staring dumbfounded at our largest pot upside down on the tile floor. The contents were splashed in a four-foot radius and pieces of chicken and noodles had plopped on both Henry's and Enrico's feet. "Never mind. Henry, let's just keep the lunch service going. Enrico, could you let Gillian know we're out of soup? I'll get a mop."

Geez.

Forty-five minutes later, the kitchen was presentable, lunch was winding down, and Walter had departed the restaurant. I breathed a momentary sigh of relief. Because although the skirmish had ended, the next time I came face-to-face with him, it might turn into an all-out war. I must have been still fuming when Benny handed me a seltzer in my back booth.

"Tough day," he said.

"Walter gets under my skin."

"I'd say." He glinted at me.

I couldn't help it. I glinted back.

* * *

By three I was antsy to leave, first to stop by the Municipal Building, and then to get on the road and head to Creston for my meeting with Sally. I checked my watch. "Benny, I'll be back in a couple of hours, okay? You can take off then."

"Sure thing. And stay away from Walter," he added.

I had no intention of running into Walter, purposely or accidentally. I huddled inside my down jacket, breathing into my scarf, and hurried to my Metro. It balked at having to wake up and warm up, and the engine rattled for a good minute before I could shift into Drive and cruise down Main Street.

I found the last empty parking spot in front of the police station next to the space reserved for the chief. It was occupied. I peeked in my rearview mirror, ran my fingers through my waves, and dabbed on a touch of lipstick. Maybe I'd have a moment alone with Bill.

A rap on the window interrupted my reverie. Archibald Alvarez blew on his gloveless hands before he stuffed them in his pockets. The wind propelled a length of his dark hair over his face. He motioned for me to wind down the window.

"Hello, Mr. Alvarez," I said politely.

"Archibald."

For a brief moment his image in the "Hottest Male Models" article flashed on my mental monitor: his shirt open to his waist, his abs a six-pack that rippled their way through the laptop screen.

"Mind if I ask you a question?" he said.

"Of course not." I opened the car door and he stepped aside.

"Just wondering if you knew anything about Sally Oldfield's background. Where she's from, what she does outside the Etonville Little Theatre. Something you might have forgotten to mention."

I shrugged. "I told you and Chief Thompson everything I know. She came to Etonville from Boston about a month ago."

He squinted at me as if seeing right through my white lie. Something about the tone of Sally's texts prevented me from saying any more until I saw her.

We walked into the Municipal Building, Archibald pausing at the town's ego wall to study Etonville's triumphs on the playing fields and in the law enforcement arena. His gaze finally came to rest on the photo of Bill from the *Etonville Standard*. He was a hero for solving the murder of Jerome Angleton. "Small town life."

I bristled in defense of Etonville. As a home it had its eccentricities, but it was *my* eccentric home. "It grows on you." I moved away and immediately headed down the right hallway to the police department where Edna was on dispatch. Archibald followed, nodded at us, and continued on to Bill's office.

Edna murmured, "He reminds me of one of those TV cops. Too handsome for their own good."

I agreed.

Her switchboard lit up and the headset crackled. Edna raised a finger, telling me to hold on. "Ralph, the chief's been looking for you." She paused. "Well, you better get a move on. There's a 586 by the Shop N Go and a 10-60 at the Parkers'. That's right. Mrs. Parker has been calling here every five minutes, and the chief doesn't have time to unlock her door."

I snickered softly. Mrs. Parker had become the bane of Bill's existence.

"10-4." Edna signed off and removed her headset. "Illegal parking and Mrs. Parker lost her keys." She leaned out the dispatch window. "Ralph's got his nose out of joint. He thought with the chief on crutches, he'd be second-in-command after Suki. But then Archibald came on board." She gave me a knowing look. "A little professional jealousy if you ask me," she whispered, then asked hopefully, "Any word on whether the show might open next week? Everybody's pretty tight-lipped around here."

"Nothing yet," I said and crossed my fingers.

Her switchboard lit up again and I waved good-bye. I moved on, stopping at Suki Shung's desk in the outer office. "The chief's expecting me. Need to sign my statement."

Suki buzzed Bill's inner sanctum. "You can go in."

I smiled my thanks, and Suki tilted her head and nodded. It was the closest she'd probably ever come to acknowledging our shared near-death experience last fall at the hands of a couple of ruthless killers.

I could hear muffled voices in Bill's office and knocked gently.

"Enter."

I stood in the doorway, taking in the scene: Bill sat at his desk, shirt sleeves rolled up to his elbows, his broken ankle propped up on a short stool. Archibald slouched in the chair opposite the desk, his tailbone about to slip off the seat, legs stretched out in front of him. If I didn't know better, I'd have said they were two buddies comparing fantasy football scores.

"Hi," Bill said and lifted his foot off the stool.

Archibald stood up, offered his chair to me, and folded his tall frame into a small settee in the corner.

"We were discussing the security at the theater. How easy it might be for someone to wander in," Bill said.

Walter had had the whole theater rekeyed last October when it became apparent that uninvited guests could enter and roam around at will. "Most of the time everyone's pretty careful about locking up. But when the ELT gets close to an opening, there's last-minute work and rehearsals, people in and out at all hours." I shrugged. "I don't think the lobby door was locked that afternoon. The victim *could* have wandered in."

Archibald squinted at me. "What time were you here again?"

"I came about four thirty and prepared the concessions in the lobby, then I went backstage to change about five or so."

"And the theater was empty when you arrived?" Bill asked.

"Yes. I think it was empty most of the afternoon," I answered.

Archibald crossed his arms and allowed his head to slump forward on his chest. Had he fallen asleep? Finally, he spoke. "So...there were a few free hours when someone could have slipped in there and committed the crime."

"I guess so."

Bill was watching Archibald. "That fits with the medical examiner's preliminary report. Time of death within a couple of hours of being discovered."

Archibald's head snapped up. He shot a look at Bill, then at me. I'd been around the theater long enough to earn the right to indulge in lingo. Walter harped on subtext constantly and Archibald's subtext was plainly written on his face: Why are you revealing facts of a homicide investigation to a civilian? What's the story?

Bill must have read Archibald's face too. "Dodie has worked with me previously. She has good instincts."

Yahoo! Bill was finally recognizing my ability to—

"Really?" Archibald wasn't buying it.

"Yeah," Bill said dryly, pulling a sheet of paper out of a file and pushing it across his desk to me. "Read this over and then I'll need your signature."

I took the paper, scanned the statement, and nodded. "Looks fine." As I scribbled my name, I could feel Archibald's eyes perforate the back of my neck. I opened my mouth. "What kind of knife was it?" I might have been pushing my luck.

Bill raised a hand. "We can't talk about—"

"A hunting knife," Archibald said, eyeing me dispassionately. "Foldable. Five-inch blade. Well-worn handle with the initials GW. Unidentifiable prints."

Bill sat up, bouncing his cast onto the stool again. "I don't think you need to go into specifics."

"You said you trusted her." Archibald smiled.

Bill squirmed uncomfortably like a worm on a fish hook.

I pressed my advantage. "That would fit the victim."

"How so?" Archibald asked.

"You know, the camouflage hunting jacket and trapper hat," I said.

"Very observant." Archibald stared right through me.

Of course, I'd had the advantage of seeing him earlier this week dressed in the same clothing. "Have you identified him?"

"Okay, that's enough for now." Bill replaced my statement in the file. "We'll talk later if there's more we need to ask you."

Rather a hasty dismissal from the man who, only recently, was snoring in his bedroom while I dozed on his couch after sitting two hours in the emergency room.

Archibald stood, ran a hand through his longish hair, and stretched, straining the seams of his leather jacket. "Do you know where we can find this Sally Oldfield? She seems to be our prime suspect at the moment."

Prime suspect? Not a person of interest? This was moving quickly and not in Sally's favor. "She has a room in town. Has Penny delivered contact information on the cast?" I asked.

"On its way," Bill said.

"Me too. Got to get on my way." I grabbed my bag, smiled innocently at the two of them, and beat it out of the Municipal Building, waving to Edna as I sprinted past.

* * *

I put the address Sally had texted me into my cell phone GPS and glanced nervously at my watch. I had agreed to meet her at three thirty. It was already three forty-five and I still had a twenty-minute trip to Creston. I prayed she hadn't given up on me. I texted her that I was running late and zoomed onto State Route 53, one eye on the road, one on my clock, my mind sorting through a clutter of issues. What exactly did Sally know about the hunter's death? She'd looked terrified when she'd darted out of the theater; understandable given the circumstances. One thing was certain. Sally knew that man, which only made her guilt more possible. But what would she have been doing in the theater that afternoon? Earlier in the week she'd agreed to help me prepare the hot drinks for the opening. But when she'd disappeared after the dress rehearsal without any explanation, I thought that she'd abandoned me.

Then there was Archibald Alvarez, buff-model-turned-PI, in an awful hurry to convict Sally of a crime for which there were too many loose ends. And what about Bill? Did he have an opinion on Sally's guilt or innocence? He was excellent at keeping his cards close to his chest.

Traffic was light—the rush hour getting underway—and I reached the Creston exit at five minutes after four, when I immediately slowed down to the town speed limit. Genie, my GPS, led me down the main drag until I passed the Creston Police Department and then had me turn right on South Central Street for a couple of miles. It was new territory for me. Not the high end of the town that had fallen victim to a series of burglaries last fall, or the bustling shopping district, which I had occasion to frequent now and then, but a residential area that was dingy and discolored. Dull gray houses with peeling paint, patches of dirt for front yards, worn-out rusted autos parked in gravel driveways. Altogether a little depressing.

"Destination is ahead on the left," said Genie.

29 South Central. A corner bodega. I eased my Metro to the curb, sliding up and over a small mound of ice, and turned off the engine. What was Sally doing in this neighborhood? Did she know someone living on the street? I checked my watch: four twenty. I was almost an hour late. Still, she had texted me, urgently pleading for me to come.

I studied the shop, a brown brick building with a colorful awning and a yellow facing that advertised sandwiches, coffee, frozen desserts, and sodas. In a corner of the front window, an ATM sign was prominently displayed. Beneath the sign, gaffer's tape formed an X, probably covering a crack in the window. A bicycle rested against a newspaper stand.

Just then an elderly man exited the store, pausing on the sidewalk to turn his collar up and check a piece of paper in his hand. Maybe a lottery ticket. Two boys pushed past him and bounded into the grocery. Other than that, the area was deserted.

I locked my Metro and slowly crossed the street. I opened the front door and bells jingled, announcing my entrance. The two boys were now at the counter, jostling each other and counting out change for sodas. The clerk, a fortyish woman, stood at the cash register, one hand on her hip, blowing out air between pouty lips.

"Let's go," she said. "I don't have all day."

The boys ignored her and continued to search the contents of their pockets. She shifted her gaze from the kids, sizing me up and down, waiting for me to talk first.

"Excuse me. I'm wondering if you know a Sally Oldfield?"

"Who?"

"Sally—"

"Now look what you did!" she yelled.

The boys had knocked over a display of Slim Jims and the meat sticks tumbled into the lottery machine.

"Get out of here," she said, scooping up their coins and thrusting the soda cans at them.

The boys screamed with laughter, gathered their drinks, and fled out the door. Meanwhile, I had picked up a Snickers bar and Peanut M&Ms. I withdrew a five-dollar bill from my wallet and lay the candy and money on the counter. The clerk eyed me suspiciously—was it the candy or my unfamiliar face in the grocery?—and made change.

"So I was asking about a friend of mine. Sally Oldfield? I was supposed to meet her here."

"Don't know anybody by that name."

She turned her attention back to the newspaper she no doubt had been reading before the boys rudely interrupted her.

"That's so strange because she gave me this address. Brown hair, thin, pretty…"

"You a cop or something?" the clerk asked.

"Me? No! I'm looking for my friend. I was supposed to—"

"—meet her here. So you said." She took off her glasses. "We don't get many strangers in this neighborhood. I own this place and I know everybody who comes in here. I'd remember if a stranger walked in."

Like me. This was going nowhere, so I nodded my thanks and left. I imagined the woman watched me cross the street, climb into my Metro, and start the engine. The heater crackled and cold air spit out of the vent. I dialed it back and pulled away from the curb, frustrated, chilled to my bones, and worried. The sun had set while I was in the store and now the streets were dark, dull light leaking from curtained windows in unfriendly looking houses. Where was Sally and why had she led me on a goose chase?

10

I texted Sally to see where she was, reminding myself to check her Facebook page later for any clue to her hiding place, and Benny to let him know I was running late but was on my way. Benny texted back: *Call me.*

On the outskirts of Creston I drove into the parking lot of a convenience store and tapped on Benny's number. "What's up? I'll be there in a few minutes and then you can leave."

"You're not going to believe it, but we just got a reservation for thirteen for seven o'clock tonight," Benny said, wheezing.

"Great. You okay?"

"Yeah, I hauled three cases of wine from storage. I think I'd better stick around tonight," he said.

"Why? A Henry problem?" I asked.

"It's good news, bad news."

"Give me the good first. I need to fortify myself," I said.

"Henry is excited and panicked, and we had to postpone your Mardi Gras theme night. So no jambalaya and shrimp boil," Benny said.

I knew Henry was a little iffy on my Mardi Gras menu ideas. "What's the bad?"

"Henry is excited and panicked and going over-the-top with tonight's specials. He's been experimenting with roasted parsnip soup, coq au vin, and baked polenta."

"What?"

"Yeah, right?" Benny said.

"We talked about putting all three on the menu next month. Why the hurry tonight? Who is this group?"

"Are you ready? They had a reservation at La Famiglia, but it cancelled on them because the owner's father passed away suddenly and they closed down for the night," Benny said.

OMG. La Famiglia patrons.

"It's Mayor Bennet and a crowd from the Chamber of Commerce," Benny added.

The closest thing Etonville had to royalty. "I'm on my way."

I stepped on the gas pedal and my Metro, in total sympathy with the culinary emergency, leapt forward. Twenty minutes later I parked illegally by a fire plug two doors down from the Windjammer—no way the fire department would be making a run here tonight, right? I grasped my jacket around my midsection and picked my way carefully around patches of refreezing slush on the sidewalk.

The Windjammer was in a frenzy. Carmen and Gillian had already prepped the dining room and rearranged a few tables to form a longer banquet table in the middle of the room. Benny had the glossy wooden bar sparkling, the beer and soda taps shiny. I waved to them and headed straight for the kitchen. Henry was hunched over the soup pot, taste testing his latest creation.

"Henry, great news!" I said.

He straightened quickly, pulling his ladle out of the pot and flipping a few roasted parsnips onto the surface of the stove. His eyes bugged out, his face was shiny from the heat of the kitchen. Yep, excited and panicked. He had stars in his eyes—as in four stars from the *Etonville Standard.*

"You heard?" he asked.

"Sure did." The coq was resting on the center island surrounded by the vin and assorted ingredients. Enrico was focused on the rest of tonight's menu.

"Are you okay in here?" I asked him softly.

"Carmen will join us and I called my cousin," he said in a whisper.

"Quick thinking, Enrico." I gave him a thumbs-up.

"Maybe we get a review tonight?" Enrico stole a quick look at Henry who had his eyes closed as he inhaled the savory aroma of his soup.

I smiled. "Maybe." I fervently pleaded with the kitchen gods to prevent any possibility of the food critic from the *Etonville Standard* darkening the threshold of the Windjammer tonight.

At six thirty a faction from the theater—Abby, her husband Jim, Edna, Mildred minus Vernon, and Penny—arrived. I hustled them to a booth as far away from the Chamber of Commerce as possible. Might as well keep their craziness and ongoing theories on the murder victim contained. The potential for chaos was high.

* * *

Of course, I was wrong. Henry's specials were a big success and the mayor called him out of the kitchen to compliment his coq au vin. The Windjammer had bolstered its reputation this evening, I thought, as the group clothed themselves in winter weather togs, preparing to exit. The mayor, the last to leave, turned to nod at me as Bill appeared in the doorway. They exchanged a few clipped words before the town's chief administrator disappeared and Bill, after waving off his chauffeured squad car, clumped his way into the dining room.

I placed a menu on a table by the front window, but Bill indicated he'd prefer my back booth.

He deposited his crutches on the bench, wriggled out of his coat, and rubbed his hands together. "I'll have Henry's special."

"That's coq au vin and—"

"Whatever." He massaged his temples, eyes closed.

I put in his order and brought him a glass of cabernet. Bill was edgy, unusual for him. Among other character traits, he'd brought a levelheadedness to the chief of police position in Etonville. He'd maintained his composure, most of the time, regardless of the tough situations he'd encountered since his arrival a year ago. But his broken ankle wasn't helping.

"Rough one?" I asked.

"Mayor Bennet again. Every time there's a…predicament…"

"You mean a…murder?" I asked carefully.

"It's like the whole thing is my fault. I'm to blame the ELT had to cancel its show. I guess I'm responsible for Etonville missing a mention in the *Star-Ledger*," he grumbled.

"Having Archibald around should help move things along," I said.

Bill paused, his wine glass halfway to his mouth. "What do you think of him?"

"He seems…capable," I said, playing the diplomat.

"Ralph's capable," he said wryly.

Gillian brought a place setting and Bill's dinner. He thanked her and dug his fork into the chicken. "What do you really think?"

I decided to keep my discovery of his modelling days to myself. "Smart guy, but I'm not sure he trusts me. He's a friend of yours?"

"We were in the police academy together. Afterwards I went to Philly to work and Archibald went back to Texas. Then I heard he worked in Trenton and Pittsburgh. He ran into some trouble there and left the force.

Took up private investigation. We've been in touch off and on over the years." The left side of Bill's mouth curved upward. "He's good looking."

You should see him shirtless. "In a way. I don't think he wants to let me in on the details of the murder even though he described the knife to me. Which has now made it onto the front page." I withdrew a copy of this morning's *Etonville Standard* from my bag and set it on the table.

Bill chewed thoughtfully. "I read it. The only thing not there is the ID."

I creased the paper. "Do you have it?" I sipped my coffee, attempting to tamp down my curiosity.

"The victim's name is Gordon Weeks. No major priors, only a single run-in with the law years ago, but his fingerprints were in the federal database. Keep that to yourself," he warned. "We haven't found any connection to Etonville yet."

My heart did a little flip-flop. "Did he have a cell phone? Probably tell you a lot." I needed to know if he'd called Sally recently, but I didn't want to seem to be prying too much.

Bill shrugged. "No. Could have used a burner phone. Prepaid, disposable, no trace." His eyes narrowed. "Why do you ask? What's whirling in that brain of yours?"

"Nothing. Just wondering," I said.

"Speaking of cell phones, have any members of the ELT heard from Sally Oldfield?"

Strictly speaking, I was only an honorary member. "I don't know. Have you spoken with the cast?"

"Penny dropped off a contact sheet. Archibald is working his way through it."

"I understand you're interested in finding Sally, but it's hard to believe she's guilty of anything," I said.

"Running away from a murder scene covered in blood is one sure way to arouse suspicion. Archibald may be right," Bill said.

"Sally's the prime suspect?"

He nodded. "We've put out a picture and description to local departments in Creston and Bernridge. I'll be sending out an APB in the morning."

So soon? "Not for nothing but Sally's about five three, four at the most. Gordon Weeks was a big guy," I said earnestly.

"Maybe it was a crime of passion. Passion can make a person capable of unbelievable stuff." Bill watched me over the rim of his wine glass.

Wasn't that the truth.

He dove back into his entrée. "But why a seemingly nice young woman would be involved with a scruffy guy like Gordon Weeks is beyond me."

Me too.

* * *

I was the last person standing at the Windjammer. I'd mopped the floor
after Gillian and Carmen had cleaned tables, did an inventory check after
Henry and Enrico had wiped down the kitchen, high-fiving each other on
a successful evening, and tallied the deposit slip. The restaurant had done
well tonight, thanks in part to the misfortunes of La Famiglia's owner.

I turned out the lights, locked the front door, and pulled my jacket hood
over my head. It was ten degrees colder leaving the Windjammer than it
had been on my return from Creston seven hours ago. The sky was clear,
thankfully, which meant no snow tomorrow. I slipped into my Metro,
grateful that I hadn't gotten a ticket for parking by the fire plug, and noticed
that the interior was freezing. Had I left the passenger side window open?

I turned on the overhead dome light and inhaled sharply. The glass
was shattered, with a hole the size of a fist at the bottom of the pane. A
few shards covered the passenger seat and the floor. Where I'd left my
bag. Had someone stolen my wallet? My address book? Luckily, my cell
phone and keys were in my coat pocket. My heart boomeranged in my
chest as I searched for my credit cards and cash. All there. Why break into
my car and then leave fifty-six dollars and credit cards in my wallet? My
little hairs trembled. It wasn't only the wind blowing through my front
seat that set them off.

A tap on my driver's side window made me jump out of my skin. It was
Archibald Alvarez. "You scared me!" I yelped.

"Sorry," he said apologetically. "I was working late at the department
and on my way home when I saw a car parked by the fire hydrant. Not a
safe thing in this weather. Thought I should investigate." He shuddered
and swiped his hair off his face. "Freezing out here." He bent down and
looked into my Metro. "Is that a broken window?"

Before I could say 911, Archibald had gotten my story, collected the
broken glass, and insisted on following me home.

"I'm really fine," I said as he shut my door.

"No sense taking any chances. Be sure to report this in the morning."
He touched my shoulder. "And don't leave your purse in the car."

Yowza. Despite the fact that I was freaked out, I couldn't help noticing that
his voice could melt rock. I had to admit it: He was easy on the eyes and ears.

I pulled out of my illegal space and his automobile—a black, late model
Ford—trailed me down Main and over Fairfield until I turned into my

driveway on Ames. He stopped long enough to see me enter my house and then he drove off.

The clock on my kitchen wall said twelve thirty; time for me to be in bed since I had a big day planned for tomorrow: First a trip to my service station to see about a window repair; and then a little snooping that included visits to Sally's residence, her place of work, and a call to my brother, Andy, to see what he knew about Sally.

I should have been wiped out but my eyes were wide open, my mind racing, the image of my broken car window popping up. What was the break-in all about? What did the intruder want? I wasn't in the mood for Cindy Collins's latest mystery novel—*Murder Came Calling*—and there was nothing on late-night television that held my interest. I pulled the *Etonville Standard* out of my bag and skimmed the article on the ELT murder. If there truly was no such thing as bad publicity, Walter should have been ecstatic to see the theater mentioned. A statement by Police Chief William Thompson indicated that his office was working on the identity of the victim. But there was no reference to Sally or Archibald Alvarez joining the force temporarily. The *Standard* would be sniffing around the Municipal Building until it had Weeks's name.

I was about to toss the paper into my recycling pile when a small article on the bottom half of page one caught my eye. The Etonville public works department had towed a vehicle with a Massachusetts license plate that had skidded off the access road by State Route 53, hit a phone pole, and wasn't drivable. Why did that trigger a déjà vu? Sally had lived in Boston... could it have been her car?

My cell binged. I checked the text. It was Sally: *Did you come? Meet me there tmr?*

No way was I going to traipse back to the bodega in Creston only to be stood up again and reminded by the owner that she knew everyone who frequented her store and blah blah blah. I typed in: *Sorry I was late. Ok tmr. But not there. Bernridge?*

I could understand why Sally would want to avoid Etonville; Bernridge was a safer place and close by. There was no return text from her so I went to bed, my brain still whirling. What if someone had been lying in wait to attack me? Still in the area watching me? What if Archibald had not appeared when he did...?

* * *

I sat in my Metro, a steady, chill wind hurling my hair to and fro. I thrust my arm through the shattered passenger window, scraping my jacket sleeve, and Archibald twisted my hand. He started to pull me closer. "Wait!" I screamed, "I can't fit through that hole!" He laughed charmingly, my face smacking the glass, and I continued to yell, "No!" Archibald disappeared, and I dissolved into thin air. My eyes shot open, my chest pounding. Another one of my alarming dreams...

I dressed for warmth in a wool sweater and slacks since the weather app on my cell flashed twenty degrees. I yanked on my boots, avoided my coffee machine, and tramped outside, ready to take on the morning's icy air. Planting myself on the plastic seat cover of my Metro was like sitting in an icebox. The engine ground, sluggish, as if resentful that it had to be working in this weather. "Sorry," I mumbled and guided the car out of my driveway.

I stopped at Timothy's Timely Service, a longtime Etonville landmark on the periphery of town and a stone's throw away from Route 53. They prided themselves on quick turnaround.

Timothy inspected the hole in my window and let out a low whistle. "Looks like someone took a crowbar to this." He scratched a straggly gray beard and tugged on his ball cap.

"How long to replace the window?" I asked, mentally calculating the difference between my deductible and the cost of replacement.

Timothy stuck his hands in his down vest pockets. "Got to check with Junior, but it'll likely take a coupla days. Got to remove the door panel and clear out the remainder of the window. Then insert a new one and test the mechanism." He looked off toward the garage. "I'd say the beginning of next week."

Not very timely. "I didn't expect to be without the car that long."

"Not to worry. Junior can take care of you. We got a coupla loaners for times like this."

I negotiated with Timothy Jr. for a used Hyundai that had a "coupla" dents in the front bumper, crickets in the motor when I cranked the engine, and the lingering odor of cigarette smoke. But it had heat and cloth seat covers so I was satisfied. Driving away felt like depositing my first-born child at summer camp without a cell phone. I missed my Metro already.

11

The Hyundai sputtered as I drove out of the service station and down the access road that ran parallel to Route 53. I gunned the motor and wound my way back into the north end of Etonville. I knew Sally had rented a room on Belvidere, a few doors down from the Etonville Public Library. I eased my car next to the curb, or where the curb would have been if there hadn't been a snowbank blocking the parking lane. I stared at 417 Belvedere. A modest olive-green Victorian with a gray slate roof that featured third-floor dormers. A wraparound porch could accommodate a number of guests on summer nights. Hanging out on a front porch in warm weather was the next best thing to squishing my toes in the sand at a Jersey Shore beach. Oh well…

I tramped to the front door, grateful for the recently shoveled walkway, and pushed the bell. A curtain on the front door fluttered and a youthful face appeared.

"I'm looking for a friend of mine. Sally Oldfield."

The eyes in the face grew round. "Sally? She's not here."

"Could I speak with you for a minute?"

The face hesitated, then stepped away from the window and the door opened a few inches. "I'm not supposed to open the door when I'm alone, but Mr. Peterson is upstairs so I guess it's all right."

I slipped inside and the door shut with a whoosh, the frigid air replaced with a blast of hot air. The temperature in the house had to be nearly eighty degrees. Never mind. Better eighty than twenty. "Thanks. Cold out there."

The young girl was maybe ten, eleven with short-cropped blond hair, a baggy sweater, and blue jeans. She looked at me quizzically. "You're a friend of Sally's?"

"Yes, I am. I helped her find this room." In a way.

"She's not here."

"When was the last time you saw her?" I asked.

The kid tilted her head upward searching for the answer. "Tuesday. That was the night of my birthday party."

Also the night of the dress rehearsal when Sally ducked out before the curtain call. "That's nice. Was Sally at the party?"

"She was supposed to come back after the play practice but she never did." She bit her lower lip.

"Was she your friend?" I asked gently.

"Mom said just an acquaintance and I shouldn't be surprised I never saw her that night." The girl hesitated. "But she promised to come."

"Is your mom here now?"

"Out shopping. She shops a lot." Then she wrinkled her nose. "I'm supposed to be cleaning my room."

"Oops," I said and laughed with the girl. "I'm Dodie. What's your name?"

"Angela."

"Angela, did Sally seem upset that morning or maybe the day before?"

"Like mad, you mean?" she asked.

"Mad, or sad, or afraid of something?"

"She was upset with that man," Angela said.

My neck hairs stood at attention. "What man? Can you describe him?"

Angela shrugged. "I didn't see him, but Sally was standing on the porch with him and Mom shook my shoulder and told me not to eavesdrop."

"When was this?"

"The morning of my birthday."

The day before the murder. "Thanks, Angela. You've been a big help."

"That's what that other man said too." Angela smiled proudly.

"Other man? The one who talked with Sally?" I asked.

"No! This one's really nice. He has a soft voice and cowboy boots. His name is..." She thought.

"Archibald, right?"

"That's it!"

Of course, he would investigate Sally's residence. "Did he ask you about Sally?"

"Uh-huh."

I looked up the stairs. "How many renters do you have here?"

Angela frowned. "There's Mr. Peterson and Janie..."

"And Sally," I prompted her.

"And the nice man."

Archibald was renting a room here? "When did the nice man rent his room?"

Angela frowned and thought. "I think the morning after my birthday party."

If Angela was correct, Archibald Alvarez had arrived in Etonville *before* Gordon Weeks's death...*before* Bill had broken his ankle. I began to sweat, beads of perspiration rolling down the inside of my sweater. I hunted inside my purse, feeling for my wallet. "Do you like to read?"

"Yes. I just finished *A Wrinkle in Time*. I loved it!" she said enthusiastically.

"I read that in school too." I held out a gift card for Books, Books, Books, Etonville's answer to Barnes & Noble. It was a Christmas present from Benny and family. "Here. Happy Birthday."

Angela looked at the card. "For me?" She beamed.

"Sure. And if you see Sally, would you have her call Dodie?"

Her head bounced up and down, and I gave her a quick hug. "Bye."

What a cute kid. I glided away from the snowbank, my thoughts crashing headlong into each other. I had no idea what to make of Angela's revelations. Who was the real Archibald? What did Bill know or not know about him? What exactly was he doing in Etonville? I checked my watch. I had about an hour and a half until I had to appear at the Windjammer. My cell pinged. Probably Sally! I intended to meet with her and find out exactly what was going on. The Hyundai's brakes squealed as I approached the light on Belvidere and Anderson. I retrieved my cell from my bag and glanced at the text. Not Sally but Lola: *Call me. Need to talk*. I was only a few blocks from her house so I hung a right on Anderson and a left on Weston, hitting a patch of ice and sliding to a stop at the edge of her driveway.

Lola opened the front door before I could ring the bell of her Queen Anne Victorian with its ornamental gingerbread detailing and intricate roofline. Dressed to kill, as usual: a tweed blazer and knee-high suede boots. Her blond hair was pulled back in a neat bun.

"That was quick. Where's your car?" She squinted past me. "Where did you get that thing? Want some coffee?"

"It's a long story, Timothy's, and let's get some in Bernridge." I stamped my boots to rev up the circulation in my feet.

"Bernridge? Why?" Lola stepped into her house, expecting me to follow.

"I'll explain on the way. Come on. We don't have much time." I headed down her front steps.

"Well, if you say so. Let me get my coat and keys. I'll drive."

Lola's Lexus was usually preferable to my Metro. "Not today. I need to get a car wash."

"In this weather?"

"It's almost thirty." I had the engine growling by the time Lola settled herself into the passenger side of the Hyundai, swathed in her Canadian goose down winter coat. "Where did you say your Metro was? Dodie, this car smells!"

I started with my discovering the hole in the passenger side window, segued to my visit to Sally's rooming house, and ended with my intention to stop by her workplace, the car wash, to poke around a bit and remove the smoky aroma. I revealed my trip to the bodega for good measure. "But this is strictly on the QT. I haven't told Bill or Archibald that Sally's been texting me."

"Dodie, you've been busy. I guess this means you'll be investigating the murder?" Lola asked hopefully.

"Not on purpose. I'm trying to straighten things out with Sally. I figure if I meet with her, maybe I can persuade her to come in and talk with Bill. Spill the beans on Gordon Weeks. How she knew him."

"Gordon who?"

Ooops. Bill had told me his name in confidence. "The dead man at the theater. His ID hasn't been made public yet."

Lola zipped her mouth shut. We'd shared a good amount of secret information during the last year and only half of it had been broadcast unintentionally. "Why do you think Sally stood you up?"

"I was late. Maybe she got antsy."

"Still, she texted a second time to make a date. So she wants to meet," Lola said.

"I'm wondering about the man she had the argument with on the porch."

"You think it was Gordon Weeks?" Lola asked.

"That makes sense."

We were on the edge of Bernridge, and my GPS took us through a working-class neighborhood. I could see a red-and-white sign ahead on the left announcing the services of E-Z Clean Car Wash. A handful of men and women swaddled in hoodies and parkas blew on their hands, jumped up and down, and darted from the washing bay to the lot where they dried and buffed the autos. I guided the Hyundai into the washing lane, careful to line up the tires with the track. I requested an extra spritz of something to eliminate the Hyundai's interior odor, and Lola and I hurried from the car to the waiting room. A television blared a cooking show on the Food Network which reminded me of the Windjammer which reminded me that I needed to find a new home for the frozen pies I'd been keeping for the ELT intermission concessions. Henry was making noises about storage space.

I stepped to the cashier and laid a receipt and a twenty-dollar bill on the counter.

The young woman picked up the money with the pads of her fingers since her pointy nails—painted blue with red sparkles—extended half an inch beyond each digit. "Four dollars change," she said.

"Thanks..." I studied the name patch on her uniform. "...Aurora." A lot to live up to there.

"Sure." She turned to the customer behind me.

"Is Sally here? I know she's only part-time and I don't know her schedule—"

"Nope. She quit."

"She didn't tell me that. When was she here last?" I asked, attempting surprise.

The guy behind us shifted his weight from one foot to the other, exasperated. The cashier held out her hand for his receipt. "Monday... Tuesday. Might have been Wednesday. I don't really know." She made change and dropped the man's bills on the counter.

He stomped off to wait for his car outside.

"Did she say anything to you the last time you saw her? I mean, did she tell you she was quitting?"

The girl laughed. "Sally? Talk to me? She barely said two words to anybody. First week she was here, she was, like, mute. I mean, the only time I remember her talking to anybody was one day last week. This really cute guy came in and Sally took her break so they could have coffee." The woman pointed a stiletto nail to the front window of the car wash. Across the street was a diner.

I started to sweat again. "Cute guy? Longish hair, killer eyes. One hot number. Cowboy boots even in this weather."

"Cowboy boots? This dude looked filthy rich." The cashier leaned across the counter. "Maybe he was her sugar daddy, if you know what I mean." She grinned. "I asked Sally if there were more like him wherever he came from. She looked at me like she was going to cry and ran to the ladies'. Sorry if she's your friend and all, but Sally did some weird stuff. Know what I mean?"

No kidding.

* * *

I was running late. Lola accompanied me to the Windjammer so that I could open up and she could get a cup of coffee. By eleven thirty Benny had the bar in hand and Gillian was checking the online reservations for this evening. Lately, weekend nights brought out all of the stir crazies who'd been indoors all day. But with the temperature supposedly hitting single digits tonight, there was a good chance we'd all be twiddling our thumbs.

Lola planted herself in my back booth with a steaming mug while I popped into the kitchen with inventory sheets. With the success of the Chamber of Commerce dinner, Henry was content to stick with old standbys this weekend. I found him up to his elbows in the business end of a twenty-pound turkey. "Something smells good in here."

Enrico grinned. "Chorizo and bacon pasta bake for lunch. You want to taste?"

"Later, Enrico. Henry, are we going to have healthy Monday specials?"

I'd been working on him since Christmas to include some light winter alternatives on the menu on Mondays: vegetarian meals, more salads, gluten-free items. I'd thought about adding a tofu option. Of course, I knew what Henry's recipe for tofu would be: step one, throw it in the garbage, and step two, grill some meat.

Henry withdrew his arm from the turkey. "Lettuce wraps and veggie burgers for lunch and salmon and quinoa for dinner."

"Yay! I'm proud of you. We're going to get Etonville eating healthier in spite of itself."

Henry grunted.

I finished an inventory of the freezer, made a mental note to remind Cheney Brothers Food Distributors about the fish order, poured myself a cup of coffee, and joined Lola in my booth.

She leaned forward. "So…Sally and an older wealthy man?"

We hadn't had a chance to talk over our findings at the car wash, since the minute we seated ourselves in the Hyundai—smelling a tad better—Lola had fielded a call from Walter. He'd delivered a diatribe on the future of the ELT if they somehow could not open *Eton Town*. Not to mention the devastation to his playwriting career. Lola listened, adding an "uh-huh" periodically, apparently eager to end the call.

"I'm stumped. Including the man she talked with at the rooming house, that's two different guys tracking her down within the same week. Not counting Archibald Alvarez, of course. He had good reason to be investigating her residence." Did he also have a good reason to rent a room at the same location? Before Gordon Weeks had even been murdered?

We sat in silence.

"What do you think about moving *Eton Town* to another venue?" Lola asked.

"What did you have in mind?" I immediately pictured the ELT crew rolling the turntable down Main Street…not a pretty prospect.

"I think there are a couple of possibilities…"

While Lola described theater options, my mind drifted off to Archibald Alvarez. I was willing to bet there was definitely more going on there than Bill knew. But how much to tell him? I had to step lightly to avoid treading on Bill's toes. I didn't want to ruffle his police feathers unnecessarily. Of course if/when he found out I had postponed telling him about Sally meeting me, more than feathers would fly.

"…so what do you think?" Lola asked, finishing off the last of her coffee.

Mine had gone cold and I'd lost the thread of her explanation.

"Moving the show?"

"Sorry, Lola. I got sidetracked," I said.

"I was saying we could check with the Creston Players, even though Walter would have a fit, or with the VFW Hall in Bernridge. I'd have to restage some scenes without the turntable, which, frankly, ought to be chopped up for firewood if you ask me," Lola said vehemently. "I think it brought us bad luck. After all, that's where the dead man was found."

I knew Lola was firmly wedged between a rock and a hard place, and I empathized with her box office anxiety. But to blame the turntable was tantamount to buying into the Banger sisters' theory that it was a deathtrap, not simply a laboriously moving, wooden platform. "Those sound like good options to me."

"I guess I'd better get on the stick and start making a few calls," Lola said.

Which reminded me that I also had an important call to make.

12

True to my prediction, as the temperature dropped so did the number of patrons dashing from the street to the inside of the Windjammer. I released Benny early and had Carmen step behind the bar. I offered to pick up the last couple of tables so Gillian could leave too. Henry's turkey and dressing were delicious, perfect winter comfort food, but there would be lots of leftovers. I was thinking turkey enchiladas, turkey fettuccine, turkey pot pie.

"Let's close the kitchen," I said to him at nine o'clock. "We haven't had a walk-in for over an hour."

Henry agreed, and at ten thirty, I watched him, Enrico, and Carmen traipse out the door with an admonition to drive carefully. I figured there might be a few hardy souls in town who needed an evening drink so I planned to give it an hour and then call it a night myself. The now unoccupied restaurant was ideal for double-duty: a little sleuthing and a sibling catch-up. I tapped a number in my cell phone contacts and waited while it rang on the other end.

"Hello?" said a familiar baritone voice that never failed to trigger a grin from me.

"Hey, little bro. What's up?" I asked. Though we were only eighteen months apart, I relished the fact that I could play big sis from time to time. And the fact that he and his wife, Amanda, and their two-year-old son, Cory, were now living in Boston. That meant we could spend more time together, as we had at Christmas, playing a marathon game of Monopoly as we used to down the shore, whipping up competing chili recipes, spending a Sunday afternoon arguing about the New York Giants versus the New England Patriots. We'd even concocted family beach plans for Cape Cod next summer. Andy and I were good friends as well as siblings, and I had missed him when he was living on the West Coast.

"It's Boston! Five degrees and Amanda's in bed with the flu. I just got Cory to sleep."

"Sorry about Amanda," I said.

"I'm keeping her in quarantine. Cory spent January sneezing and coughing," he said.

"That's what you get for trading sunny San Diego for Beantown. Maybe Amanda should have refused the fellowship." If she had, I'd have been really disappointed.

"Yeah. But I'm liking sharing a practice with other therapists. What about you? The Windjammer closed for the weather?" Andy asked.

"No, but I sent everyone else home. Nice and quiet."

"How's Bill?" he asked slyly.

I'd divulged the status of our relationship over Christmas—and Andy had been tormenting me ever since. "Funny you should ask, being a doctor and all."

"I'm not that kind of doctor. What's wrong?" He sounded worried.

"Black ice accident. He broke an ankle."

"Wow...sorry," he said.

"So in your capacity as that other kind of doctor..."

"I can't do remote diagnoses, although it sounds like Etonville is full of potential clients." He laughed.

"I'm not calling about an Etonville resident," I said coyly.

"So you *are* interested in a diagnosis," he teased.

"One a little closer to your home. Sally Oldfield."

The line went quiet. When he spoke, Andy was serious, all business. "What about her?" he asked, guarded.

"Is there something I should know? I helped her out on your recommendation—"

"*My* recommendation? What are you talking about?" Andy was truly surprised.

"What are *you* talking about?" I asked.

"Let's start over," he said. "How do you know Sara?"

"She came to Etonville last month and goes by Sally here. I helped her find a room. And she's in the current theater production. At least she would be if a man she apparently knew wasn't murdered on the turntable and the show had to be cancelled."

"What?" he practically yelled.

I proceeded to explain Sally's showing up five weeks ago and her integration into the Etonville community. "She has a job too. Part-time cashier at a car wash."

I could hear Andy exhale sharply. "A car wash? Do you know who she is? And what's this about a murder?"

My brother listened silently to the details of Gordon Weeks's death and Sally's disappearance. I skipped over my investigative snooping and the fact that Sally had been texting me.

"You're not getting involved in this, I hope." It wasn't a question. He'd acted like a big brother when he'd discovered my previous investigative activities.

"Not really." Not too much. "So what aren't you telling me?"

"First of all, I didn't recommend she look you up. I probably mentioned having a sister in Etonville but that's all," he said hastily.

"So she is one of your patients?"

He hesitated. "Professional ethics prevent me from giving you specifics, but yes, I was seeing her for a month or so. Until she stopped coming several weeks ago."

"Probably about the time she showed up in Etonville," I said.

"Did she tell you about herself? That she's a member of one of Boston's old money families? She didn't need to be working at a car wash. She's worth millions."

"You're kidding! Sally never let on. She told me she came to Etonville because she was looking to get a fresh start," I said.

Andy paused. "I'm not telling you anything that wasn't in the *Boston Globe* or local scandal sheets, but her mother passed six months ago. Sara had a tough time with her death. They were very close."

"Did she have other family? She said I was lucky to have a brother."

"No siblings. I got the impression she and her father didn't get on very well. Look, Dodie, I don't know what's going on with Sara, but this murder thing…steer clear of it. Anyway, she's probably back in Boston by now getting lawyered up. That would be the smart thing to do, and Sara, though she can appear a little helpless, is brilliant. She dropped out of MIT last semester. She was a physics major."

We said our good-byes, me promising to let him know if and when I heard anything else about Sally. He promising to call our parents this weekend since they bugged me when they hadn't heard from him.

I sat in my back booth with a cup of coffee fortified by a shot of Jim Beam. So Sally-aka-Sara Oldfield was a Boston Brahmin with a penchant for playing fast and loose with the truth. There was definitely more to her story than she was letting on. And I had better be prepared when we meet. I downed the end of my drink.

I turned out the lights and locked up, pausing at the entrance of the Windjammer to study the sky: inky black with pinpoints of light. I felt warm inside from the Irish coffee and warm outside from my winter wear. Henry had distributed fistfuls of rock salt on the pavement adjacent to the restaurant before he'd left, but there was still a film of ice that made movement treacherous. My cell rang from the confines of my bag and, with gloves on, I rummaged around clumsily to retrieve my phone. I checked the caller ID and tapped the green button.

"Hi," I said as sexily as I could, considering that my face was starting to freeze. It wasn't *that* late and maybe we could rendezvous at Bill's place…a crackling fire, another hot toddy, the roads so bad I had to spend the night—

"Why didn't you tell me someone burglarized your car?" Bill demanded. Or not.

"Guess you were talking to Archibald."

"We're sharing an office! Of course, I talked with Archibald. He told me your window was broken. Was anything stolen? Why didn't you come down and fill out a report? Where are you?" He sounded put out and exhausted.

"Slow down. Chill. Nothing was taken. At least not that I could tell. My cash and credit cards were still in my wallet. I'm not sure what they were after. Maybe they wanted to hot wire my Metro. Good luck with that."

"Dodie! We've got a murderer on the loose. You need to be careful."

I stamped my feet to keep the circulation going. "Speaking of which…?"

"It's been a long night on the telephone and in front of the computer. Nothing new on Gordon Weeks. Sally Oldfield still unaccounted for. Archibald is pursuing some angles with a detective friend in Boston."

Uh-oh. I needed to find her. It was only a matter of days, maybe hours, before Archibald discovered Sally's connection to Gordon Weeks. Whatever it was.

"So I guess you aren't in the mood for a little company tonight?" I asked. "I'm just leaving the Windjammer." The cold was beginning to penetrate my winter weather clothing.

"I have about another hour of work and then I need to get some sleep. I have an early meeting with the medical examiner tomorrow morning," he said, weary.

"On a Sunday?" I asked.

"Crime never sleeps."

"You need a ride?" I offered.

"Thanks but Archie is dropping me off on his way home later."

I wondered if he'd heard that his private investigator buddy had rented a room in Etonville. "Take it easy tonight. Stay off the black ice and your broken ankle."

"I'll check in tomorrow," Bill said and clicked off.

Check in! Check in? That sounded like I was running a hotel or an airline. Not very personal. I wasn't cold any more. Irritation tended to warm one up significantly. Warming up reminded me that I'd still not rescued my favorite fleece pullover from the women's dressing room backstage. Strictly speaking, the theater was off-limits as per Bill's directive. But feeling rebuffed by him and discouraged in my efforts to connect with Sally left me flirting with defiance. I still had a master key to the front door. I could slip in, grab my clothes, and slip out. A five-minute job. No one would be the wiser.

I shuffled across the surface of the slick sidewalk and paused outside the ELT. I wasn't thrilled to be visiting the place, given recent events, and seeing the scene of the crime would be unsettling. But I ignored any misgivings and entered the theater, careful to lock the door behind me. I scrambled across the lobby, flicking on my cell flashlight. The house was pitch black except for the illuminated Exit lights, and I picked my way down a side aisle to the stage. I waved my flashlight back and forth, the onstage tumble of furniture forming a kind of skyline: chairs, tables, and a ten-foot ladder all cast eerie shadows. I climbed the set of stairs leading to the stage and stepped over the yellow crime scene tape.

I should have given this area a wide berth; *Gordon Weeks died here*. I stared at the dark circle of dried blood where his body had lain. I crouched down and scrutinized the stage floor. The CSI unit had gone over everything with a fine-tooth comb. Did they miss any miniscule piece of evidence? As I stood up, the back of my neck tingled—my little hairs were at it again. I was creeped out and hurried through the green room to the dressing room. I pushed open the door, spied my fleece pullover and stretchy slacks. I grabbed them, closed the dressing room door, and, guided by my flashlight, fairly sprinted through the green room.

With my hand on the door to the stage, I stopped. A sliver of light was visible at the bottom edge of the doorframe. Someone was onstage and if I could see remnants of their light, they could also see mine. I clicked off my flashlight, slipped behind a sofa that usually accommodated lounging actors waiting for Penny to blast her whistle and call them to work. The footsteps outside pounded against the wooden floor of the stage…snow boots? Work boots? Clomp, clomp, clomp, then silence. A pause of five seconds. Then clomp, clomp, clomp again, growing louder. He or she was moving around the stage, back and forth, away from the spot where Gordon Weeks was murdered?

The pacing ended and the light at the periphery of the door disappeared. I screwed up my courage and tiptoed to the center of the green room. I stopped. The silence was weighty, dense. I hugged my clothes to my chest and eased the door open. Whoever had been examining the stage was gone. I scrunched down by the main drape and waited five minutes to give whomever time to exit. And then I lit out of there, bumping my way from the stage to the house to the lobby, forgoing my flashlight for fear of detection.

I stepped outside the theater into a freezing puddle of slush at the border of the ELT welcome mat. Main Street was empty. Adjacent to the mat was a strip of virgin snow, untouched by salt or shovel. In the arc of light thrown by an exterior lamp on the façade of the theater I could make out a partial, pointy print of a boot or shoe. A cowboy boot? There was only one person I knew in Etonville who traipsed around in cowboy boots. Why was he sneaking around the theater after hours? He had every right to be there. Something tickled the recesses of my mind and the thought surfaced: Did Archibald have another agenda other than aiding Bill in solving the murder of Gordon Weeks?

13

I awoke to the sound of pelting sleet rattling my bedroom window. I shivered involuntarily and buried my face in my down comforter. Sunday! The Windjammer was closed. No need to rise this early, I told myself and closed my eyes firmly. After twenty minutes, the last bits of sleep eased away, and I found myself staring at a crack in the ceiling which I'd been reminding my landlord needed repairing for months. I surrendered to the day and threw on my terry cloth robe and Giants slippers.

It was going to be a dreary, gray day, I decided, after sticking my hand out the front door for my Sunday *New York Times* and scanning the sky. In another lifetime, I'd thought of persuading Bill to join me at Etonville's town park for a bout of sledding today. That was last weekend…before the broken ankle, before the murder, before the cancellation of *Eton Town*. I fixed a cup of coffee and toast, and hunkered down at my kitchen table.

I skimmed the front page of the paper, reading about the Greek economic crisis and a regional story about two New Jersey teens stopped by local police because they were shoveling snow without a permit. Reminded me that my driveway required some attention. I saw a recipe in the Living pages for spur-of-the-moment risotto. Basically an upscale mac and cheese with rice, butternut squash, onion, saffron, three cheeses, and bread crumbs. Even at nine in the morning, it sounded delicious. Maybe Henry would be interested. I was tearing out the recipe, ready to tackle the Arts and Leisure section, when my eye caught the Society page. Announcements of engagements and weddings filled several columns. Glancing at them forced me to evaluate my own matrimonial status. Never mind matrimony; someone to curl up with on a winter night instead of a book would be sufficient. Could Bill be that someone? I looked down at the paper again. A young couple was getting married on Long Island. He was from Manhattan, she was from Boston...blah blah blah. Boston!

I put the *Times* aside and powered up my laptop. I started with Sally's given name and typed in *Sara Oldfield Boston*. Up popped a series of links: the recent death of her mother, Olivia Holmes Oldfield; the family history, dating from the Mayflower; and one article on the wealth produced by generations of Holmes via shipping, banking, and shrewd investing. Lots of Harvard alums. Old money indeed on Sally's mother's side. No wonder Andy was surprised she had part-time employment at a car wash. Exactly what was Sally doing in Etonville? Who did she know besides myself and the ELT bunch? What did she do with her time away from rehearsal and the car wash?

I sat back and stared at my computer screen. Sally had not yet returned my text about a possible second meeting, and Archibald Alvarez was hot on Sally's trail and her connection to Gordon Weeks. What did I know about Weeks? Sally's conversation on the porch of the rooming house with a man the day Gordon Weeks died; Sally freaking out when she spotted Weeks, dressed in the hunting cap and coat, on the street earlier in the week; Gordon Weeks found dead—hunting knife protruding from his chest—on opening night. A hefty, scruffy, outdoorsman. Polar opposite of the petite, quiet, fragile-appearing Sally, especially now that I knew her Boston upper-class pedigree. I typed *Gordon Weeks* into the search engine and watched as links appeared: there was a banker in Texas, a software engineer in Silicon Valley, and a magazine editor in New York.

I felt drowsy. I needed either another jolt of caffeine or fresh air. Despite the overcast sky and frigid temperature, I slipped into my down jacket and pulled on my waterproof boots. The sleet had stopped, leaving a sloppy residue on the ground. No matter, my body was aching for physical exercise, and since fooling around in the snow was off the table, a brisk stroll was the next best thing. I tucked my hair into a knit hat and locked my door.

I moved down Ames, waving at my neighbor across the street who was shoveling his driveway, and tramped onto Fairfield. Within five minutes I'd worked up some heat and was actually warm, my leg muscles enjoying the bounce in my stride. I allowed my mind to wander, reviewing everything I'd learned from my brother, Andy, and my Internet digging in the last twenty-four hours.

Twenty minutes later I turned onto Main Street, my mind still occupied, my body headed straight to Coffee Heaven. I pushed open the door to the tinkling of the welcome bells and was hit with a wave of hot air—some from the heater, some from the animated conversations drifting out of the booths. It was Sunday brunch in Etonville.

I sidled up to the counter. Since I'd already eaten breakfast, I was thinking a light snack.

"Hi, Jocelyn," I said as I slid onto a stool.

"Hey there, Dodie. The regular?"

"Sure and throw in a—"

"Hot cinnamon bun. Got it." She scribbled on a pad, then stuck her pencil in the pile of hair on top of her head. "Anything new on the murder of that homeless man?"

There was no use explaining that Gordon Weeks was not a homeless man.

"Because I heard at Snippets that he might have been a friend of one of the actors," she said knowingly.

"Whose friend?" I asked.

"Abby."

Abby had had a checkered career at the ELT lately. A disappointed Lady-in-Waiting in *Romeo and Juliet*, but one of the murderous Brewster sisters in *Arsenic and Old Lace*, and now a village matriarch in *Eton Town*. Things were looking up for her. She could replace Lola as the next ELT prima donna. Though she'd be a pudgy, moody one.

"Why would anyone think that? Has Abby said something?"

Jocelyn set a caramel macchiato and warm roll in front of me. "Well… word is, the man was seen with her at the Valley View Shooting Range." Which Abby managed.

"Are they sure?" I asked. "I mean—"

"Eye witness. Abby was flirting with a big, burly guy in a one of those hunting jackets."

"That could also describe Jim. Her husband," I reminded Jocelyn. Jim was a patient, genial, bear of a man, usually with a smile on his face. And it was challenging to envision Abby—with the perpetual scowl—flirting with anyone.

"You know what they say," Jocelyn said.

I couldn't imagine. "What?"

Jocelyn leaned in. "Love may be blind, but jealousy has twenty-twenty vision."

"So people think Abby's Jim murdered Gord—uh, the stranger, because Abby was flirting with someone who was dressed like him at the shooting range?"

"Love makes strange bedfellas! Gotta run." Jocelyn waltzed away to pour coffee for another customer.

I sipped my drink and nibbled on my roll. Crazy rarely took a day off in this town. I knew, by now, that it took practically nothing to stir up the gossip machine—one spontaneous comment, a feverish fancy, and Snippets was off to the races. But this one was a stretch even for the Etonville rumor mill. Still, as nutty as this latest theory was, it appeared to make as much sense as Sally killing Gordon Weeks.

My cell phone binged. It was Lola: *Call me.* I finished my bun, left money for the check, climbed back into my jacket, scarf, and gloves, and headed outside. "Hi, Lola. What's up?"

"Hi, Dodie. Well…Walter thought we should have some kind of rehearsal because the actors get disassociated from the play if they are away from it for too long so I scheduled a line-through, you know, we could sit and have everyone in a circle doing lines to whomever they share a scene with, and thought the basement of the Episcopal church would be ideal because it has plenty of room and folding chairs and no one is using it this afternoon once the Sunday service is over but then the minister called me—"

"Lola!"

She gulped, then picked up more slowly. "The furnace broke. There's no heat in the church."

"Oh no. That's too bad. Do you have a plan B?"

She paused. "I was wondering…well, since the Windjammer is closed today…I know this is a lot to ask, but the restaurant has heat, right?"

I closed my eyes, envisioning Henry's face as I approached him about the Etonville Little Theatre holding an afternoon rehearsal in the restaurant. He'd barely gotten over my Sunday baking classes for the colonial intermission desserts.

"I'll call Henry."

"Thank you," Lola said appreciatively.

"But I might need a favor."

"Anything!"

I knew I could manipulate Henry, grousing nonstop, into permitting the rehearsal, but it would be soooo much better if he was enthusiastic about the venture. I tapped Pauli's number. After two rings he picked up.

"Hey."

"Hey, Pauli. What's up today?" I asked.

He cleared his throat and did a verbal shrug. "Zip."

"No digital forensics homework?" I asked.

"Done." He lowered his voice. "You got a job for me? We're studying these search engines and tracking devices in my digital forensics class. Like really awesome stuff."

"No, Pauli, nothing like that," I said hastily. "But I was wondering if you'd like to take some photos this afternoon at the Windjammer. Something we can put on the website and maybe use for promotion."

"Awesome. What time?"

I told both Lola and Pauli I'd get back to them, hurried home, and jumped in my loaner car. Within the hour I had turned up the heat in the Windjammer and phoned Henry. Predictably, I'd gotten him in a less than cheerful mood—his mother-in-law was in town from Delaware and Henry's wife had forced him to go to the Museum of Modern Art in the city this afternoon. When all he really wanted to do was chill on the sofa and surf ESPN for some sporting event. I plunged into the ELT's predicament and, before he could cut me off, I dangled a hook with tempting bait. I'd gotten Lola to agree to take a full-page ad in the *Etonville Standard*, touting the community spirit of the Windjammer in providing the restaurant for the rehearsal. With pictures of the restaurant and the cast in action. I assured him this was something La Famiglia would *never* do.

* * *

I had the coffee brewing, dining room furniture organized to accommodate the large cast, director, and stage manager, and the bar open—in case someone needed something stronger. Like Lola or me. Lola was the first to arrive, closely followed by Penny and a semi-grateful Walter. He had trouble meeting my stare, and, with a cup of coffee, busied himself with the script in a corner of the dining room.

I wondered who would take Sally's place, if anyone.

"Hey, O'Dell, you want to fill in for her?" Penny cracked, slapping her clipboard against her pink ski pants–covered leg.

I still had no idea how she managed to infiltrate my brain.

"No thanks. Besides, assuming the show goes on, someone has to run the refreshment stand." Assuming there would be any early American pies left after today.

"The show always goes on, haven't you learned that yet? As soon as they clean up the blood," she said, sliding her eyes in Walter's direction to make sure he was otherwise engaged. "But too bad about the Creston Players," she muttered.

I refilled my mug of coffee. "What about the Creston Players?" I asked absentmindedly as I calculated how many apple pies I'd need to thaw out to offer a snack to the probably-a-little-disgruntled cast. After all, they were giving up their Sunday too.

"*Our Town*? The real play?" she said. "You haven't heard?"

"Penny, enough with the twenty questions. What are you saying?" I asked.

She hooted softly. "The Players decided to do *Our Town* in April. You think anybody in Etonville is going to want to see *Eton Town* when they can see the real thing next door?"

"Does Walter know?"

"O'Dell, you don't ask a drowning man for a glass of water," she said.

Huh?

"Especially one who is—"

"Tri-polar. I know. Maybe we should get this rehearsal going before word gets out." I spotted Lola talking with Vernon by the bar and Pauli fiddling with his digital camera.

"Got it." The sound of Penny's whistle bounced off the walls of the Windjammer and hung in the air.

Actors held their ears, cringed, and moved to the circle of chairs. Walter rose from his corner and solemnly made his way to the seat reserved for him—between Edna, who played his wife, and Narrator Vernon.

"Let us sit quietly and meditate," Walter said.

Romeo and several younger cast members snickered, the Banger sisters nodded and closed their eyes, probably headed for slumberland.

"What?" Vernon asked.

"Quiet!" Penny yelled.

"Turn up your hearing aids," Mildred whispered to him.

Lola joined the cast. "Okay, everyone, let's focus before we begin," she said firmly, avoiding Walter's gaze.

"Uh, like, you want a picture of this?" Pauli asked me sotto voce, snapping away.

"I think we can bypass the meditation and get a few shots of the actors running lines. Make them look good," I said.

Pauli grinned and nodded, a hank of brown hair flopping over his forehead.

Without warning, in the silence, a low rumble worked its way to the center of the room. Eyes popped open, a few people squirmed in their seats. It was Walter. Softly chanting a mantra that sounded to me a lot like "end this show." Penny shushed the actors and most of them swallowed their giggles, respecting Walter's position as the theater's former head honcho.

Lola rolled her eyes and mouthed, "Oh brother."

By the time Walter had meditated the cast into submission, I was jitsy, ready to get the show on the road. In my back booth I nudged Pauli, who was playing a video game on his phone. "I think we're about to get started."

Pauli sucked on a straw jammed into his Slurpee. "Sweet."

The actors woke up, stretched, went to the rest rooms, fidgeted in their seats, and prepared for the line-through.

"I had to browbeat people to show up for this rehearsal," Lola said, glancing wistfully at a bottle of red wine I'd placed on the bar. "But Walter's right, they need to brush up on their lines if we're going to open later this week." She paused, studying my face as if trying to decipher a code. "Do you think that's a possibility? Because we've got a very narrow window with the *Star Ledger* reviewer."

I couldn't confide in Lola about my unauthorized visit to the theater and near run-in with Archibald now. It would have to wait until after the cast had thrashed the life out of *Eton Town*. "Let's talk later," I murmured.

Vernon adjusted his hearing aids and the rehearsal began. "Ladies and gentlemen, the play you are here to see this evening is about the founding of our village, Etonville, named after the American Revolutionary war hero Thomas Eton." Vernon looked to Romeo, who smirked and gave a quick salute to the "audience." Vernon continued, describing Etonville's location, vis-à-vis New York City, the Jersey Shore, and the Pennsylvania border, and the shops on Main Street—the general store, the blacksmith, the hotel where the ELT now stood. He pointed out the newspaper office of the *Eton Town Press*, the precursor to the *Etonville Standard*. And the clinic where Doc—aka Walter—served the community.

I stifled a yawn. Pauli crept around the periphery of the acting circle to shoot the cast at work—Abby slumped down in her chair, Edna doodling on her script, Romeo texting, and the Banger sisters not even pretending to be alert.

Vernon paused and Lola stepped in. "Let's pick up the pace, everyone."

Abby and Edna started their scene, talking about the home front during the Revolutionary War, exchanging domestic tidbits and general worrying about when the fighting would end and the soldiers return home. Abby started to speak faster than normal and Edna, still feeling competitive from *Arsenic and Old Lace*, kept up, matching her tempo, cutting her off in the process. Abby fought back. The lines flew!

"I declare, is that Doc I see coming up the—"

"Have you seen Doc? He's been out all night—"

"He delivered twins, did he? I can't imagine—"

"You're right. That family at the other end of town—"

The rest of the cast began to watch the proceedings eagerly. Finally something interesting was going on. Pauli skipped around the room, seizing the opportunity as other actors got into it. *Eton Town* was a racehorse heading down the home stretch. The play made less sense, but at least it was moving faster than it ever had during rehearsals in the theater.

Lola's jaw dropped, and Walter—when he realized what was happening—jumped up. "Enough! Enough!" he shouted, striking a theatrical pose. "Penny!"

"On it!" She tooted her whistle. "Take ten."

The actors collapsed in fits of laughter and Walter stomped off to the men's room.

He was fast losing control of the Etonville Little Theatre. I watched Lola work the room, attempting to settle things down. I put on another urn of coffee.

"O'Dell, better make that decaf." Penny looked over her shoulder. "They're already on speed."

"Guess they took Lola at her word. Keep the show moving."

Penny snorted. "As if that would help."

"Have you heard from Sally, being the stage manager and all?" I asked. I already knew the answer, but it didn't hurt to confirm my suspicions.

"Nada."

"Is Walter planning on replacing her?"

Penny tapped her clipboard. "She didn't have many lines. Just a Townsperson." Penny pushed her glasses a notch up her nose. "She'll probably show up. 'Course Walter doesn't like to reward unprofessionalism. Nobody misses curtain call *and* rehearsal, even if it is a line-through." She surveyed the dining room. "Yep. Walter is losing control."

Penny was in my head again.

A scream from one of the actors brought the room to a silent standstill. A young woman pointed to a ghostly pale Walter who had sagged against the doorframe of the men's room, clutching his chest.

Was he having a heart attack?

Edna plowed through the knot of stunned actors, both business-like and alarmed. "Call 911," she yelled, and people whisked out phones and tapped the numbers. "Let me in. Back away. What do we have here?" she said and helped Walter to a sitting position on the floor. She looked around, mumbling to no one in particular. "Looks like a 10-43 to me. Need a doctor. Not sure about 10-45...serious or critical..." Then she shouted suddenly, "Walter, can you hear me? Are you in pain?"

"Walter...Walter? Speak to me!" Lola pleaded on her knees next to him.

Walter groaned and raised his head, grasping Lola's hands gratefully, his lips curving in a desperate smile.

Penny directed traffic. "Move to the other side of the room," she commanded the actors. Then turned to me. "He should have been on a watch list."

"Penny, it looks like a heart issue. He didn't try to off himself," I said sternly.

"O'Dell, duh, how many times do I have to tell you? Theater people take their work seriously. Life's more than a bowl of rotten cherries," she said knowingly.

14

The EMS team had determined that Walter's vital signs were excellent and that he had probably suffered a panic attack, but trundled him off to the emergency room anyway. What there had been of the creative balloon had deflated. Lola and Penny debated calling it an afternoon versus trying to finish the rehearsal, while Mildred suggested an acapella run through of "Blest Be the Tie That Binds," and blew into her pitch pipe. The actors gathered around, more sober now after Walter's incident—even Romeo and his onstage love interest were on their best behavior—and followed Mildred's lead. Her soprano wobbled a bit, then headed straight into the hymn. The momentum picked up and voices slipped into the two-part harmony that had been rehearsed for weeks.

I sat at the bar quietly examining meat inventory sheets for next week, trying to get a little work done while I was captive in the Windjammer, but when the cast hit their musical stride on "...*fellowship of kindred minds...*," I shifted my attention to the singers. Not bad. In fact the hymn was downright inspirational. When they sang "...*share each other other's woes...*" and "...*mutual burdens bear...*" I was actually touched. I felt my eyes fill and glanced across the room at Lola, who brushed her hand across her face. Even Pauli had stopped taking photos in deference to the hushed mood of the song. By mutually supporting each other in the hymn, the cast of *Eton Town* had accomplished something on their own that Walter had been harping about for weeks: They'd formed a true ensemble with a common goal.

Apparently deciding to end things on an upbeat note, Lola dismissed the cast after a few directives about reviewing lines and watching their email and Facebook for updates on rehearsals later in the week. They wrapped up against the cold and wind and trudged out the door.

"Good rehearsal, Lola, even if we didn't get to finish the play," Mildred said.

"Maybe we should end it with Act One and the hymn," Vernon added helpfully.

Mildred elbowed Vernon gently. "Sorry about Walter, though."

Lola nodded gratefully and closed the door after them, the last of the cast to leave. Pauli, Penny, and I reset the tables and chairs, swept the floor, and cleaned up coffee spills on the bar.

"Penny, you'd better check on the Episcopal church. Maybe the furnace will be in working order in the next few days," Lola said.

"What do we do about the Creston Players?" Penny asked.

Lola shrugged. "Nothing. Everyone will find out about their *Our Town* sooner or later."

"It's probably already on Facebook," Penny said.

"Let's keep it secret as long as possible."

"Mum's my word," Penny promised, tying the flaps of her winter cap under her chin. "Secrets are safe with me."

The cap reminded me of Gordon Weeks's trapper hat.

Lola collapsed on a stool at the bar, while I poured us a couple of glasses of red wine. Pauli declined a soda, content to sit in my back booth and flip through his afternoon of work while he waited for Carol to pick him up. He'd only recently gotten his driver's license and coping with winter streets in the dark was not on his mother's agenda yet.

"Lot on your plate, girlfriend," I said softly to Lola.

She took off her boots and massaged her feet. "Every show is a potential catastrophe, but this…we've never had to work without a theater. And now Walter."

"He'll be fine. At least he hasn't resigned yet, has he?" I asked.

"No. But he's been threatening nonstop since the body was found."

"Speaking about the murder, I had a chat with Andy last night and—"

"Oh! That's nice. How are they liking Boston? Talk about the cold! One winter, I travelled up there three times because—"

"Lola, wait until you hear this," I said, dropping my voice and glancing at my back booth. Pauli was still occupied with his digital camera. "Sally is worth a fortune."

"What? She works at a car wash."

"And guess who's her therapist?" I asked.

Lola stopped kneading the soles of her stockinged feet. "No! Andy?" she cried.

"Shh. Yes!" Pauli looked up and I waved. "I agreed to keep that little bit of information under wraps. Guess I'll need to tell Bill or Archibald sooner or later."

"Details," Lola begged, forgetting her feet and the *Eton Town* disaster for the moment.

I described my phone conversation with my brother: Sally's family history and the death of her mother, the moneyed background, her visiting Andy for therapy, and then the sudden departure.

"So he had no idea she was coming to Etonville?" Lola asked.

"Nope. She just disappeared from Boston," I said.

"Andy thinks she's back home?"

"I guess so. 'Lawyering up' in case she needs a criminal defense."

Lola studied my expression. "But you don't agree."

"She texted me twice to meet her. I don't think she'd do that if she was four or five hours away by car."

We sipped our wine in silence. It felt much later than five o'clock.

Lola's cell beeped. A text from Walter. She pulled on her boots. "Guess I need to pick him up from the hospital."

"He's okay?"

"Yes. They're releasing him with a prescription for Xanax." Lola's loyalty to Walter was touching; of course, he was an ELT partner and a former romantic interest.

"At least nothing's wrong with his heart," I said.

"Nothing that a personality makeover won't cure," she said.

She caught my eye and we exchanged smiles.

Lola left and I rinsed our glasses in the bar sink. "Pauli? You still awake?"

"Huh?" he asked groggily.

I slid onto the bench of the booth next to him. "Got any useable pictures? I know it didn't last long, but hopefully there's something we can put in the ad and on the website."

"Like, yeah." Pauli started to swipe through photos of actors sitting in the circle, eyes closed meditating, speaking to one another before the rehearsal collapsed into chaos, then laughing hysterically as Abby and Edna tried to top each other in the pace department. If you didn't know any better, you'd think *Eton Town* was a hilarious farce. Which wasn't such a bad thing, come to think of it...

"Send me the best ones and I'll pick a few we can use. Also send me an invoice for your time," I said, ruffling his hair.

He blushed and whipped the hood of his sweatshirt over his head. "Okay," he croaked, his voice still in the process of changing. "You know what you need?"

Many things: Sally's location, the identity of the murderer, a savings account, a night out with Bill—

"A Facebook page and Twitter account for the Windjammer," Pauli said. "Like, yeah, most businesses have them. You could post stuff about the restaurant and people could follow you," Pauli said eagerly.

I admired his enthusiasm. Most of the time he was an average teenager, a nice, respectful kid, his face buried in his cell phone, probably with the same raging hormones as most boys his age. But mention anything digital and Pauli came alive, a virtual encyclopedia on how to manipulate the Internet. Digital forensics, deep searches, even email hacking.

"You know, that's a great idea. Everybody's on social media these days." Even my parents got with the program to see pictures of Andy, Amanda, and Cory. Of me? Not so much. "I'll talk it over with Henry." The Windjammer's website was only a year old; Henry was a technophobe.

"Yeah, because, like, even the Windjammer could use a few more friends," he said sincerely.

So true. "Great. Let's set one up."

Outside Carol's horn honked and Pauli stowed his camera in his backpack. "Gotta bounce."

"Right. Say hi to your mom and I'll text about a time to meet on the Facebook thing."

He shuffled out the door and I stood alone in the middle of the dining room. Facebook...I needed to get home, commune with my laptop, and do a little online surfing.

I switched off the lights, surveyed the dining room to make sure it was shipshape and ready for the morning, and stepped outside to face the weather. I pulled the hood of my parka over my head, treading carefully on the sidewalk that ran adjacent to the restaurant. There were still patches of black ice despite Henry's continuous salting of the cement. Black ice reminded me that Bill hadn't called to "check in" all day. Had he been that busy with the medical examiner? My borrowed Hyundai was cranky, gasping and coughing for a few moments before coming alive. Much the way I was feeling...frustrated, tired, and not thrilled being out on this unusually cold February night.

I swung the car into my driveway, picked my way across the snowy porch, and unlocked the front door. I stared into the darkness of the interior, flipped on the overhead living room light, and shut the front door, stamping winter sludge off my boots. I shivered and popped my jacket onto a coat tree by the door. Then I switched on the table lamp. It had belonged to my great-aunt Maureen. A simple ceramic stem with a now-faded lampshade, it held sentimental value and brought a halo of warmth into the room. I needed something hot to warm up.

* * *

Within fifteen minutes, I was in sweats, a bowl of Henry's chicken noodle soup thawing in the microwave. Perfect for a night like this. I settled in at the kitchen table, ran through my email—mostly junk plus a couple of messages from my father wanting to know if I'd heard from my brother lately and an online university encouraging me to register for a distance learning master's degree. Advanced education…maybe I should consider going back to school.

The microwave signaled my dinner was ready. I dipped a spoon into the bowl. The soup needed another minute so I plopped into a chair and turned my attention back to the laptop. I began to scroll through messages and, for no apparent reason, the nape of my neck tingled. Goose bumps formed on my shoulders and ran down my arms. My radar system was warning me about something…but what? I glanced up at the curtainless window across from the kitchen table and gasped. There was a flash of white with dark features staring into the kitchen. I sat still, glued to the chair, my heart pounding. Was it my feverish imagination, simply a reflection of my own face in the glass? I ignored the microwave binging a second time and forced myself to stand and step closer to the window. I peered outside. I saw only the silhouette of my neighbor's house illuminated by the moon. I retrieved my soup, and settled in once more. I guessed I was jittery these days, what with my car being broken into and a potential murderer on the loose, as Bill had reminded me.

I shifted from my email to my Facebook page. I was interrupted by the muted ringing of my cell phone, which I'd left in my purse in the living room. I thought about avoiding a conversation—there were only so many crises I could handle at one time—but then reconsidered. It might be Bill. I leapt to my feet and bounded to the living room, stubbing my shoeless toe on the corner of the sofa. "Ouch!" I yelled out loud and then felt a breeze on my neck and my little hairs quivered. Again. What was going on?

I scrounged around for my phone. "Hello?" I said quickly.

"Hi. How are you?" asked Bill.

"Fine." My mind raced.

"I meant to call earlier, but then I got a text from Suki who heard from Edna that the ELT was holding a rehearsal at the Windjammer today." He chuckled. "That must have been an event. Seriously, though, I hope it all went well. I do feel bad about the theater being off-limits for the time being."

Something was wrong. A streak of movement blew by the living room window, which was only partially covered by sheer drapes. There was no mistaking a face this time. Someone was watching me.

"Dodie?"

"Yeah," I sputtered out.

"What's the matter?"

"I'm not sure. I think I have a Peeping Tom," I whispered.

"What?" The question exploded out of my cell. "Where are you?"

"In the living room. But—"

"Lock the doors. I'm sending someone over," he shouted.

"Okay, but—"

"Now." He clicked off.

I stuffed my cell in the pocket of my sweatpants and clicked off the living room lights. Both my snoop and myself being in the dark created a level playing field. I wondered if someone had been spying on me at other times as well.

An Etonville police vehicle, lights flashing without a siren, sped down Ames and came to an abrupt stop at my curb. Probably Ralph. It wouldn't be the most efficient interview, but at least I could file a report. The car door opened and a figure alighted. Across the street a couple of neighbors stuck their heads out. I opened the front door and waved to them.

Archibald appeared at my side. "What's going on here?"

"Not Ralph?" I said.

"Nope." That smile creased his face.

"So you think you saw a face at the kitchen window—"

"—and in here," I said.

"That's it?"

Of course, my hairs were jumping, but *that* I could not disclose to Archibald Alvarez, who sat on my sofa, boot-clad feet crossed over one another. He stroked his stubble of a beard and focused his dark, brooding eyes on me. "Yes."

Archibald swept his hair off his forehead. "Any reason to suspect neighbors? People from town? Someone who's a little bit too curious?"

Hard to explain the close-knit Etonville community to a former city cop. "None."

"Maybe someone playing a trick on you?" he said.

A trick? Really? "I don't think so."

"I'll file a report and update Bill. Meanwhile, keep your doors and windows locked."

"I always do."

He smiled lazily, his eyes dropping to my feet and moving slowly to my face again. "Bill says you're one smart cookie."

Whoa. I blinked.

"He said that?" I asked, my voice skittish.

Archibald laughed. "Not in so many words. I think he appreciates your initiative."

Bill's word? "I guess I am a little proactive..."

Archibald leaned forward, his eyes fastened on mine. "You two are a couple, yes?"

Startled, I coughed on a sip of my tea. No one in Etonville had ever put it so bluntly.

"Didn't mean to surprise you. Just checking out the territory," he said evenly.

I felt a warm flush spread from my face to my neck. What did that mean?

He handed me his mug. "Thanks for the coffee."

"Sure." I needed to shift this awkward conversation. "Have you made any progress locating Sally Oldfield?"

"She's a friend of yours, yes?" he asked.

"I'm concerned about her," I answered.

"Have *you* heard from her?"

"No." Technically I hadn't *heard* from her. Texts were silent.

"I'm sure Bill will keep you posted on any progress. Have a good night," he added charmingly and left.

Archibald Alvarez was one slick dude. A real hottie...no denying it. His attention was flattering, but it also put me on edge. What was it about him that made me suspicious? Not for the first time, I considered the contrast between by-the-book Bill and shoot-from-the-hip Archibald. Maybe opposites really did attract.

I'd never been afraid alone in my home. Tonight was a different story. I rechecked all the doors and windows.

15

By the time Archibald left, my soup was cold, my seltzer was warm, and I was out of the investigation mood. No matter. I opened my Facebook page. I hadn't posted anything since the beginning of February when I'd added pictures of the baking class creating colonial desserts. I'd gotten quite a few "likes" from some of my 856 Facebook friends. I scrolled through my home page and laughed out loud at Andy's latest post of Cory singing "Rubber Duckie" in the bathtub, skimmed a few other posts of friends' travel pictures, and then went in search of Sally's page.

On her timeline, she'd posted some shots of ELT auditions and rehearsals from late January with cute captions including the Bangers, Mildred, Vernon, and one of Penny and her whistle. She'd also posted a beautiful picture of a snowy Etonville morning on February 9. Funny, if she wanted to remove herself from her past and all its complications, why post pictures of the town where she was now staying? Maybe someone in Boston was monitoring her Facebook page. Maybe Archibald as well? There was no other personal information on her page, no mention of Boston.

Sally's winter morning photo had generated "likes" from Etonville folks and a few comments: "beautiful"; "winter in NJ!"; "no wonder I'm in Florida." I scrolled farther down her timeline and saw a picture of the two of us. I sat back in my chair. I didn't remember it being taken. We were standing outside the entrance to the Windjammer and Sally was threatening to throw a snowball at me.

I flipped back to the top of her timeline where she'd posted, most recently, the day before Gordon Weeks was murdered. It was an unattributed quote: "I like to be alone…but I hate to be lonely." What was she saying here? Then it struck me. Sally's Facebook page began when she moved to Etonville. There was nothing before January.

I went back to the search bar and typed in *Sarah Oldfield*. There were six or seven listings, but not one that matched Sally's profile. Then I retyped Sara without the H. Bingo! Sara Oldfield attended the Massachusetts Institute of Technology and lived in Boston. No mention of a job or work experience. I scrolled through her timeline. There were pictures of Sally with groupings of various generations. Probably extended family. Sally with a woman who had to be her mother given the startling resemblance; Sally sitting in a leafy green setting backed by academic buildings; Sally with a nice-looking guy. Wonder what happened to him?

Nothing on either Facebook page suggested the recent turbulent life Andy had hinted at, other than the lonely quote. And certainly nothing that told me anything about her current situation. I was stumped.

My cell rang and I checked the caller ID. "Hi."

"Everything okay? Archibald called in," Bill said.

"What did he tell you?" I was curious.

"What you told him, I assume. You thought you saw a face in your kitchen and living room windows." Bill sounded distracted. "I'm going to have Ralph swing by your place later to keep an eye on things. Between your car break-in and tonight's unwelcome visitor, looks like someone is interested in you."

"How well do you know Archibald?" I asked on a whim.

"Why?" He sounded weary.

"Just wondered. You two seem so...different."

Bill chuckled, suddenly more relaxed. "We are different. He was an ace detective, always closed his cases. A little unorthodox in the way he approached investigations, though."

Also in the way he competed as hottest male model. "Did he ever get in trouble?"

"Sometimes. So why the questions? Something you don't like?" Bill asked.

Was now the time to tell Bill about Archibald's late-night visit to the theater? Of course, I was trespassing there myself... "No, no. Like I said, just curious about you two. I don't think he took my peeper all that seriously."

"Look, Dodie, Archie doesn't know you. I do. And if your instincts are telling you something is wrong, I'm listening."

Wow...he believes me!

"...because there's a murderer on the loose."

Right.

"Well, guess I'll get going," he said slowly. "Be careful, okay? Keep your doors and—"

"—windows locked. Right. By the way, what did the medical examiner have to say?"

"Not much. The preliminary finding was pretty predictable. He confirmed the wound was made by a five-inch-blade that severed arteries and nicked the victim's aorta."

Which everyone knew.

"There was one other thing. Of course, I shouldn't be divulging this information…"

"But…" I said quickly.

"I'm telling you only because I know it will eventually leak to the *Etonville Standard* anyway."

"Is that the only reason?" I asked teasingly.

He dropped his voice into his sexy zone. "What do you think?"

"What do you think I think?" I countered.

"Dodie!"

"Okay. What else did you learn?" I asked.

"Gordon Weeks suffered head trauma possibly from a blunt object."

"What kind of trauma?"

"Subdural hematoma. There was a swelling and deep bruise on the back of his head."

"Maybe he was knocked out before he was stabbed?"

"Let's don't jump to conclusions. His head could have hit the floor in the course of the attack. He was a big guy and would have gone down with a bang," Bill said.

Or he could have been hit from behind by someone not capable of overcoming him with a knife. Someone smaller than Gordon Weeks. Someone like Sally. If this line of reasoning occurred to me, chances are it had occurred to either Bill or Archibald. Or both.

"Would you like a ride home? I can be there in ten—"

"Suki's here and she'll drop me off," he said.

"If there's anything you need…?"

His voice slipped back into sexy mode. "Once this cast is off, a little company would be nice."

Yikes.

* * *

Still no return text from Sally about meeting in Bernridge. So before I went to bed, I returned to Sally's Facebook page and commented on her loneliness quote: "So touching...hate to be lonely too." Maybe she'd see it.

I awoke on my own at seven a.m. I was happy that all signs of my cold had dissipated during the last twenty-four hours and now, finally, I was sniffle-free. I vaulted out of bed, energized by a good night's sleep, despite my worry about the peeper, and benign dreams. I indulged in a warm lavender bubble bath while I sorted out my day. First, a call to Lola to check on Walter—he wasn't my favorite person, but he'd had his attack in the Windjammer so I felt I needed to rise above petty feelings. His and mine. Then I needed to stop by Snippets for a trim and to catch up on Etonville gossip. Maybe someone there had heard something about Sally. I submerged my shoulders, the bathwater up to my chin, and weighed my options with regard to her: She wasn't at home or work. Had she gone back to Boston? What about the older "sugar daddy" at the car wash? Maybe I needed to stop back there and get a better description—

My cell binged. I reluctantly rose and stepped out of the tub, swaddling myself in a large Turkish towel. I padded to my bedroom and seized the phone. Lola: *Are you up?* I texted back that I'd call soon and tossed the phone onto my unmade bed. I rifled through my closet. These days I dressed for comfort—corduroy trousers and a cable-knit sweater. I slipped on alpaca socks my mother had sent as a reminder that the weather was in the 70s in Florida, and headed downstairs. I had taken my first sip of coffee when another text came in. Lola was impatient this morning. Fingers crossed there was no more bad news about Walter. I snatched my phone off the kitchen counter and tapped Messages. It wasn't Lola. It was Sally and Andy was wrong; she hadn't left New Jersey to "lawyer up": *OK to meet in Bernridge.*

She supplied another address that I wasn't familiar with so I texted back: *OK but no repeat of Creston.*

I had no desire to waste time at another backstreet bodega. I suggested a meeting at seven tonight. I was due for an evening off after last week and Benny had agreed to pick up some nights this week.

I texted Carol to see if I could pop in for a trim at eight thirty—I could—and then called Lola.

"Hey what's up? Walter okay?"

"I think the Xanax is going to make a new man out of him. He was so pleasant and agreeable when I picked him up. Of course, he was also woozy. I was tempted to steal a few pills," Lola said.

"That bad?"

"Still trying to figure out what to do about the show. The Creston Players are out of the picture now that they're doing the same show in a few months," Lola said huffily.

"Well...it's not *exactly* the same show," I said carefully.

"You know what I mean. Small town, same theme, similar characters," she said.

"Different time period, dialogue, and setting," I countered.

"True. Oh, I don't know. Maybe Walter gave himself an attack so he wouldn't have to deal with all of this," she said.

"What you need is a good hot meal. I'm headed to Snippets for a quick cut and then how about breakfast at Coffee Heaven?"

"You're on. I'll meet you there at nine thirty."

* * *

I bundled up in my down jacket even though the temperature had risen to a balmy thirty-five. The roadway slush was melting and rivulets of mucky water ran down the gutters to the storm drains. My Hyundai was balky, jerking when I stepped on the gas, shuddering when I stepped on the brakes. I couldn't get my Metro out of the shop soon enough; Timothy had promised tomorrow at the latest. Parking on a side street half a block from Snippets forced me to walk in the bracing air. It felt good.

The hair salon was just opening. Carol was on the phone, her employees, Rita and Imogen, setting up the color and cutting stations, and two customers paging through the latest issues of *People* and *Cosmopolitan*. Carol motioned for me to head to the sinks in the rear of the shop where Imogen shampooed my hair, applied conditioner, and did a final rinse, sending a layer of suds down the drain.

"Heard you had a rehearsal of that play at the Windjammer yesterday," Imogen said, tilting her half-shaven head, this month's style, to get a better look at my face.

"Yes, we did."

"Then Walter had a heart attack," she said.

"Not a heart attack. A panic attack."

Imogen squinted at me. "Probably his cholesterol or blood pressure."

"Since it wasn't a heart attack, I don't think—"

"My uncle had a heart attack and they put him on a ton of drugs." She wrapped my head in a towel.

"Really." No sense fighting City Hall.

"Walter should take it easy. Heart attacks are serious stuff." She texted her way to the front of the salon.

Carol led me to a chair in her cutting station and eyeballed my head. "How about an inch and a half?"

That was more than usual, but I was in a frisky mood. "Go for it."

She cut away, pruning my waves and bangs and thinning the clutch of hair at the nape of my neck. "Heard about Walter. That man should take a vacation."

"He has." I shifted in my chair to meet her eyes. "Xanax."

"Poor Lola. She has her hands full with him," Carol said.

"And the play." Carol worked in silence for a moment. "Did you know Sally Oldfield?" I asked.

Carol frowned. "Sally...?"

"She was in the show. New to Etonville. Only been here since January."

"Sally! Sure. Chrystal had a fit because she had the wrong costume for the dress rehearsal," Carol said.

"She seems to have disappeared."

So far, except for Lola, Walter, and the Etonville Police Department, the connection between Sally and Gordon Weeks had been kept under wraps.

"Really? Wait a minute." Carol walked to the front desk, scanned her appointment calendar, and came back. "She had an appointment here the morning of the opening."

Hours before the murder?

"She wanted to clean up her length," Carol said, blowing and brushing my mane that was now shorter and bouncier.

"How did she seem? Was she okay? Or, like, disturbed?"

"Disturbed? I don't think so. In fact she was talking about a cruise she was taking in April."

Something was wrong with this picture. Sally was upset seeing Gordon Weeks and another man earlier in the week and yet here she was, chatting up Carol about a vacation after the show closed.

"Did she mention anything about having visitors from home? From Boston?"

"Boston? Is that where she's from? Oooh talk about cold! Weather Channel said it's ten degrees there today."

"Sally?" I nudged Carol back to the subject.

"She never mentioned anyone visiting her. Except for her father. She said he might be coming in town for the play."

* * *

Carol had divulged all the information she had on Sally, so I viewed myself approvingly in the mirror, paid my bill, and coaxed the Hyundai to travel the mile or so to Coffee Heaven.

Lola was waiting for me, her eyes widening when she saw my new 'do. "Very nice. Maybe you should pop next door and see if the invalid needs anything."

I giggled. "Bill's not an invalid but maybe you're right. I should check up on him."

"The regular, Dodie?" asked Jocelyn.

"Sure. No, wait! Make that black coffee and two eggs over easy." Out with the old, in with the new. My hair, my breakfast...

Jocelyn shrugged and filled a coffee cup at the booth next to ours.

"I picked up some scuttlebutt at Snippets," I said quietly.

"From the staff?" Lola asked.

They'd been a great source of chitchat in the past. "From Carol."

"Share!"

As we ate, I brought Lola up-to-date. "It seems odd. She has this stormy week with two different men, one of whom ends up dead, and she's planning a cruise?"

"But she didn't know Gordon Weeks was going to die later that day when she was at Snippets."

We munched in silence.

Jocelyn refilled our cups. "Lola, you think the show is ever going to go on?"

"I hope so. We're looking into alternate venues," Lola said.

"Because the word is, maybe you could do half of it now and the other half next month. Kind of like a series. Part one and part two," Jocelyn said, trying to be helpful.

"That's an idea," Lola said weakly.

"That would handle the three-hour problem." Jocelyn left our checks.

"See what I mean about the town not coming out?" Lola was frantic.

I patted her hand. "Don't panic yet. Leave that to Walter. Things might work out." I gave her an encouraging smile and took her advice. I strolled next door to the Municipal Building.

16

Edna was on dispatch. "Ralph, you better get a move on. There's a 10-14 at the library. That's right. Citizen with a suspect. They caught a kid throwing snowballs into the basement windows." She paused. "You're going to have to put the fear of God in him even if he is only ten years old. And don't forget there's an 11-26 in the parking lot at Lacy's Market."

I was betting that was a vehicle issue.

Edna lowered her voice. "Don't let the chief know you stopped at the Donut Hole. You're supposed to be patrolling the south end of town and he's in a snit. Yeah. 10-4."

"Busy morning?"

Edna stuffed a pencil behind one ear. "The usual. Suki's in Creston on department business, Archibald is running some errands for the chief, and Ralph is supposed to be on duty in town."

"So...a snit?"

Edna removed her headset. "He threw kind of a hissy fit this morning over some missing paperwork. I think he's had it up to here with the broken ankle, if you know what I mean."

"Wow. Poor guy."

"Maybe you can get him to snap out of it," she said with a grin and a wink. "Nice haircut."

I hated to think to what degree Etonville discussed Bill's and my relationship on a regular basis.

"I'll try." I turned away from the dispatch window.

"Sorry about the rehearsal at the Windjammer yesterday. We got carried away," she said awkwardly.

"Hate to tell you, but the play didn't make much sense," I added.

Edna stiffened her spine. "Abby brings out the competitor in me. We have a history."

I'd say. They nearly came to blows during *Arsenic and Old Lace.*

"What's the lunch special? Henry have something fun up his sleeve?" Edna asked hopefully. Her appetite was legendary in Etonville, though how she maintained her rail-thin physique was beyond the town.

"We're going with the Mardi Gras theme. Seafood po'boys," I said.

"What's in them?"

"Shrimp, oysters, and crabmeat—"

A familiar clunking as Bill stepped out of his office and smashed a crutch on the doorframe. "Edna!" he yelled.

"—on a French baguette. Gumbo for dinner."

"Save me some." Edna stuck her head out of the dispatch window. "Yes, Chief?"

Bill thumped down the hall. "Get Ralph. The library is calling my private line about that kid and the snowballs."

"Copy that, Chief." She went back to work.

Yep, it was a snit all right. "Do you have a minute?" I asked.

Bill nodded and made his way back to his office. He waited for me to enter and settle into a chair opposite his desk before he bumped his way from the door, around the desk, and into his seat. He practically threw his crutches onto the floor. Whew. I decided to pretend I didn't notice. The injury *was* wearing on him. Circles under his eyes attested to little sleep, and the spikes of his brush cut were pointed every which way. Had he been tugging on his hair?

"Tough day?" I asked gently.

"Everybody is out and about but me," Bill complained, pouting like a kid forced to stay inside and do his homework.

"You're supposed to take it easy for a few weeks, right? Besides, you've got Archibald leading the murder investigation."

Bill looked up at me. "Have you been talking with him?"

"No," I said hastily. "Not since last night. I assumed..." I let the thought that Archibald was doing the legwork dangle in the ether. "Gives you more time in the office."

"To shuffle paperwork. And some of it is missing," he grumbled.

"Yes?"

"A report from the CSI team on the evidence at the crime scene. There were three sheets and one of them is gone. I guess I misplaced it somehow. And that's not like me." He frowned.

"I picked up some information on Sally Oldfield." I wanted to be helpful but didn't intend to share anything that would incriminate Sally any further than her behavior already had. And I definitely did not plan to violate Andy's confidence. I also knew that anything I told Bill would end up with Archibald.

His face brightened. "Yeah? Nothing's come in from the APBs we put out in Creston and Bernridge."

"You know about her background? The Boston Brahmin thing?"

"I heard." He whistled softly. "An inheritance worth millions after her mother died."

"Odd that she was living in a rooming house and working at a car wash. Of course, she told me she wanted a change in her life," I said.

"Archibald has made inquiries at both locations. Nothing much to go on."

"Sally and I are Facebook friends. I checked her timeline."

Bill sat forward. I had his interest now. "Oh?"

"She mostly posted pictures of ELT rehearsals on her personal page, which she created in January when she moved to Etonville. And a quote on loneliness posted the day before the murder."

"Poor little rich girl?" he asked.

"Maybe. But I never got the feeling Sally was a loner. I mean, she meshed with the ELT, fit right in," I said.

Bill laughed. "Not sure that was such a good thing."

I laughed too. It was nice feeling comfortable around each other.

"I also heard at Snippets…"

Bill groaned.

"Still a great source of information," I pointed out.

"Yeah. So?"

"Carol *said* Sally *said* she was planning on taking a cruise after the show closed. That doesn't sound like someone in a crisis," I said.

"Who said she was in a crisis?" Bill asked.

Uh-oh. Was I helping or hurting her case?

"I mean, that sounds pretty chill for someone…who might be…involved in a murder…" I finished lamely.

Bill studied my face, those magnetic eyes searing right through me. "Is there something you're keeping to yourself?"

"What makes you think that?" I asked.

"History. One of these days, you're going to learn you can trust me."

Ditto.

"Anything new on Gordon Weeks?" I wanted to change the subject.

"Nothing. What he was doing in the Etonville Little Theatre is beyond me and Archibald." He paused and looked me in the eye. "What about you?"

"Me? I have no idea what he was doing there."

Edna's voice shot out of his intercom. "Chief, Ralph's on the line. He responded to the 10-14 and wants to know what to do with the suspect?"

"The ten-year-old? Take him home and turn him over to his parents. He's truant anyway. It's a school day," Bill said.

"Copy that."

I was thinking fast. I had an appointment with Sally at seven in Bernridge. Depending on how that went, it could last five minutes or an hour. I had no idea what would happen after our meet-up. But either way, I would probably be back in Etonville by nine. "How about that nightcap you owe me? I'll be off work by nine tonight. I could swing by and give you a lift home?"

Bill smiled slowly. "Maybe I'll take Archibald up on his offer to man the office this evening." He nodded. "Sure, why not?"

I checked his wall clock. I had to scoot. "It's a date."

I needed the hustle and bustle of the Windjammer to keep my mind off tonight—both the meeting with Sally and the prospect of a late-night rendezvous with Bill. I was wound-up about both events.

The Mardi Gras theme lent a carnival atmosphere to the restaurant. Enrico had hauled in a carton of beads that I'd ordered from a party store in New York and now Carmen and Gillian were distributing the green, purple, and gold strings, as well as lunch, to customers.

"So pretty, don't you know," said one of the Banger sisters.

"It matches my ensemble," said the other, who wore a purple sweater over a green blouse.

"It sure does," I agreed. "More coffee?"

They both nodded. The po' boys were a hit.

"Dodie, the sandwiches are delicious, but what does pobboy mean?"

"It's not pobboy, it's po' boy. Like 'poor boy,'" I said.

"Oh, that's too bad. What happened to him?" one asked.

"Nothing. It wasn't a real boy," I said slowly.

The sisters squinted at me as if I were responsible for the fate of the child.

"The name came from a New Orleans sandwich that was invented during the Depression and given out to striking workers who were considered 'poor boys' so…" I looked from one to the other and gave up. "The boy ate the sandwich and lived to a ripe old age."

"Oh, that's such a nice story. We're so happy for him." They clapped their hands in appreciation.

Geez. "You ladies have a good day." I rang up their bill at the cash register. "Those two are a couple of sandwiches short of a picnic," Benny said.

"Tell me about it. Sure you're okay closing tonight?" I asked.

"Oh yeah. Got a hot date?" he teased.

"I think I'll probably spend a nice, quiet evening at home." No sense in stirring up anybody's imagination.

In the kitchen, Henry was stirring up a pot of gumbo, his arms moving rhythmically in a full circle. He was in a particularly good mood: True to Lola's word, she'd bought a full-page ad in the *Etonville Standard* promoting the Windjammer's community spirit. It would be published tomorrow. The editor called to get a quote from Henry and he laid it on thick, how he was thrilled to help the theater in its time of need, that businesses in town had to think about more than their own success—a dig at La Famiglia—when disasters hit. The newspaper claimed they had to bump a story on the mayor's plans to change the street-cleaning schedule. Not that they weren't happy to have the ad revenue. Given the finances at the theater, I had the feeling that some of the revenue came out of Lola's pocket. I couldn't wait to see the ad.

I spent part of the afternoon doing general inventory for the week— vegetables, fruit, and seafood. And then I counted the frozen apple pies for the concession stand. There had been two dozen, but what with the giveaway the night of the murder and yesterday's rehearsal, we were down to six. Of course, if the show never opened, intermission desserts were a moot point. I made a mental note to mention this to Lola; theme food seemed a little less critical at this moment.

17

I shouldn't have been surprised at the address Sally gave me for our meeting: the diner across the street from the E-Z Clean Car Wash in Bernridge. Pretty smart of Sally. If anyone was looking for her, they would have already scoped out her place of employment and moved on to other territory. I was learning new things about Sally Oldfield every day.

I drove through the working-class neighborhood until I saw the neon sign ahead that advertised the now-closed car wash. I slowed down and pulled next to the curb at a spot where I could see into the Primrose Diner. Interior lights were bright, illuminating the entire front section of the restaurant. Booths lined the wall that faced the street and I could see heads, arms, occasionally a body as someone leaned forward on the bench. But no sign of anyone who resembled Sally.

I locked my Hyundai—who would want to snatch it, but still—and walked briskly across the street, easing my parka up around my ears. I pushed open the glass doors, and from the waiting area, scanned rooms on either side of me. No Sally. I checked my watch: 7:05.

"How many?" asked the waiter, a Mediterranean type with a bushy mustache and a full head of slick black hair.

"Two. I'm supposed to meet someone here. Mind if I take a look around?" I asked.

He shrugged, returned menus to a holder by the cashier, and resumed watching a reality talent show on the television. I stepped to the edge of the room on my left. Six tables of family groups—adults and children discussing the menus, spilling water, and sharing plates of food. In the recesses of the booths I could see a couple arguing quietly but vehemently and an elderly twosome, silent, staring at the remains of their dinners. I turned around and headed to the other dining area. Less crowded, there were singles having dinner alone at the counter and a scattering of twos and threes at the tables. Everyone was engrossed in eating, minding their own business, reading the newspaper, generally unwinding at the end of the day.

Was this the bodega all over again? Annoyance was rearing its tired head. My shoulders slumped and I shifted my focus back to the entrance. No latecomers walking into the diner. I checked my cell; no texts apologizing for being late. That's it, I was done playing "meet-up" games with Sally. I'd head back to Etonville and kill an hour until I picked up Bill. Maybe I had time to stop home and change…something a little sexier, a little less Nanook-of-the-North.

"Dodie," a soft voice said at my back.

I whirled around. It was Sally. I blinked and stared: a knit cap pulled low over her forehead, a black, scruffy coat, and work boots. She looked girlish, homeless, and frightened. "Sally!"

Her eyes darted around the diner. "We can't talk here. Come on."

I tailed her out the door and down the street. She cut through an alley and ended up on a block that looked deserted. No lights in the houses and hulking shadows of trucks and autos in driveways.

"Where are we going?" I called out.

No answer from Sally, who shot down a sidewalk. I ran faster than she was speed-walking and stepped in front of her, putting out an arm to halt her progress. "Sally! Stop! What are we doing here?"

She was breathing raggedly and pointed to a car ten yards away. It was a nondescript, fairly new Chevy. She'd obviously ditched her sporty Jeep Cherokee. Sally climbed into the front seat, but not before she scanned the street—it was deathly still. We sat in silence for a moment as she cranked the engine to generate some heat.

"Talk to me," I said quietly. "Tell me what's going on."

She closed her eyes. "I'm sorry I didn't wait for you at the bodega."

"You know the police are looking for you?"

She nodded.

"In fact, I think you might be the prime suspect in the murder investigation."

Sally pulled the cap off her head, her hair was matted in clumps. Her eyes looked hollowed out. "I didn't do it."

"Then come in and talk to Chief Thompson. He's a fair guy. He'll listen to you."

"I can't. No one will believe me," she said.

"I believe you," I said.

Sally regarded me warily. "I don't know why."

"I have good instincts and those instincts tell me you aren't capable—physically or emotionally—of stabbing that man. And then watching him bleed to death."

She swallowed. "I'm not."

"Even though you know the victim," I added.

She rotated in her seat to face me. "What?"

"Sally, we spotted Gordon Weeks, that's his name, although I guess you know that, Sunday afternoon across the street from the theater. You were shocked to see him. So tell me what happened in the theater," I pleaded.

Sally twisted her still-gloved hands. "I wanted to meet to tell you I was innocent. I wanted to explain everything to you but…" Her voice faded away to nothing.

I went for a different, less direct tactic. "Where are you staying?"

"I have a room," she said.

"Here in Bernridge?"

She didn't answer.

"You can trust me," I said, the same words Bill had said to me hours earlier.

"Please don't push me." Sally's words were thrust into the space between us.

I exhaled slowly. "All right. Let's start from the beginning. I know about your family background, your mother, the inheritance."

"It was only a matter of time before word got out."

"So you were running away from home when you arrived in Etonville?" I purposely avoided mentioning Andy and entangling him in Sally's predicament, whatever it might turn out to be. Besides, he'd warned me to stay out of the whole mess.

"I told you. I needed a change in my life," Sally said.

"And everything was going well. You had a room, a job, you were a part of the theater, and then Gordon Weeks came to town."

She hesitated. "Yes."

"And you freaked out."

"Yes."

"And he came to visit you at the rooming house," I said.

Sally gasped.

"Angela was helpful. And she really likes you a lot."

Sally started to cry, burying her face in her hands. I tentatively reached for her and, startled, she cringed.

"It's okay. Things will work out if you'll come back and talk with Chief Thompson."

Sally sniffed. "He wanted to meet me so I went to the theater and saw him...like that...and I panicked...and then you came in and I ran."

A car cruised down the street past us, slowing ahead at a stop sign. Sally ducked down and recoiled into her coat. "I have to go now," she said, eyes on the vehicle down the street.

"Go? But we haven't settled anything and you haven't told me who Gordon Weeks is."

"I'm not sure who he is," she said, sobbing again.

"I don't believe that. I saw the way you looked at him last Sunday. It was the look of someone who—"

"Please!" Sally begged.

"Why did you want to meet with me if you won't tell me anything?" I asked, frustrated. I clutched the door handle.

"I wanted to tell you in person I'm not guilty. And I need a favor." She'd stopped crying, her voice low and steady.

"A favor? Look, Sally—"

"I dropped something that day. I need it," she said vehemently.

My neck hairs tingled inside the collar of my jacket. "What is it?"

"A photograph. It was small, like maybe three inches square and folded. I had it in my hand but when I ran, I was so scared...I must have..."

I flashed back to the day of the murder. I remembered Sally had been holding something. "But why are we talking about a picture when you might be facing murder charges?" I asked.

"Please. Text me when you find it. It's got to be in the theater," she said, desperation creeping into her voice.

I gave up. "Promise me you'll at least think about coming in."

Sally's head bobbed vigorously.

I slipped out of the car and had barely shut the door before she took off, speeding down the street. I stood on the sidewalk, discouraged. What had been the point of the meeting? Other than to ask me to search for a photo. There was no way she was appearing at the Etonville Police Department and admitting she knew Gordon Weeks. She couldn't even admit it to me and I saw proof of their association.

The temperature was dropping and the wind was picking up. I flipped up the hood of my jacket and stared down the street. It wasn't late—not even eight o'clock—but the darkness felt as if it was well into the night. I began to retrace my steps up the street. A few yards into the alley I noticed shadows to the right of me. The backyards of houses that faced the street where Sally and I had sat in her car and talked. A few bare trees with snow-laden branches dipped to and fro like dancing skeletons. I hadn't noticed how eerie this back lane was earlier. I was too busy trying to keep up with Sally. But now, a spooky sensation creeped me out. The only sound, at first, was the scraping of my boots on the slushy gravel, stones and chunks of ice rubbing against each other. Then I could swear I heard an echo of my footsteps. I turned backward and saw nothing; never mind, I told myself, and broke into a light jog. My hairs began to twitch and my heart pounded. Every step I took seemed to be answered with another one, a fraction of a second behind mine.

I was puffing heavily, cold air painful in my lungs as I increased my speed. I could see the end of the alley ahead and almost laughed. In my relief, I didn't detect the sheet of black ice in the middle of the lane. I'd missed it trailing Sally, but now I was moving quickly and carelessly. Unknowingly, I placed one foot on the ice and skidded forward, landing facedown on the gravel and freezing mud. I could taste the muck on my lips and my left cheek felt raw and sore. My ears were ringing; I knew I wouldn't be able to hear someone stalking me. I rolled onto my back and faced the night sky, the moon covered in a sheer layer of clouds, and battled to stand up and regain my footing. I gingerly moved to the end of the alley and onto the street. The diner was up ahead on my left, the car wash on my right. I must have looked a fright—two young guys left the diner and stared at me. I ignored them and ran across the street. I fumbled with the door key and collapsed into the front seat, gasping. The street was uninhabited now. The diner had posted a Closed sign in the window. Could it all have been a figment of my overactive imagination? Bill would probably think so…

I turned the key in the ignition and the engine sputtered as it had done on many occasions in the last few days. But this time as I cranked the motor, it wouldn't turn over. I pumped the gas pedal and tried again. The Hyundai stubbornly refused to start. My dread returned. I didn't feel safe in a deadbeat car on a street that was deserted in a town I wasn't too familiar with. If I had to call for help, how was I going to explain my presence here? Meaning, what would I tell Bill if I got caught texting and meeting with Sally? Not to mention how mortified I'd feel with my face in this state. I switched the ignition key to Off. The evening had been a bust and all I had to show for it were a scraped cheek and a split lip that was swelling slightly. I rested my stinging face on the steering wheel and my great-aunt Maureen's words came to mind: *Dorothy, you must accept that some days you are the pigeon and some days you are the statue.* Right now, I swore I could hear wings flapping.

As if the Hyundai took pity on me, I cranked the engine again and it sparked to life. I limped back to Etonville, careful to keep gunning the engine even at red lights. No sense giving the car the opportunity to stall.

It was a quarter to nine by the time I pulled into my driveway. I'd argued with myself all the way home from Bernridge: cancelling on Bill versus cleaning up and creating an excuse for my appearance. Date night won out and I decided to suck it up, no matter how Frankensteinish I looked. I'd laugh it off as though falling on my face were an ordinary event.

I texted Bill that I was running a little late and confronted my bathroom mirror. I had to promise myself an extra caramel macchiato in the morning to get me to open my eyes. I squinted at first; maybe if I couldn't see well, I'd miss a few marks…no luck. My cheek was red and scratched with a bruise that might turn some shade of blue by morning. My upper lip was cut with bits of dried blood clinging to the perimeter of my mouth. Altogether not a pretty sight. I needed to compensate. I washed my wounds gently, applied ice to my mouth, a bandage to my cheek, and slipped into a red silk blouse. With my black leggings, I thought I was looking pretty hot from the neck down. I gave my hair a once-over, grabbed my coat, cashmere scarf, and purse, and prayed that the Hyundai had forsaken its balky behavior. The car gods were listening and we made it to the Municipal Building without incident.

I pulled in front and texted Bill, as he'd instructed, and within a minute he was bumping down the hall and allowing Suki to open the front door as well as my car door for him. I pulled my hair around my face and kept it slightly angled away. If I could keep my eyes on the road ahead, maybe my secret would be safe until we arrived at Bill's.

"Hey there," I said as cheerfully as I could with a puffy lip.

"Thanks, Suki," Bill said. "Have a good night."

She nodded and patted the car door. "See you tomorrow." Suki smiled enigmatically. As a Buddhist cop, it was her calling card. That and her om-like expression even under the direst of circumstances.

I eased away from the curb. "Sorry I'm late."

"Busy night at the restaurant?"

I fervently hoped so. "The usual."

"Pretty wild in the department too."

Bill described Suki having to handle a traffic accident down on the highway while Ralph had to contend with Mrs. Parker's security alarm that went off because she'd mistakenly set the motion detectors forgetting her cat, Missy, was busy running in circles.

"I spent the evening on dispatch," he said ruefully. "I *cannot wait* until this cast comes off."

"Only a few more weeks," I said. "Patience!"

"Yeah. Not my strength." He turned sideways in his seat. "You took off early from the Windjammer?"

"Benny likes the extra shifts. Archibald's not covering the office this evening?" I asked casually.

"He had some personal business to take care of in New York."

I wondered about his "personal business."

"Have you?" Bill asked.

"Sorry?"

"I said, have you eaten?" He chuckled. "I know you work at a restaurant, but I've seen you get so involved in a job that you forget about food."

I'd been so focused on Sally and a stalker tonight that I hadn't noticed my stomach growling until now. "Actually I was too busy to eat. What do have in mind?"

He thought for a moment. "How about an herb-and-cheese omelet?"

My mouth watered. "Sounds heavenly. You can cook and hop around at the same time?"

"Is that a challenge? Watch me."

I helped Bill out of the Hyundai and guided him hobbling to the front door. He was so fixated on his crutches that he hadn't paused to look me in the face. Once inside his house, I closed the door and fortified myself for what was to come. I didn't have to wait long.

He tossed his uniform jacket onto a chair in the foyer. "Make yourself useful. There's a nice bottle of pinot noir on the center island. It won't take long for me to whip up—" He turned to smile, then he stared at me. "What the—? What happened to you?"

"Don't go all ballistic. I fell on some black ice on the sidewalk in front of the Windjammer. *You* know how treacherous that stuff can be—"

"Why didn't you tell me? We could have cancelled," he said sympathetically.

"And miss your herb-and-cheese omelet? Not on your life." I attempted to sound upbeat and energetic.

I didn't fool Bill. He regarded me uneasily. "Is that the whole story? The black ice?"

"Yep." My great-aunt Maureen informed me at a young age: *It's only lying if one doesn't have a good reason. Otherwise it's just fibbing.* I couldn't bring myself to share the Sally story until I could sort out a few loose ends. Definitely a good reason.

I watched him whisk fresh herbs and grated cheeses into the eggs and milk while I uncorked the wine. It needed a moment to breathe and so did I.

"Mmmm. Looks delicious," I said.

"The trick is a mixture of Parmesan and Asiago cheeses," he said while chopping fresh chives.

"Maybe you need your own cooking show," I teased.

"What, and give up policing Etonville?" he said in mock disbelief.

"You wouldn't have to deal with the 11-26s and 20-20s and 10-40s."

Bill lifted his head from the cutting board. "Or the homicide investigations."

"Those too."

We were silent for a moment. "Any new leads?"

"Since a few hours ago? We're looking into Gordon Weeks, but frankly nothing so far ties him to the ELT. The only thing to go on is Sally Oldfield. We got in touch with family members, but no one knows where she is. It's like she fell off the face of the earth. Archibald is planning to speak to a few people up there."

"In Boston?" I asked, cautious.

He hesitated. "Uh-huh." Bill sprinkled a pinch of salt and some pepper into his foaming liquid and poured the mixture into an omelet pan.

My back was beginning to ache and I had a crick in my neck. It was either the fall on the ice or my fear that Archibald Alvarez would discover Sally's hideaway before I did. We made ourselves comfortable on a couple of stools at the center island, the corner of Bill's mouth ticking upward impishly as I moaned aloud at the first taste of his omelet. We devoured the fluffy egg-and-cheese concoction as if we hadn't eaten all day, washing it down with the red wine.

"That was delicious," I said, wiping my mouth as Bill refilled our glasses.

"Let's move to the living room," he said.

"Are you sure I can't clean up? After all, you did the cooking..."

"It'll keep." He smiled.

I picked up our glasses and obediently followed him as he crutched through his early American dining room and into the comfy living room. A fire was already laid in the fireplace and, as Bill struck a match, I could feel myself oozing into the cushions of his sofa. The food, the wine, the glow from the snapping flames...

Bill hit a switch on a CD player, lowered the lights, and joined me on the couch, laying his crutch to one side. The mellow, sexy tones of Norah Jones singing "Come Away with Me" melted into the room. Was Bill trying to tell me something? His eyes sparkled in the red-yellow light from the fireplace.

"I love this CD," he said and sipped his wine.

"You're a country western guy." At least that's what he'd told me so I had gifted him a couple of Garth Brooks CDs for Christmas.

"I am. But a guy can like different artists. Besides, some occasions call for something a little more..."

Romantic?

"Relaxing...at the end of a hectic day," he said.

Oh.

And then he slipped his arm around my shoulders, giving them a squeeze. "This is nice."

Which part, my fuzzy brain wondered: Norah Jones, the fireplace, my shoulders? "Yeah."

Bill angled my head slightly to get a better take on my face and his finger grazed my injured cheek with a whisper of a touch. "Does it hurt?"

Ouch. "Not really."

He tilted my head upward and moved in, brushing my damaged lips with his. "Does this?"

Of course, but who cared? I shook my head numbly. Norah sang on, my head spun, and I closed my eyes as he pressed his mouth against mine again. Sure, it wasn't the first time, but it had been a while, and nothing quite matched this tenderness, this concern—

I heard a soft ringing. Bill relinquished my lips and sat up, jamming his hand into his pocket to retrieve his cell phone. He cleared his throat, wiped the edge of his mouth. "Yes?"

I smiled inside. This could be the night...

"Hanging out."

I opened one eye.

"No problem. It's okay," he said,

That didn't sound good.

"What? No kidding. Sure."

He listened for a minute, then became alert and my little hairs—that had been taking a snooze, like a few other parts of me—were now vigilant. Bill clicked off and leaned back into the sofa. "That was Archibald."

Why was I not surprised? "Oh?" I said, trying for casual.

"Seems like Sally Oldfield has been hiding in plain sight."

My heart slid to the bottom of my stomach and then rebounded. "Boston?"

"No. Bernridge."

"Bern...wow...Archibald...found her?"

"Said he tailed her there earlier this evening."

My insides were fidgety but my outside was cool and composed. Archibald had tailed Sally to Bernridge? From where? More likely he had tailed me. Now I was really stressed out. Had I led Archibald to Sally? Where else had he followed me? What else did he know? Questions were bouncing around my brain like buzzing bees.

Bill was staring at me. "What's wrong?"

"Nothing...I was wondering where Sally was...when he...picked up her trail." My explanation was flimsy at best.

"He didn't say. Only that he found her in Bernridge near the car wash and was keeping an eye on her."

I swallowed a mouthful of wine to cover my worry. If Archibald found Sally, then it was my fault. "Uh, excuse me. Need to use the powder room."

"Sure. I'll freshen up our glasses," he said.

"Great." I sent Bill a bogus grin and dashed to the bathroom. I had to warn Sally. Whatever her reason for concealing herself in Bernridge, it had to be her decision to meet with Bill. Not mine. And definitely not Archibald's. I snatched my cell from the depths of my bag and tapped on her number: *Detective has found you. Could be watching u now. He's smart. Text me later.*

I peeked in the mirror. My cheek was still red and my upper lip looked raggedy—partly from scraping the ground when I took a header on the ice and partly from smudged lipstick. Which reminded me that Bill was still waiting on the couch. I smoothed my blouse and repaired my lips.

He was texting when I returned, tossing his cell on an end table when he caught sight of me. He touched his face. "Looks painful."

I smiled weakly.

"Would you like some coffee and dessert?"

I was sobering up quickly and felt frazzled. It was going to be impossible to focus on Bill's chiseled face and blue eyes, as well as other parts of his anatomy, while I was simultaneously irritated with Archibald and stewing about Sally. "Fine."

Bill laid out cream and sugar, even though he knew I didn't use either—and neither did he. No doubt about it: He was as distracted as I was. Our minds separately on Sally Oldfield and Gordon Weeks. Garth Brooks had replaced Norah Jones, the mood had shifted substantially.

"Great dinner," I said.

"Thanks." He sipped coffee. "Hope the ELT gets rehearsals straightened out."

"Me too."

"Getting the Metro back soon?"

"Tomorrow morning."

Enough of the small talk. I needed to get home and think through my next steps. Bill must have felt the same.

"Early day for me too," he said.

We stood at the center island awkwardly. "Okay, well, I should be going," I said.

He kissed me sweetly on the good cheek. "I'd suggest turning the other one but under the circumstances…"

"Right." He followed me to the foyer where I got into my coat and wrapped my scarf around my neck. "Let me know when Sally is picked up?"

"Will do. I've got to get back to Archibald."

I nodded and proceeded out into the piercingly cold night, my thoughts as scattered as the patches of snow on Bill's driveway.

18

It was midnight when I crept up Fairfield and turned onto Ames. Though it was chilly in the Hyundai once I shut off the engine, I remained seated behind the wheel. I needed to drill down on Sally's background, her relationship with Gordon Weeks, and the identity of the "sugar daddy." I hadn't heard back from her yet.

I took the plunge and opened the car door, picking my way gingerly across icy areas of the front walk, wary of unwanted visitors creeping around my yard. I unlocked and relocked the door, undressed, and climbed into bed, my laptop by my side. I'd had a notion to go back to Sally's Facebook page and google Gordon Weeks again. Maybe there were things I'd missed.

I was asleep in minutes.

* * *

The wind whistled around the eaves of the roof while bright, buttery sunshine blasted through the window panes. It was almost seven a.m. I'd only slept a few hours, but I was wide awake. Must have been that dream about traipsing through a jungle chased by a team of doctors in white coats trying to get me to stop and be examined. I tentatively patted my lip—still sore, but with good memories from last night—and my cheek, crusty where the skin had been rubbed raw. My plan had been to pick up the Metro as soon as Timothy's Timely Service opened at eight thirty, swing by Lola's to see if she wanted to get a bite of breakfast, and mull over yesterday's events. But sleep was impossible and I was too early for Timothy's. I could do some Internet sleuthing, or...

I hopped out of bed, determined to face my face, jump in the shower, and be out of the house by seven thirty. The bruise on my cheek had transitioned to a light shade of blue. Some makeup would help, but the scratch would be visible. My mouth was in better shape; lip gloss would cover up the cut and the swelling had gone down. I luxuriated in the hot steamy water for a full five minutes, washing off the soreness from last night's encounter with the black ice. I dressed quickly, leaving coffee until later. There would be plenty of time to caffeinate myself after I'd collected my Metro. But at the moment I was a woman on a mission.

The Hyundai gave me no trouble, no doubt ready to rejoin Timothy Jr.'s assemblage of used cars waiting to be trotted out for desperate customers. I wasn't sure what I was expecting to find, but my "good nose for detection," as Bill had referred to it last spring, was leading me back to 417 Belvidere Street. I drove past the house where Sally had rented a room. I spotted Archibald's black Ford adjacent to a snow pile, along with several other cars stashed at odd angles against the curb. Good. I hadn't been certain he'd be at the rooming house this morning. But what was I going to do if I saw him come out and jump in his car? Follow him? To where? I had no answers, I just knew my stubborn intuition wanted to know what he was up to.

I pulled into the Etonville Public Library parking lot, across the road and several houses away from 417 Belvidere, and came to a stop in a corner of the lot, tucked between a sizeable embankment of snow on one side and a dumpster on the other. But still within viewing distance of the house. At this hour the neighborhood was noiseless, the only traffic besides my Hyundai being a fruit-and-vegetable delivery truck probably rumbling by on its way to the Shop N Go. Which reminded me I needed to call Cheney Brothers about missing items on yesterday's order. I clicked off the motor, leaned back in my seat, my vision clearing the dashboard, and waited.

Ten minutes passed, then fifteen. The door to 417 opened and I snapped to attention. *The house was waking up.* A woman walked out of the rooming house with Angela. They got into a car and backed out of the driveway. A few minutes later a man exited the front door and walked down the street past the library. Nothing there. Even with my microfleece gloves my fingers were becoming chilled. Maybe this was a silly waste of time. Maybe Archibald slept in, after a night of surveillance. Had he found Sally and brought her to the station? It was eight fifteen; I could text Lola, drop off the Hyundai—

The door opened again. It was Archibald. Leather collar up around his ears, hands jammed in his pockets, he hurried down the porch steps to his Ford. Instinctively, I scooted down in my seat; but I needn't have bothered.

Archibald was also a person on a mission. He looked neither right nor left but climbed into his car, started the engine, and maneuvered off the pile of frozen snow and drove down Belvidere. I waited a couple of seconds, then eased out of my parking space, and headed in the same direction. A school bus moved in front of me and I hit the brakes. Irritated, I craned my neck to see around the bus, but there was no point. I had lost Archibald. Or so I thought. The bus trundled on, making a right on Anderson, revealing Archibald's car ahead, his blinker indicating he was turning left. He was heading toward Route 53...to Bernridge? He picked up speed and entered the highway. Off to my right I could see Timothy's service station with Timothy unlocking the door. I pressed the accelerator and moved into a line of traffic on Route 53. Bernridge was only a couple of exits up the road. I passed an SUV and a pickup truck and slid into a spot two car lengths behind Archibald's Ford. We were a quarter of a mile from the Bernridge turnoff. I waited for Archibald to move to the right lane to exit. But he passed the exit and drove on. Fully committed by now, I kept pace and stayed with him for another two miles. Past the U-turn to Route 3 and New York City. Where was he going?

Archibald suddenly decreased his speed and moved to the slow lane, exiting at a roadside diner. I slowed up, allowing several cars to pass me before I pulled onto the shoulder of the road, flicking on my emergency blinkers. I waited. Archibald's Ford moved into a parking space next to a dark-colored sedan. A man alighted and met Archibald, who had jumped out of his car. Though I could only see his profile, there was something about the man that felt familiar. I snapped a picture on my cell phone. The two shook hands and went inside.

Unless I intended to wait here until they'd finished their breakfast, the only sensible course of action was to return to Etonville. I took the next exit, did a U-turn and drove home. Was he on Etonville police business... or something else?

* * *

I'd picked up my Metro, new window working perfectly, left the Hyundai to the care of Timothy Jr., after warning him about the car's obstinacy, and texted Lola to meet me at Coffee Heaven. We sat in a booth waiting for Jocelyn to take our orders.

"So the good news is you found Sally," Lola said. "But sorry about your face."

"Thanks. At least she actually showed up. But the bad news is she won't talk. She says she's innocent, doesn't deny she knows Gordon Weeks, but definitely won't go to the Etonville police station." I didn't mention the fact that Archibald also knew she was in Bernridge or my surveillance of him this morning. I needed to keep that information secret until I knew what he was up to. Because I felt certain he was up to something.

"You gals ready to order?" Jocelyn asked, then stopped and stared. "Whew, Dodie, what'd you run into?"

"A patch of ice. It was dark and I was hurrying and didn't notice. Did an ass-over-teakettle as my great-aunt Maureen used to say."

Jocelyn tittered. "You gotta start staying home at night where it's safe."

Right. And worry about a voyeur.

Lola requested her standard scrambled eggs and whole wheat toast. My resolve to change my eating habits went by the wayside. "The usual for me," I said.

Jocelyn looked up from her pad. "Back to the cinnamon bun?"

"With extra icing."

"You got it. Hey, nice ad in the *Standard*. Those are some funny pictures!" She hooted and moved off.

Something about her laugh was unsettling.

"Does Sally's family know she's in New Jersey?" Lola asked.

I shrugged. "According to Bill, the department contacted them, and Archibald's doing a little digging around."

"I'd like to know his backstory," Lola said dreamily. "Now he's what I call a stone-cold fox."

"I guess," I said skeptically. "If you go for that type." I hadn't shared his modeling days with anyone.

"You mean the tall, dark, mysterious type?" Lola asked all atwitter.

"You've given up on Walter for good? No more romance?" I asked.

"Ugh. I'm not sure what I ever saw in him," she said dismissively.

"He's attractive. You had the theater in common...you worked together," I said.

"When *Eton Town* is over, the board needs to rethink the staffing of the Etonville Little Theatre," Lola said a tad haughtily, her inner diva rearing its royal head.

"You mean as in replacing Walter? Talk about something that will make him tri-polar. Any decisions about the opening?"

Lola shook her head. "I've made calls to a few possible venues but nothing definite. Time is running out. The reviewer leaves for his vacation soon."

"If I could only convince Sally to come in, maybe she could offer something that would explain Gordon Weeks and his being in the theater, and maybe it would be enough to convince Bill to allow the show to open." I knew my logic might be flawed.

"Whatever you can do, Dodie," Lola said desperately.

Jocelyn dropped off our food and placed a copy of the *Etonville Standard* on the table. "In case you haven't seen it."

I usually read Benny's copy at the Windjammer, but I needed to see the ad. I took a bite of my cinnamon bun and skipped the front page. I went straight to the advertisements in the back of the paper. There it was. Page 15. The ad. OMG. It's not that the full-page public acknowledgment of the Windjammer wasn't complimentary. A picture of the restaurant and a caption below it announced that community spirit was alive and well. But under the caption was a quote from Henry that must have gotten garbled in the transition from his mouth to the copy editor. "WELCOME TO THE FUNHOUSE!" it read.

Scattered around the quote were the pictures Pauli had taken. Actors goofing around, laughing and making faces, Walter waving his arms at the cast to quiet them down, Penny tapping her clipboard, Lola with her head in her hands, and finally, Edna and Abby face-to-face, mouths open, apparently talking simultaneously. Making the ELT look like a cartoon.

How did they end up with these? Now I remembered...Pauli was supposed to send me the best pictures and I was going to pick a few, but I'd gotten waylaid that night by a Peeping Tom and Sally's Facebook account. I'd told Pauli to go ahead and choose what he thought would work. I groaned. And to add insult to injury, La Famiglia had taken out a half-page ad opposite the Windjammer ad touting its winter specials in a sophisticated and serene layout. Henry would not be pleased.

I shoved the paper across the table and watched Lola's optimistic expression evolve into the-second-shoe-had-fallen.

"You know what they say...any publicity is good publicity."

"Whoever said that didn't live in Etonville." Red blotches formed on Lola's cheeks.

"I should have been more specific with Pauli," I said.

"The ELT looks like a bunch of clowns. Who is going to take this play seriously?" she wailed and pushed her breakfast away.

"It's not that bad." It was and worse. "I'd better get to the Windjammer and soothe Henry's no-doubt ruffled feathers."

We paid the check and left the uneaten remains of our food on the table. I gazed at my half-eaten bun wistfully.

* * *

Henry moped his way through lunch. Not even glowing reviews for his tomato cheddar soup and lobster rolls could cheer him up. I'd wanted to experiment with kale chips, but his constitution couldn't handle anything outside the box today.

"What I said was…welcome to the Windjammer, the ELT's home away from home." Henry slapped the newspaper and continued chopping the tomato and onion salad for the dinner special.

It was a good thing he didn't venture into the dining room as he sometimes did during lunch. The ad was a source of great amusement for Etonville. The spectacle of actors horsing around, with Walter and Lola in despair, generated giggles throughout the noon hour.

"…that play must be a farce…"

Well, almost.

"No wonder Walter had a heart attack!"

The rumor mill.

"…Henry said that? Oh my…"

Geez.

It would take a while before the ELT and the Windjammer lived this one down.

"Dodie, we like our photo in the *Standard*," said one of the Banger sisters.

"You do?" I took a twenty-dollar bill from them. As I recalled, their picture featured the two of them with closed eyes nodding off. Probably what many citizens were prepared for if *Eton Town* ever saw the light of day.

"We were doing Walter's exercise, don't you know. Meditating. It's good for our brains," the other sister said.

I smiled.

"Cheney Brothers at the back door," Benny said behind me.

"Thanks. I'll see you ladies later." I turned the twenty over to Benny and headed for the kitchen.

I checked delivery items off the inventory from the food distributor. "Yesterday we were missing the red cabbage and eggplant and fifteen pounds short on the fish."

The driver—a kid in a Yankees cap and bomber jacket who blew on his fists as he unloaded the crates—glared at me. "I don't load the truck. I drive it."

"Pass the word on. I'll be calling your boss," I said seriously.

"Yeah. Yeah." He waited for my signature, then took the form and stuffed it in his pocket. "He's on vacation. Aruba."

I walked back to the dining room, thinking I could use a vacation. Hot sun, crystal clear water, powdery sand...

"Hey, haven't seen him in here before," Benny said. It was Archibald. Bareheaded, unwinding a length of green crocheted material from around his neck, stamping his cowboy boots on the welcome doormat, and warming his hands. "Wonder where he eats?"

"Who knows?" I said and grabbed a menu. I knew one place he ate breakfast. I motioned to Gillian. "I'll take care of him."

Archibald sat in a booth near the front door.

"Hi. First timer!"

He looked up at me from under his shaggy hair. "I wanted to see what all the fuss was about."

Was he referring to the food or the ad?

"Henry's famous for his soup. Today it's—"

"I'll have one of those special burgers Bill raves about," he said.

"Great. Anything to drink?"

"Beer on tap?" he asked.

"Sure." I rattled off three brands and Archibald made his choice. "It'll be a few minutes."

"No hurry. I've got lots of time," he said lazily, as though he planned to spend the afternoon.

Did that mean he had Sally in custody? I was dying to ask, but my little hairs had been on alert since Archibald's arrival and I needed to play it cool.

I put the order in while Archibald checked his cell phone. Which reminded me I hadn't heard from Sally yet. Of course, if she was in the police department being grilled, texting me might be the last thing on her mind. And if she was in the Municipal Building, what was Archibald doing in the Windjammer guzzling a beer and a burger? I texted Bill: *Any word on Sally?* I texted Sally: *Where are you?*

Edna stopped in for her takeout order. "Two soups, a lobster roll, and a BLT. Hold the avocado."

"Right. So the Etonville police are hungry today," I said.

"Suki and I are."

"Where's the chief?" I asked, a little nervous. Had he taken Sally some place—

"With Ralph. He had an appointment." She squinted across the dining room. "Is that Archibald?"

I nodded. "First time he's ever been in here." I rang up Edna's order. "If the chief wants to order lunch later, give me a call and we'll deliver. I know how busy the department can get."

"Not today. Just an 11-85 and a 10-91A. That's a tow truck and stray dog," Edna said.

My pulse ratcheted down a few notches. Sally probably wasn't in custody. Archibald, head down, was concentrating on his cell, sipping his beer. I handed Edna her change and told her to keep warm. Then I picked up Archibald's lunch and walked to his table.

"Thanks," he said without looking up.

"Edna was in here picking up for the department. Guess you're not working at the station today."

I finally had his full attention. "I'm not?" That voice again, low and sultry, challenging and inviting at the same time. He raised his arms above his head and stretched, flexing his biceps.

I gulped, flashing back to his modeling body displayed on the Internet. It was distracting. "I thought maybe you two would be...dealing with Sally. I was with Bill when you called last night."

Archibald dumped a large dollop of ketchup on his sandwich. Henry would have a fit if he witnessed this desecration of his cilantro-and-avocado burger.

"Well, we would be *dealing with Sally* if I'd gotten to her, but somehow she managed to slip away in Bernridge. How do you think that happened?" He bit into his sandwich, staring hard at me.

My face flushed as if I was in the principal's office being called out for some infraction. Did it give me away? "Not a clue." I stared back.

"She's certainly one slippery suspect." He wiped his mouth.

"Well, good luck finding her," I said coolly.

"Anyone else peeking in your windows lately?" he asked with his trademark grin.

I smiled and moved away from the table. What was it about that man that made him so attractive and so annoying at the same time? He might have something on me but I had more on him, right?

19

Between my irritation with Archibald and my exasperation with the *Etonville Standard* ad, I was ready to escape. I had some errands to run. I'd planned to drive to the Shop N Go for a few items, then stop by JC's Hardware for furnace filters. And maybe stick my head in Betty's Boutique next door and check out any new sexy lingerie. I had shoved my arms in my coat sleeves when my cell pinged. Sally or Bill? Lola: *Stop in the theater on your break? Having meeting with Walter and Penny.* The last thing I felt like doing was hashing over the demise of *Eton Town* with Lola and her staff. But a BFF was a BFF and Lola needed my support now.

"Back in an hour or so," I said to Benny.

"Don't hurry back. I'll be here. Rereading the ad," he joked.

I grunted.

Though the air was brisk and a light wind had kicked up, the late afternoon sunlight brought the promise of warmer weather. If only. I buried my face in my scarf. The lobby door of the ELT was unlocked. I could hear a rumble of voices in the theater office, Lola's light but resolute, Walter's vehement but halting. I knocked on the door. Penny opened it.

"Hey, O'Dell."

"Hi, Penny."

"Some ad," she cackled. "Those pictures are gonna put the ELT on the map."

"Penny, could you go to the box office and sort tickets?" Lola asked serenely.

Penny blinked. "I did that yesterday."

"I know but there are some loose stubs in the drawer under the counter," Lola said.

Penny shot a look at Walter who waved his arm in a "go" motion. "I'm the production manager. I should be in the room for any meeting about the production." She pushed her glasses up her nose and slapped her clipboard against her leg. Clearly not happy, Penny raised herself to a full five foot two. "I'll be in the box office," she said huffily.

The minute she left the office, Lola shut the door firmly. "I'd like to keep our decision under wraps as long as possible."

"*Our* decision?" Walter asked bitterly.

Lola gestured toward a chair and I sat. "I needed another reasonable person in the room with me," she said.

Walter looked desperate. "Why can't we wait until the end of the week?" he whined.

Lola was in full artistic director mode. "The board agrees with me. If we can't find a definite venue by the end of tomorrow, we will postpone the production. Indefinitely."

Oops. No wonder Walter was frantic; the futures of both his opus and the production were in doubt. "So none of the places worked out?" I asked tentatively.

Walter turned his head toward me and glowered, as if I was solely to blame for the cancellation of his play. "No. And we have a narrow window. The Creston Players are scheduled to produce *"Our Town"* in April." He spat out "Creston" and *Our Town* as if they were evil twins.

"But before we announced it, I wanted to see what you thought," Lola said anxiously.

I knew she wasn't referring to my theatrical knowledge but rather my investigative skill. Lola was asking me in code if there would be a break in the murder case by tomorrow night. Or even the promise of a break.

But Walter had no such insight. "I still don't see why her opinion matters." I was "her."

"Because I trust Dodie to tell me the truth," Lola said.

"You don't trust my opinion? I won't tell you the truth?" Walter was about to go ballistic. Hadn't he taken his Xanax today? Rapping on the door interrupted his tirade.

Lola raised her voice in exasperation. "Penny, I'll come and get you when we're finished."

I looked up from my lap where I'd been tracing the wide wales in my corduroys and racking my brain to find a way of gently notifying Lola that, as far as I knew, the investigation was at a stalemate.

The door inched open. Walter, Lola, and I dropped our jaws simultaneously. It was Sally, her face partially obscured by a scarf, her head covered in the same knit cap she'd worn when we'd met in Bernridge. For that matter, she was still wearing the ratty winter coat and looking like a vagrant.

"May I come in?" she asked timidly.

The three of us gawked and might have stayed that way indefinitely if Penny hadn't sauntered across the lobby and materialized in the doorframe behind Sally. "Hey, Oldfield, what's the deal with skipping out on curtain call? Nobody misses a curtain call on my watch." Penny stood there, a stack of papers in one hand, her clipboard in the other. "Lola, what do you want me to do with these old audition forms?"

As if Penny's question was a wake-up call, we came alive. I jumped up and escorted Sally into the office while Lola prodded Walter to shove over on the couch and make room for her. Our reactions had wildly different motivations. Walter was glad to see an errant actor return to the company, even though said actor should receive a scolding, while Lola saw Sally's appearance as a good omen that perhaps Gordon Weeks's death might be resolved sooner rather than later. I was astonished that Sally had decided to come in on her own, apparently taking my advice, and was willing to speak with Bill. We all spoke at once.

"Sally, where have you been?" Lola asked, distressed. "We were worried about you—"

Walter chimed in. "Penny's right. You shouldn't have cut out on the curtain call at final dress rehearsal. It's not professional. Of course, with that man dying on the turntable and the show on hold—"

"I am so glad to see you!" I sent Sally a reassuring smile.

"We had to redistribute your lines." Penny tapped her clipboard. "If you had an emergency, you should have texted me before you left the theater—"

"What are you wearing?" Walter studied Sally's outer clothing. "You look like..."

Sally looked overwhelmed. It occurred to me that if we peppered her with further questions, she might let something slip about the murder or Gordon Weeks or her whereabouts for the last few days.

"Okay let's stop!" I said vigorously.

Walter and Penny glowered at me, surprised at my authoritative tone. But Lola understood and nodded. I didn't want to take a chance that Bill was still away from the police department, leaving Sally at the mercy of Archibald's questioning. I was more convinced than ever that he had other fish to fry. But I needed to get back to the Windjammer.

"Lola, maybe you could take Sally to your place for something to eat?" I prayed she didn't question the logic of my request and picked up on the subtext.

Lola's eyes narrowed. She wasn't a diva for nothing; subtext was her middle name. "Of course. Come on, Sally. Let's take a coffee break." She extended a hand and Sally rose, following Lola to the door.

"Lola? We haven't finished discussing *Eton Town*," Walter cried in a panic. "When are we going to announce our decision?"

"Walter, take it easy. Do you want to have another attack?" Lola asked.

"What decision?" Penny demanded. "I'm the production manager and I should know if the ELT is planning something." She put her hands on her hips, blocking the entrance.

"Walter. Penny. We will talk later." Lola placed a hand politely but firmly on Sally's back and guided her past Penny.

I hurried out of the office after them. Sally leaned into me and whispered, "Did you find the photo yet?" It was a desperate plea.

"I'll look later."

"I could search for it now," Sally said and took a step toward the theater.

"No! Leave that to me." We needed to get Sally out of here. I murmured in Lola's ear, "Keep her at your place until I text later, okay?"

"Will do. Maybe she knows something?" Lola asked hopefully.

"Maybe. I'll stop by this evening, but meanwhile she could probably use a bath and some decent clothes."

"I'll take care of her," Lola said reassuringly.

I watched them walk out the door and get into Lola's Lexus, Sally's Chevy nowhere in sight. Then I scooted next door to the Windjammer.

* * *

The hubbub about the ad in the *Etonville Standard* had died down, even though someone had snipped it out of the newspaper and left it by the cash register. Benny wiped down the glossy surface of the bar, dunking a cloth into sudsy water to remove grease and crumbs.

I picked up the ad. "Someone's idea of a joke?"

Benny snorted. "Probably one of the actors. There were a crew of them in here for lunch getting a real kick out of themselves."

I crumpled the paper. "Glad someone's enjoying it." I tilted my head in the direction of the kitchen. "Henry?"

"Hasn't been in the dining room all day."

I left Benny to his dinner preparations and treaded apprehensively to the kitchen. Henry had planned tonight's special last week, before La Famiglia's rival ad appeared side-by-side with the Windjammer's in the *Etonville Standard*: chicken saltimbocca and roasted vegetables with a balsamic dipping sauce. For a long time he'd resisted adding Italian dishes to the menu and that included most entrées with prosciutto and mozzarella cheese. But we'd ordered the chicken and laid in the ingredients, and he was not to be deterred. With the appearance of the ad, Henry was more competitive than ever.

I pushed the swinging door open and paused inside the kitchen. Mallet in hand, Henry was pounding the life out of the chicken breasts. We'd be lucky if a trace of the meat was left on the cutting board. I cut my eyes to the center island where Enrico was chopping the veggies for roasting. "Can't wait to try it!" I said cheerfully.

"Henry has a new recipe," Enrico confided. "Better than La Famiglia."

My cell rang so I backed out of the kitchen, hopefully leaving well enough alone. The ID read Pauli. "I was about to call you. What happened with the pictures?"

"Uh, what?"

"Pauli, we wanted to make the ELT and the actors look…" Professional? Talented? Like they knew what this play was all about? "It was supposed to be a tribute to the theater and to the Windjammer."

"Like, I thought these showed the actors and everybody like real people." I could almost hear Pauli shrug. "We talked about cinéma vérité in my photography class. Like, how it's cool to show people in real life."

Cinéma vérité? I couldn't come down too hard on the kid. He was taking initiative and trying to create art. It wasn't his fault the ELT members were up to their eyeballs with *Eton Town* and took advantage of the opportunity to fool around.

"Okay. But maybe the next set of photos could be a little…"

"Less real?" he asked.

"Exactly." One thing the Etonville Little Theatre could do without was reality. I paused. "Pauli, you said you were learning about deep searches in your digital forensics class. Search engines and websites the average person wouldn't know about?"

"Like, yeah. Some really awesome stuff. Last night we—"

Benny flagged me down from the cash register. "Pauli, gotta go but can we talk later?"

"When?" His enthusiasm was touching.

"I'll text you tonight. And remember the first rule of digital forensics…"

"Confidentiality," he said solemnly.

* * *

The chicken saltimbocca raised a few eyebrows, but mostly garnered positive reviews. Mildred and Vernon shared an order. "My, Henry is getting experimental," Mildred said. "We've had this dish at La Famiglia."

"Really?"

"I don't care for it much. Whether I eat it here or at the other place. Who needs ham on their chicken?" Vernon asked.

"It's called *prosciutto*," Mildred informed him, with a trilled "r" and a heavy accent on the second syllable. "Very continental."

"I don't care what it's called. You can leave it off my plate."

Vernon was testier than usual these days; it didn't seem to matter whether the show was opening or closing. "I'll pass your review on to Henry." I forced a smile.

Vernon pushed his plate away. "By the way, I like that picture of me in the ad. I look like George Washington."

* * *

The Windjammer was nearly empty by eight thirty. I'd texted Lola and she'd responded that Sally had taken a shower, took a two-hour nap, and scarfed up an enormous plate of pasta. Poor thing. Benny had offered to close up so I checked the seafood inventory, offered a few words of encouragement to Henry and waved good night.

Outside the Windjammer, the cold air was refreshing, its bite a pleasant change from the warmth and stuffiness of the restaurant. Breathing in the icy night obliged my senses to sharpen, my mind to quicken. I had to be alert and on-my-toes in order to question Sally. I still felt she was innocent. But her ability to evade Archibald and tempt me with a version of a bait-and-switch at a Creston bodega, proved she was more wily than I imagined. For that matter, why did she come to the theater today? The photo?

I drove down Main Street to the upscale end of town. The streets were still lightly coated in a slushy mixture of ice and snow. Spring could not come too soon for me. I tapped the brakes gently to avoid sliding into the intersection at Anderson and Main and waited for the light to change. I was weighing potential questions when red turned to green and I started to turn left. I was halfway through the crossing when a black Ford approached from the opposite direction, facing me head-on. My heart thudded. It was Archibald racing down Main, above the speed limit, and potentially headed to the Etonville Police Department. He was probably traveling too fast to identify me. At least that's what I hoped. I stepped on the gas and flew to

Lola's house. My tires spun as I wrenched the steering wheel to the right and shot into her driveway, sliding a couple of feet before I came to a hard stop.

Before I could grasp the knocker or hit the bell, the door was whisked open by Lola, looking, as usual, as if she'd prepped for a fashion shoot. Despite the chaos and tension of the day, Lola had managed to maintain her clothing composure and now wore green silk lounging pajamas, her blond hair swept up in a top-knot.

"What's the matter?" she asked. "You hit my driveway like a—"

"Where's Sally?" I glanced over her shoulder.

"In the family room. Why?"

"I'm afraid Archibald may be on to us. Let's go." I strode past her, stripping off my gloves, muffler, and parka.

"Here. Give me those."

Lola held out a hand and I deposited my winter gear into her arms. I moved through Lola's entrance hall, past her immaculate kitchen—that reminded me for the hundredth time that I needed to give my kitchen a good cleaning—and into her family room where a fire was blazing and Sally Oldfield sat in a recliner, a soda can in one hand, the TV remote in the other. When I entered, she quickly turned off the television and set her can on an end table.

"Hi, Dodie." She smiled.

Apparently the "coffee break" had been a good idea. Sally was swathed in Lola's white spa robe, her hair and face scrubbed clean of the grime she had previously worn, her expression relaxed.

"Sally. Wow. Big change," I said.

"Lola is a terrific host. And very generous with her wardrobe." She tucked her legs up under her. "Thanks for getting me here."

"I was happy to help you escape the theater. Though neither Walter nor Penny may get over your missing the curtain call," I said.

She laughed quietly.

I sat on the sofa next to her chair. "But now we need to talk. I think there's a good possibility the Etonville police may come calling tonight."

Sally pulled on the recliner's lever and the seat back popped upright. Her face fell as she tightened the robe's ties as if protecting herself from that possibility, looking suddenly dispirited.

"If you tell me everything I might be able to help you. The police chief is a good friend." I deliberately avoided mentioning Archibald at this point.

Sally nodded. "What do you want to know?" she asked innocently.

Could she be that naïve? I had to work quickly, but I knew from my last experience questioning Sally that the indirect route might be the most effective. "So you've been staying at a rooming house in Bernridge?"

Sally swallowed a sip of her soda. "It was cheap. I had to share a bathroom and there was practically no heat. That's why I looked like a street person. I was afraid to take a shower."

"And the clothes?"

Lola had crept to the entrance of the family room and perched on the arm of a matching recliner.

"There was a Salvation Army down the street from the house."

I tiptoed into the topic. "Sally, I have to ask…your family…the money? You didn't need to stay in a place like that."

"I was hiding. I figured people would be looking for me to spend money," she said.

"So let's start at the beginning. You're here in Etonville and everything is going well and suddenly on the Sunday before *Eton Town* opens, you see Gordon Weeks on the street across from the theater. And he scares you." It wasn't a question this time.

On the periphery of my vision, I could see Lola's disbelief. I'd have a lot to fill her in on eventually.

Sally nodded reluctantly. "That's right."

"And then he appears at the rooming house and you two have a discussion on the porch that Angela happens to overhear."

Lola dropped into the recliner, making no attempt to hide her surprise. Her face was half shock, half you-go-girl.

"Uh-huh," Sally said.

"Now I know you *said* you didn't know Gordon Weeks. So what were you frightened of?"

"I didn't know him. But I'd seen him before," Sally said.

I felt like a dentist extracting teeth. "In Etonville?"

She shook her head. "In Boston."

I felt a twinge of elation. Now we were getting somewhere!

"I saw him on a street outside our home in December," Sally said.

"Beacon Hill. What was he doing there?" I asked.

"I don't know. And then I saw him again hanging around a week later," she said. She scrolled through photos on her cell. "I took a picture of him in case he showed up again."

I stared at the face on her phone. Gordon Weeks in the same camo jacket minus the trapper hat. His face was barely visible with the full beard, his squinting eyes merely slits in the folds of flesh.

"And then he shows up in Etonville. You think he followed you here?"

"Maybe."

"Why? What did he want?" I asked.

"When he came by the rooming house, he was talking about my mother, and he scared me so I started to cry. He told me he needed to talk to me in private and I said okay let's meet at the theater." She looked at Lola. "I didn't know where else to go."

Lola nodded sympathetically. This was sounding more and more bizarre. What would Archibald make of it? Or Bill for that matter?

I'd been here fifteen minutes. Archibald could be on his way.

"So what time did you agree to meet him at the theater?" I asked.

She tipped her head upward and examined the crown molding on Lola's ceiling as if the answer were engraved there. "About three o'clock. I'd heard you say…" she glanced again at Lola "…that the theater would be empty for a couple of hours before the evening call. The door's always unlocked lately. But I was running late so it might have been closer to four when I got there. He wasn't in the lobby so I went into the theater. I called out and no one answered so I walked up to the stage and then I saw him…"

My thoughts rebounded from one fact to another. I'd arrived at four thirty; by that time the murder had been committed and Sally had stumbled on Gordon Weeks's body.

Sally closed her eyes, her lips quivered. "He stared at me and his mouth was moving. I saw the knife and touched his coat and it was all bloody…I wanted to call the police but then he opened his hand and it had the photo in it." She broke down. "Then he went all…quiet."

Lola jumped up and put her arm around Sally's shoulders. "It's okay. Things will be fine."

"I took the picture and then I heard someone come in, and I was afraid so I stayed onstage behind the turntable. But then I saw it was you." Sally looked at me.

Lola scanned my face. *Now what?* she seemed to be asking.

I was at a loss. Far from confirming Sally's innocence, our conversation only raised more questions and, frankly, didn't position her in a very positive light. Sally had agreed to meet with Gordon Weeks at the theater, she'd conveniently arrived late, she'd found him dead. And there was no evidence anyone else was in the theater.

A loud knocking at the door, followed by an insistent ringing of the bell, startled all three of us. "Sally, do you know someone named Archibald Alvarez?" I asked quickly.

"No."

She'd know him before too long. "I'll go," I said, before either Lola or Sally had a chance to rise. "Text me the picture of Gordon Weeks?"

Sally nodded.

I could see red and blue flashing lights through the glass panes in the door. It wasn't only Archibald who'd come to call. I opened the door to see Bill leaning on his crutches. Archibald was a step behind him while Ralph was waiting by the squad car for crowd control, since house lights were popping on up and down the street. Lola's neighborhood would rival Snippets by morning.

"May we come in?" Bill asked politely but firmly, all business, no trace of his quirky smile.

"I can explain—" I said.

Bill raised his hand to silence me. I stepped aside and he thumped his way into the house trailed by Archibald. I couldn't meet his eyes. In the family room, Sally was on her feet, Lola's arm still offering protection. Bill, speaking softly, explained that he had some questions for her and that she'd need to come down to the station to answer them. Sally stared wild-eyed and nodded. Lola walked her upstairs to get dressed and Bill and Archibald left, wordless, to wait on the porch. I was definitely persona non grata.

Within minutes, Sally emerged in borrowed jeans and a sweater, both a little baggy on the thin young woman.

"Can I call anyone for you?" I asked. "Your family?" She needed a lawyer.

Sally shook her head vigorously, smiled gratefully at Lola and took the winter jacket she provided. "Thanks."

"The police chief's a fair man. Tell him the truth." Whatever that turned out to be.

"I will," Sally said simply, then mumbled. "Please find the photo."

I watched her open the door and join the Etonville police on the front porch. The squad car drove off with Sally in the back seat, perp-like, followed by Archibald's black Ford. House lights snapped off and the neighborhood reverted to darkness once again.

Lola closed the front door. "I don't know what to think."

"I agree. Something's not right. I'd go to the station, but somehow I don't think I'm welcome there tonight," I said.

Lola clasped her hands. "Please let there be a resolution to this whole thing! We have *got* to make a decision about the play by tomorrow."

"Don't do anything drastic yet, okay? Give me a day?" I requested.

Lola nodded. "I'll do my best to hold off the board."

I texted Pauli as I left Lola's at nine thirty. I'd resisted her offer of a glass of wine in favor of going home. But first I wanted to confirm a date with my tech guru. Pauli had mentioned deep searches on the Internet before, using lesser known search engines to dig into the backgrounds of folks. I had decided I needed to find out exactly who Gordon Weeks was. Pauli texted back: *4:30 good at Windjammer.* Before I turned in I decided to check my Facebook page. I'd been so busy I hadn't had time to like or post anything—from my laptop or cell phone.

I brought my computer to bed with me, set a mug of hot chocolate on the bedside table, and burrowed into my down comforter. I clicked on home to see what my friends had posted—pictures from *Eton Town* rehearsals that looked a little more civilized than the *Etonville Standard* ad, Andy and Cory playing in the snow, my parents at a restaurant on the beach. Then I typed in Sally Oldfield—she hadn't posted anything in recent days either. Understandable. But something I'd seen on Facebook when I'd initially searched for her earlier was nipping at the back of my mind, tickling my imagination. What had I missed?

I erased Sally and replaced it with Sara and visited her timeline again. I remembered the photos of what appeared to be a family grouping with several generations. In one picture, an elderly white-haired woman was surrounded by a group of kids, with a handful of teens or twenty-somethings. In another, Sally was flanked by a man and a woman. Probably her parents. I clicked on the image and held the screen closer to my face. There was the woman who Sally resembled. I shifted my attention to the man. I hadn't really noticed him before. Extremely handsome, a bronzed face, a full head of hair...

My little hairs danced wildly. I knew that man. He'd been the fellow in the silver Lincoln with the Massachusetts license plate that I nearly plowed into the day of the baking class. If the woman was Sally's mother, he had to be her father. If he'd followed her to Etonville, why hadn't Sally mentioned him? From the far corners of my memory I heard the cashier at the car wash: *...dude looked filthy rich...maybe he was her sugar daddy...I asked Sally if there were more like him...she looked at me like she was going to cry...*

He was her daddy all right. But not the kind the cashier had thought. What had Andy said? *...no siblings...only a father and I got the impression they didn't get on very well.* My mind was leapfrogging over the events of the past days, springing from one fact to another: Sally seeing Gordon Weeks in Boston; talking with him in Etonville; Gordon Weeks dead; Sally, bloody, in the theater, supposedly to meet with him; her father in town the week before the murder. So Gordon Weeks wasn't the only one following Sally to Etonville.

20

I flung myself back and forth in bed, tangling the comforter, dreaming, then waking, then dreaming again. I was locked away in jail when I awoke for the last time, shaking the bars and yelling at my captor. A good-looking man with hair combed off his forehead—Sally's father—and a ruddy face that sported a quirky grin—Bill. The combination character laughed and laughed at me. I blinked and he disappeared, but the after effects were obvious: I had to breathe slowly to calm down.

I was the victim of too much information. But revealing all to Bill included confessing my DIY investigation, trying to meet with Sally while Archibald was hunting her down. I'd also have to admit to witnessing Archibald in the theater and tracking him to the diner. Things Bill would definitely not appreciate. After all, they were colleagues from way back and Bill had confidence in Archibald.

I shivered, partly because, as usual, the temperature in my bedroom was hovering in the mid-sixties, and partly because I was anticipating Bill's reaction. He was becoming more accustomed to my investigative instincts, but did I go too far this time? I shivered again and convinced myself to fling back the cover. I had to face the day.

The hot shower revived my spirit, the water splashing down on my head and streaming over my shoulders was invigorating. I toweled off and ran a brush through my snarled locks. I inspected my face in the mirror. My cheek was healing nicely, only the barest discoloration now, and my mouth was almost back to normal. Which reminded me of Bill...our lips locked gently while the fire glowed and Norah Jones sang "Come Away with Me."

I was afraid that ship had sailed for the present.

Never mind. Bill would come around once the Sally/Gordon Weeks situation was sorted out and the killer caught. I was feeling optimistic so a visit to Coffee Heaven was in order. I slipped into my black jeans and a stretchy red knit top. Red was my power color and—

My cell phone binged and then rang. Wow. I was popular this morning. The ringtone was insistent so it earned my attention first. The text would have to wait. I checked the caller ID. *Yikes.* I hadn't expected to hear from Bill this soon.

"Hello?" I said, my tone neutral as though I had no idea who was on the other end.

"Dodie." His voice was leaden.

"Hi, Bill." Had he gotten a confession out of Sally?

"I need to speak with you. Today." So maybe no confession…

"Okay. Well, I can stop by during my break at three—"

"This morning." He expelled air, releasing his gruff attitude with it. "Things are not good here," he said quietly. "Sally didn't have much to say but did tell us you'd been in contact with her."

Whoops.

"Can you get here at nine?"

I gulped. "Sure."

He rang off. Now I definitely required a visit to Coffee Heaven for courage. I checked the text; it was Lola.

* * *

The clamor at Coffee Heaven was to be expected. A cast member of the Etonville Little Theatre being picked up at the artistic director's house in connection with a murder was big news. I had planned to steal into a booth at the back of the restaurant, hoping no one would pay any particular attention to me.

Wrong. Heads swiveled as I slinked to my haven, a few nodded, a few looked about to ask questions.

"That must have been some night at Lola's," Jocelyn said and placed my drink in front of me. She lowered her voice. "Hard to believe that sweet Sally was related to the homeless man."

"Sally's not related to the dead guy."

Jocelyn lifted an eyebrow. "Are you sure?"

She left me hunkered down in the booth uncertain. That was one possibility I hadn't considered. I visualized Gordon Weeks—cap, jacket, bearded face. It didn't seem likely in addition to the fact that Sally claimed she didn't know him.

The restaurant was suddenly deathly still. I looked up to see Lola standing in the entrance like a deer caught in headlights. I motioned to her and she ducked her head, scrambling to my booth. The minute she sat down, the place exploded in chatter.

"I can't believe how fast the word got out," Lola whispered.

A couple in the booth next to us were craning their necks to hear what we had to say so I whispered back. "I can." Been there, seen that. "Bill wants to meet me at nine." The wall clock said eight forty-five.

"What did Sally tell them?" Lola asked.

"Apparently not much. Listen, I've got to come clean about my communicating with her," I said.

"Bill won't be pleased."

"I know. But I've got a bigger problem." I proceeded to share my near run-in with Archibald at the theater and following him to the diner.

Lola listened wide-eyed, speechless.

"Should I share all of this with Bill?" I asked.

"I don't know." Lola wound a lock of blond hair around her index finger. A nervous habit I'd seen before.

"Maybe Andy can shed some more light—"

My cell binged. It was Bill: *Are you on the way?*

I downed the rest of my coffee. "Wish me luck," I said to Lola and picked up my bag.

She crossed her fingers. Heads rotated again as I walked to the door. I didn't envy Lola on her own in Coffee Heaven.

* * *

"So let me get this straight. You texted Sally Oldfield and asked to meet," Bill said sternly.

"Yes." I could feel his laser-like eyes piercing my protective armor.

"More than once," he confirmed.

"She gave me an address in Creston. Turns out it was a bodega and she never showed. I was late and I guess she got scared."

"And then Bernridge," he said.

"Right. We met at a diner." I eyed Archibald who was leaning back in a chair, legs stretched out in front of him. Eyes hooded. The diner reference failed to elicit a reaction. "And then we sat in her car for a few minutes."

"What did she have to say?" he asked.

"Not much. Just that she was not guilty of murdering Gordon Weeks and was afraid no one would believe her," I answered.

"For good reason."

They were the first words Archibald had uttered since I walked into Bill's office. I stared at him, deciding immediately that I would keep my evidence about his questionable behavior to myself. "That attitude is exactly why she wouldn't come in. Why she eventually came to the ELT. She felt she couldn't trust anyone in this office." I knew I was tarring Bill along with Archibald, but a good offense was the best defense in this case.

"Let's get back to Sally and you," Bill cut in. "She showed up at the theater and you still felt you shouldn't phone it in to us?"

"She needed a bath, food, and some clothes. She was in no shape to be interrogated."

"Sally was not interrogated last night. Only questioned. We need to know if she played any part in Gordon Weeks's murder." Bill's voice rose a few decibels.

"Did you find out?" I asked.

"Did you?" Archibald's chair tipped forward and landed with a clatter.

"I have to admit her story sounds bizarre. Seeing Gordon Weeks in Boston, him showing up here and wanting to meet with her. Then discovering he'd been stabbed to death." Had Sally mentioned the photo in the dying victim's hand?

Archibald rose and stretched. "I'm going out for coffee."

I was shocked; Bill looked surprised. Why would the primary investigator walk out of a meeting where his primary suspect's motivations were being explored with the only person the suspect really talked to? I didn't get it.

"Anybody else?" Archibald asked.

Bill shook his head. Archibald left.

"What is with that guy?" I fumed. "He has Sally tried and convicted."

Bill slowly turned to me. "Okay let's get to the bottom of this."

"Fine."

"We've been through this before and I presumed we had an understanding. Your investigative instincts are sharp and I appreciate them. But you have to communicate with me. I have to know what you're doing," Bill said.

"I felt Sally wasn't going to get a fair shake from Archibald. I wanted to get her side of things and—"

Bill exploded. "That's not your job. That's my job!"

"I understand but since you aren't able to get around…"

"That's why I have Archibald," Bill said evenly.

I had an unexpected impulse. "Did you call Archibald or did he contact you about helping out?"

"What? Why?"

A knock on the door interrupted us.

"Enter," Bill barked.

Suki opened the door and crossed to Bill's desk, extending a file. Bill took it, Suki nodded—without even acknowledging my presence—and left.

"Guess I'd better go." I stood.

Bill focused on a sheet of paper in the file. "It's not good news for Sally Oldfield."

I sat back down.

"The medical examiner's final autopsy report. Depth of the knife wound is consistent with the upper body strength of a female. Angle of the wound is consistent with someone five foot four to five foot six." Bill dropped the file on his desk.

About Sally's height. "Or maybe someone was off-balance, you know, struggling, bending over. Maybe Gordon Weeks was hit on the head first and then stabbed while he was on the ground."

Bill inclined his head skeptically. "I didn't say he'd been hit on the head. Only that there was blunt force trauma—"

"Everything you have on Sally is circumstantial. Sure, she was in the theater about the time Gordon Weeks was killed. Yes, she had blood on her hands. Okay, so she ran off and hid for almost a week. None of it proves anything. No hard physical evidence," I said.

"Can you hear yourself? A prosecutor would have a picnic with that much circumstantial evidence," Bill said, frustrated. "Anyway, if your theory is correct, *Sally* could have knocked him out and stabbed him."

Bill was right. "But what's her motivation? Why would she want Gordon Weeks dead?" Every suspect in the mysteries I read had to have both motive and opportunity. Bill had only established the latter.

"I don't know. She's not saying much," he admitted.

"There were no witnesses and she didn't confess to anything." I paused. "Are you holding her as a person of interest?"

"Not yet. But I don't want her doing a disappearing act again. Archibald is going to keep an eye on her."

Maybe I should keep an eye on Archibald. "Have you spoken with her father?"

Bill regarded me warily. "Charles Oldfield? Why do you ask?"

"Sally said he was coming in town for the show."

"Archibald's been in touch with her father," Bill said.

"About your friend...I know you have a lot of faith in him, but on a couple of occasions, he did some strange things and—"

"Enough, Dodie! No more digging around on your own." He drummed fingers on his desk. "There are aspects of any investigation that can't be shared with civilians. You've got to let us do our jobs."

I stood. "I know you might not agree with me, but for what it's worth, I truly believe she's innocent," I said quietly.

He looked up, studied me, an overnight stubble covering his face. Had he even slept last night?

"I hope you're right. For both your sakes." He shifted in his chair, swinging his bad foot out from under the desk, and plopping his cast on the top of the low stool.

I wanted to say more, ask after his broken ankle, offer a little encouragement on the investigation but his expression was like a crossing guard's paddle: Stop!

I left without a word. As I moved down the hallway, I could hear Edna on dispatch. "Ralph, you better hightail it over to the cemetery. We have a 594. That's right. A gang of kids are playing hooky." She adjusted her headset and lowered her voice. "The chief is in no mood to talk about your pay raise. 10-4."

"I recognize 594. Malicious mischief." I was getting used to Edna's codes.

Edna removed her headset. "A snowball fight on the graves of Etonville's forefathers." Edna shook her head in disbelief.

"Edna, were you here when Sally left last night?"

Edna frowned. "Nope. Poor kid. I don't think she could murder anyone."

"Me neither."

"Especially not on opening night. I mean, she was in the cast, for goodness' sake," Edna said sadly.

Right. I rested my arm on the counter. "So does Archibald check in periodically during the day? You know, where he's going, who he has appointments with, that sort of thing," I asked casually.

Edna smiled slyly. "You'd like to keep tabs on him?"

"Well..."

She leaned up to the window. "I don't blame you. If I was twenty years younger..." She batted her eyelashes.

"I'm not interested that way—" I said quickly. That's all I needed—another rumor about my love life spiraling out of control.

"Your secret's safe with me. Of course, the chief might feel differently," she said archly, observing me over the rim of her glasses.

I forced a laugh. If I wanted information, I might have to take one for the team. "Just wondering where I might find him later in the day. You know...when I'm on my break."

"You youngsters! I'll text you if he calls in," Edna whispered, delighted to be a potential romantic conspirator.

"Thanks," I whispered back. "But it's between you and me."

Edna winked. "Copy that."

I prayed that Edna's offer to play Cupid didn't spread to the ears or mouths of the Snippets crowd. I texted Sally: *Where r u? OK?*

* * *

Lunch was crazy. Gillian called in distraught over breaking up with her boyfriend again, so I took her place, running from kitchen to table to cash register. It had started to flurry with three to five inches expected before nightfall, but the weather didn't seem to deter Etonville from venturing out. The opportunity to natter on about Sally Oldfield and the murder of Gordon Weeks was worth a trek through the cold and snow. Of course, the town was engaging in unbridled speculation after seeing the headline in the *Etonville Standard*: ELT ACTRESS INTERROGATED FOR MURDER.

"Sally Oldfield was from Boston. A stranger in town..." said Vernon.

"One of those rich outsiders." JC tsked.

"I heard she was related to the man," said Jocelyn. "Guess this means *Eton Town* is cancelled."

"Probably a good thing...heard it ran over three hours...I'll see the real play in Creston in April." The nail in the coffin.

Geez.

The article was brief, not much to tell. Background on Sally and her Boston life, the death of her mother, her father's business ventures, and her recent arrival in Etonville. And being picked up at the home of the ELT artistic director. Lola would hate that; Walter, too, but for a different reason. He still considered *himself* the artistic director.

Below the fold was *ETON TOWN* ON HOLD INDEFINITELY, an interview with Lola, where she tap-danced around the show's opening, and a quote from Penny: "Doesn't matter if it's a tragedy or comedy, the show always goes on. Unless it can't. Even though the ELT would like to be up a stream with extra paddles, this is a no win-win situation. But we're team players. Trying to think inside the box."

Huh?

Henry's specials for lunch included a popular beer-battered-fried-shrimp-and-curly-fries option, tasty comfort food that Etonville scarfed up in between spinning motivations for Sally's supposed crime. His other special—French onion soup in a bread bowl—received a decidedly mixed review.

"You eat the bowl too?" asked Abby.

"I kind of like my soup in a regular bowl," said Vernon.

"Don't you think Henry is getting a little too New Yorkish for Etonville?" One of the Banger sisters.

Too bad the town didn't have any strong opinions. I smiled through its culinary assessment, as I usually did, and escaped to the kitchen to check on a few orders. Henry and Enrico were whirling dervishes, churning out plate after plate.

At three o'clock I collapsed into my back booth with a plate of pasta and a side serving of curly fries. I needed carbs for moral support.

Benny handed me a cup of coffee and whistled. "Sally was friendly and kind. She even offered to babysit one time." He hesitated. "Probably good that never worked out. You okay? Seem a little preoccupied," he said.

"Just worried."

"Hey, one good thing. If she's arrested, she can afford the best legal defense money can buy," Benny said.

"Right." I nibbled on a fry.

"Wonder if her father will show up."

He already has.

Those little hairs again...Andy said Sally inherited her mother's fortune. Where did that leave her father? And more importantly, how did he feel about it? I was mulling over possibilities when my cell phone binged. I fished it out of my pocket, hoping for a return message from Sally. It was Lola: *Any news?* I texted back that there was nothing to report; Sally was released from the police department with the warning to stay in town. And I was spinning my wheels waiting to hear from her.

"Mmmph."

I looked up. It was Pauli outfitted in a hooded down jacket with a muffler wrapped around the lower half of his face, stifling his speech.

"Hi. Have a seat."

He scooted onto the bench opposite me, slung his backpack off his shoulder, and removed his scarf and coat. "It's, like, zero out there."

I smiled at his exaggeration—I knew it was in the high twenties—and asked if he'd eaten.

"Only lunch and a snack."

That meant he was ready for some pre-dinner nosh. I set him up with a Coke, fries, and whatever dessert was left over from lunch. Today it was chocolate cream pie. I checked in with Henry, where the kitchen was busy prepping for scalloped potatoes and a roasted corn casserole. I poured myself a seltzer.

Pauli was already at work on his laptop.

"So deep searches," I said.

"Okay, like, what are you looking for? Like, there's this database we learned about for public records. Really sweet. You can even download an app for it."

"What kind of records?"

"Email, phone numbers, addresses…" He took a big bite of pie.

That information wouldn't be much help in digging into Gordon Weeks's background. Bill said he probably had a burner phone and no known home address. "What else?"

He shrugged. "Traffic tickets or, like, if you went bankrupt."

"Okay, let's check him out."

Pauli logged into his special database and typed in *Gordon Weeks*. We were confronted with two dozen names—among them a college professor, an IT engineer, a magazine editor, and several with no profession listed. We eliminated some by birthdate. The medical examiner estimated Gordon Weeks's age as late forties. But we skimmed through them all, none seeming like the scruffy outdoorsman who died on the ELT stage. Without knowing anything about his background, this was going to be impossible.

Leave it to my tech guru. "So, like, this is the dead guy," Pauli said cautiously.

No point in not confirming what was already in the *Etonville Standard*. "Yes."

"At Snippets they're saying he's probably a homeless man—"

"I don't think he's—"

"—with a police record."

I paused. Bill said a search of law enforcement databases revealed a minor run-in with the law years ago.

"Pauli, what are you suggesting?"

"Let's check to see who's been in trouble with the police. Like who's been arrested. Maybe something will pop."

Pauli went to work. We waded through the list of names, stopping to investigate backgrounds and shady pasts of anyone in the forties, early fifties age range. Nothing looked promising until we hit on a Gordon Weeks with no known background information. As if he was off the grid.

No bankruptcies, no reported traffic tickets. But he did have an arrest for burglary in 1997 in Beacon Hill. The part of Boston where Sally lived. Was there a connection? If so, it was tenuous…but tenuous was better than nothing. I made note of our finding and checked my watch. "Guess it's time for you to be shoving off."

"Mom's coming by." He screwed up his face.

"Spring will be here soon and then you can tear around Etonville with your own wheels," I said.

Pauli grinned. "Yeah. Cool." He packed up his laptop. "So if you want to do any more searches…"

"Thanks. I'll let you know. Pretty amazing what you can find out there on someone."

"Yeah. Like, on yourself too," Pauli said.

"I guess so. But at least I don't have any bankruptcies or arrest records. Yet."

Pauli nodded his head wisely. "Data fusion."

"What's that?"

"There's a company that combines public records with purchasing and behavioral data. Like, what you bought at the Shop N Go last week and who your neighbors are. Like, when was the last time you did Chinese takeout."

"Wow. Really?"

"Yeah like profiles can even have pictures of cars using automated license plate readers tagged with GPS coordinates and time stamps," he said, excited.

"Time stamps. Pauli, this is some heavy-duty stuff. I'm impressed."

He ducked his head. "Like, yeah."

Carol's SUV pulled up in front of the Windjammer. "Your ride's here."

Pauli wrapped up and marched to the entrance, with me close behind. I opened the door to a blast of cold air and Carol waved to me. She wound down the passenger side window and yelled, "Stop by Snippets in the morning. Got something to share."

"Sure." I waved back.

21

Dinner was well underway when Edna texted: *Arch. checked in... off for the night...appt. in NYC.* Then she inserted a row of hearts. *PS. Chief is in...?!*

Edna was taking the Cupid thing seriously. If I didn't have Gordon Weeks's murder on the brain, I might have tried to make plans with Bill. I shook myself back to the present. Edna's text gave me an idea.

"Benny, interested in trading closings? Swap tonight for tomorrow night?" I asked.

"Sure. Might be a light evening." He inclined his head in the direction of the front window where the snow was coming down gently but steadily. "Maybe Henry will close early again."

"Maybe." I texted Lola: *Can u talk?*

Within a minute, she'd called me. "My home is like a prison. I'm afraid to leave. Everywhere I go, I get buttonholed about Sally. 'What did I know? Why was I sheltering her? Did she really do it?'"

"Look, I think it's time to take this investigation to the next level."

"What does that mean?" Lola asked eagerly.

"A couple of things. First I'd like to get into the theater tonight. Are you up for joining me?" I said.

"I guess so. What are you going to do there?"

"A little reconnoitering. But in case someone stops by, I'd like some cover."

"I'm your alibi!" she said.

"Yes. No chance of Walter coming in?" I asked.

"I think he's having another panic attack. I told him to take a pill and go to bed."

"Have you eaten? I can bring dinner for you. Meet me in front of the theater at eight?" I asked.

Lola agreed.

I juggled a cup of coffee, my bag, and a takeout container of scalloped potatoes, roasted corn casserole, and honey-baked ham for Lola. Her Lexus glided into a parking space as I exited the Windjammer. The wind had picked up, but the snow had stopped; I stepped gingerly on the pavement in front of the theater, still wary of black ice everywhere. Lola unlocked the door of the ELT, flicked on lights, and we sat down in the office. As Lola ate, I filled her in on my meeting with Bill and then reminded her about my almost-run-in with Archibald at the theater.

"So you think he was here looking for something?"

"I assume. I couldn't see him since I was hiding in the green room. But it sure sounded like someone was pacing back and forth, searching or inspecting," I said.

"He has a key, you know. The chief requested one so that Archibald could come and go during the investigation," Lola said, scooping up the last of the potatoes. "These are so yummy."

"One of Henry's favorite dishes," I said.

"So where do we start?" Lola asked.

"Onstage."

Of course, there was also Sally's insistence that I find a photo she'd dropped the day of the murder. Maybe I could kill two birds...

"What about the crime scene tape? The chief said we needed to stay out of that area," Lola warned me.

"I'll be careful. If we're going to get anywhere, we need to start with the scene of the crime. I feel as if something is missing."

Lola stood and smoothed her white cashmere sweater and designer jeans.

"I'll do the crawling around and dirty work. Maybe you could find a flashlight? Better to leave off the house lights."

Lola produced a utility lantern and we made our way furtively to the stage. Everything was as it had been since the last time I was in the theater. The flashlight sent eerie shadows dancing around the curtains and on the wall that divided the turntable into Acts One and Two. Lola provided illumination as I made my way to the location of the murder. I slipped under the yellow crime scene tape and knelt slowly, examining the wooden floor. I avoided the conspicuous dark stain and focused on the furniture that had been sitting on the stage both before and after the killing. Chair by chair I worked my way across the turntable, picking them up, feeling around the seams of the seats and checking the undersides.

"Find anything?" Lola stage-whispered.

"Nothing yet." The CSI unit had, no doubt, done a thorough job of scrutinizing the area where the body was found, the area that functioned as the graveyard for the second act of *Eton Town*. I sat on the floor and scanned the turntable once more. Examining this part of the stage presupposed that Gordon Weeks wasn't in any other part of the theater. But Sally was a theater geek; she understood stage etiquette, despite Penny's assumption that anyone new to the ELT was totally uninformed. I'd heard Penny often enough warn actors to stay off the stage before and after rehearsal. Sally might have heeded this advice and intended to meet with Gordon Weeks elsewhere in the theater. Except that he was dying when she got here.

"What are you doing?" Lola asked nervously.

"Sally said she walked into the theater and came up to the stage. Of course, no one knows if Gordon Weeks was anywhere else in the theater. Just that he died on the stage," I said.

"Maybe we should get out of here," Lola said.

"Okay." There didn't seem to be any point to searching the rest of the theater if Sally was telling the truth. "While we're here, let's take a look around for the photograph Sally claimed she dropped that afternoon. She's really anxious to get it back."

"Let's hurry," Lola said quickly, waving her flashlight across the stage floor. "What's it look like?"

"Three-inch square. Folded in half, according to Sally. She said she probably dropped it when she ran out of the theater."

"That makes it easy. Let's scan the aisles and see if we find anything." Lola hurried up the left aisle.

"Sounds good." I treaded softly around the crime scene tape and joined her.

"I don't see anything," she said. "Which aisle did she run up when she left the theater? Left or right?"

I closed my eyes and tried to visualize that afternoon. Sally frantic, my confusion at her appearance, her disappearing from the stage, my tripping in my colonial outfit…I stiffened. I never actually saw Sally run through the house. I had fallen forward and when I looked up she was gone. I *assumed* she'd run through the house. I hurried back onstage. "Come on!" I yelled to Lola.

"What? Where to?"

"The emergency escape." I knew about the relatively hidden hallway that ran from the backstage to the lobby since I'd used it during the sting to catch Jerome's killer last April.

Lola flicked the flashlight over the Act One furniture stacked in a haphazard pile by the main drape. "Penny left the scenery in a mess," Lola mumbled.

The unmarked door in the offstage right wing creaked when it opened, a musty, damp smell permeating the air.

"We never use this. I even forget about it." Lola waved her hands over her head briskly to bat down cobwebs. It was a week's worth of cardio. "Doesn't seem like anybody's been in here."

"Let me have the flashlight." I swung the light back and forth, skimming the cement floor and cinder block walls. Lola was right. It didn't look as though anyone had been moving through this area. Of course, a shorter person could run the length of the escape and leave most of the cobwebs undisturbed.

Lola scurried after me. "You think she left the theater through here? Would Sally know about this escape?"

"All of the actors know about it." In the past, I'd seen a few sneaking out of rehearsal via this hallway. I shined the flashlight ahead of me and lit up the door at the end of the passageway, the one that opened into the lobby. I didn't see anything, not a scrap of paper, or food wrapper, or soda can. "Might as well check out the other entrance," I said, and Lola followed me to the end of the escape.

I took a look at the floor. Something caught the light from the lantern. Something pale in color that lay flush to the cinder block wall. I crouched down. It was a small photograph, dog-eared and creased where someone had folded it. "Got it," I said.

"The photo?" Lola asked.

I trained the light on its surface: a young couple smiling and holding each other. They looked very happy staring into the camera.

Lola leaned over my shoulder. "Who are they?"

"I have no idea but Sally was dying to get it back."

A door slammed in the lobby. I jumped up. Archibald was supposed to be in New York, according to Edna.

"Oh no!" Lola gasped.

"Shh! Let's stay put for a minute. It's the safest place," I said and stuffed the picture into my pants pocket.

We hunkered down. Someone was opening and closing doors in the lobby—the office, the box office, the entrance into the house. We had to get out of there. When everything was quiet for thirty seconds, I inched the door open. The lobby was dark, save for the security light.

I motioned to Lola. "Let's go. Whoever it was is either gone or on the stage."

She nodded and tiptoed into the lobby behind me. We had crossed the distance between the escape and the theater office, and I was congratulating myself that we had avoided an altercation with Archibald, when, without warning, a piercing shriek split the silence.

"Aaaah!" we yelled in unison. I braced myself for the worst and Lola put up her hands as if we were caught in a robbery.

"Hold it!" a familiar voice screamed.

The lobby lights flashed on. I blinked. "Penny?"

"Lola?" Penny said, whistle in hand. "What are you doing here?"

"What are you doing here?" I asked in return.

She shoved her glasses up her nose. "I asked you first."

Lola stammered, "We...uh..."

I jumped in. "We were in the office and thought we heard some noise backstage," I said.

Penny looked skeptical. "O'Dell, you're not supposed to be in the theater."

Lola had regained her composure. "Penny, you shouldn't be in the theater either."

"Walter wants me to keep my ears open. After all, I am the production manager." She eyed us smugly. "Now that they're releasing the body, maybe we can get this show onto the road again."

"They're releasing the body?" I asked. "How do you know?" Bill hadn't said anything to me.

Penny zipped up her jacket. "Keeping my ears on the ground." She chuckled. "I also heard some of the ELT actors are auditioning for the Creston Players. Guess that's show..." She shot a look at Lola and stopped herself. "I'm outta here. Lock up."

Lola and I watched Penny exit the lobby.

Red spots appeared on Lola's cheeks. She was fired up. "That does it. I'm calling Walter and the board and the police department. I refuse to lose the membership of the Etonville Little Theatre to the Creston Players. I don't care what production they are doing and who died on the ELT stage. I'm not going down without a fight."

"You go, girl. I have to stop by Snippets in the morning, but let's meet up afterwards to see Bill together."

We made plans, wrapped up, and braced ourselves for the wintry night; the wind had subsided, the sky was a clear, inky black, and the remnants of the earlier snow shower had stuck to the sidewalk. I said good-bye to Lola, peeked into the darkened Windjammer, where Henry had indeed closed up early, and cranked the engine of my Metro. The picture I'd found in the corridor was burning a hole in my pocket. Who were those two people and why was Sally so eager to have it back?

Swathed in my terry cloth robe, sweatpants, and wool socks, and fortified with a glass of chardonnay and a jar of peanut butter, I was ready to work at my kitchen table. First I wanted to check out Gordon Weeks's arrest for attempted burglary in 1997 in the Louisburg Square of Beacon Hill. My digging revealed that it was one of the most prestigious addresses in Boston, and one of the most expensive residential neighborhoods in the United States. In recent years, townhouses sold for over ten million dollars. Whew!

I googled the *Boston Globe* and discovered I had to subscribe online to have access to its archives. I followed through and searched the Metro section for a 1997 burglary in Beacon Hill. It was tedious work, scrolling month by month through articles. I had just begun the October archive. My eyes were scratchy, weary from staring at the screen. I yawned. It was almost midnight and I was starting to think this was a wild goose chase. But I was determined to finish 1997 so I traded my wine glass for a mug of hot tea and settled in again.

Forty minutes later I was approaching the last week of December. Then I saw it. December 24, 1997. Bingo! A man named Gordon Weeks was arrested for a forced entry through the back door of a Greek Revival townhouse in Louisburg Square. When arrested, the perpetrator was in possession of personal items belonging to the occupants of the house who were out of town at the time. Personal items? My eyes popped open and I was exhausted no longer. The house belonged to Olivia Holmes Oldfield and Charles Oldfield who lived there with Olivia's mother and her three-year-old daughter, Sara. Purely coincidence? That Sally was a suspect in the killing of a man who had attempted to rob her home when she was a child? *Did* she have a connection to Gordon Weeks even though she claimed she didn't know him?

A dull ache was growing at the back of my skull. I swallowed two aspirin to quell the throbbing, but questions continued to pile up: What exactly was going on here? I ran to my bedroom and retrieved the picture from my pants pocket. I dug out my magnifying glass from a miscellaneous drawer in the kitchen and scooted into bed under my down comforter, photo and magnifier in hand.

The picture was unremarkable. A young man and woman, probably in their early twenties, grinning animatedly. Both wore dressy outfits: He was in a suit and tie, she in a beige dress with a lacy bodice. It had to be spring or fall. No outerwear.

I adjusted the glass and pored over every detail. In the background were a set of steps, that fronted a large building, and people who moved behind the couple seemed oblivious to the photography. Doubled over, it was small enough to fit inside a wallet. Someone had carried this with them for years, maybe folding and unfolding, possibly staring at it endlessly. For some reason, I felt sad studying the picture. Who were these people and why had someone treasured it for so long? And what was its significance to Gordon Weeks and Sally? Given its condition, someone had hung onto the photo for dear life. I hesitated texting Sally, knowing that Bill and Archibald were now keeping an eye on her. Facebook was my only option. I private messaged her: *I have the photo. Who are they?*

I set the picture aside and turned out the light.

22

"Maybe Sally was a little…" One of the Banger sisters twirled her forefinger next to her ear in the universal sign for "crazy."

Takes one to know one.

"But murdering a poor homeless man? Who would do such a thing?" said the other.

"Number one, she hasn't been arrested for murder. Only questioned about her whereabouts in the theater that day. And number two…" I scanned the group waiting eagerly for any nugget of gossip I could offer. The Banger sisters, Mildred, Georgette, Carol, and Snippets' staff—Rita and Imogen—surrounded me. It would be pointless for the nth time to repeat that Gordon Weeks was not a homeless man. "Well, let's stick with number one."

"I knew some Weeks from Bernridge," Imogen, the shampoo girl, said helpfully, cracking her chewing gum. Everyone looked at her with interest, nodding their heads approvingly; maybe there was some connection to Gordon.

"Sally had a lovely singing voice," said Mildred. "I was glad she was in the chorus of *Eton Town*."

"Well, I liked her. She gave me a huge tip last time," said Rita, assistant manager at the salon.

"She certainly could afford to," said Georgette. "She's worth millions."

A brief pause while the women contemplated the magnitude of having a chorus member of the ELT wealthy enough to buy the theater lock, stock, and barrel.

"I liked her too." I smiled at Rita and corrected myself. "I guess I should say I like her. She's still with us."

"For the time being," said the first Banger sister ominously.

"Okay, ladies, let's get shampooed." Carol broke up the grapevine, Imogen escorted the sisters to the sinks in the rear of the salon, and Rita started in on Mildred's hair.

"Let's talk up here. I have a minute," Carol said and motioned for me to follow her to the reception desk.

The shop would be busier in half an hour. But at the moment Carol could afford to take a short break.

"I can see that the scuttlebutt on Sally has made the rounds," I said.

"That's all anyone can talk about. Sally murdering that Gordon Weeks. Even if she is just a 'person of interest.' But that's not why I had you come here."

I sat on a stool behind the counter. "Okay. Give."

"Remember when I said she talked about taking a cruise next month?" Carol asked.

"Sure."

"And she said maybe her father was coming to the show?"

"Right."

"There was one thing I forgot and I only remembered it when I read the article in the *Etonville Standard* about how Sally was from Boston and had this unbelievable background and her family came over on the Mayflower and then they lived on Beacon Hill and—"

"Carol!"

"Okay. So I'm rethinking that morning in the shop," Carol said.

"The day *Eton Town* was supposed to open," I reminded her.

"Yes. She received a phone call as she was on her way out." Carol lowered her voice. "I couldn't help overhearing even though she tucked herself away in the corner." Carol pointed to a small waiting area with padded benches, shelves of cosmetic products, and a stack of magazines.

"What did you hear?" I could feel a shot of adrenaline kickstart my nervous system.

"Sally said something that sounded like 'I want to be alone' or 'leave me alone' or something like that. Then I heard 'at the theater.' And before she ended the call, I ducked my head so it wouldn't look like...you know..." she said.

"Like you were eavesdropping?" I prompted her.

"That's right. And Sally said 'I don't care about the money,'" Carol said. "It was the money part that I remembered after I saw the article."

"You're sure? She said 'I don't care about the money?'"

Carol nodded. "Do you think she was talking to Gordon Weeks?"

"I don't know, but I'm going to have to tell the chief. He may want to interview you," I said. Had Bill confiscated Sally's cell phone to track her calls?

Carol's revelation added fuel to the Gordon Weeks fire. Maybe she was negotiating with him to stay away from her. And offering him money to do so. Still she had agreed to meet him at the theater later.

Lola and I had decided to meet at the Municipal Building at nine thirty. I'd stayed at Snippets longer than I'd anticipated and now had to hurry. I parked on a side street that was clear of snow drifts and avoided patches of ice as I made my way to the police department. My head was tucked into my scarf to dodge the gusts of cold air that were blowing through Etonville, so when I yanked on the front door, I didn't see Archibald opening it from the other side.

"Somebody's in a hurry," he said, a cocky smile on his clean-shaven face. A shirt, tie, and overcoat had replaced his leather jacket and jeans. Only his signature cowboy boots remained.

"A meeting with Bill," I said in what I hoped was a friendly, neutral fashion.

"He's waiting for you."

Was that a look of triumph? I'd texted Bill last night that Lola and I wanted to meet with him this morning. I couldn't help myself. "Liking your new digs?"

"The rooming house? Not bad." His eyes narrowed as if he knew what I was up to. "Good vantage point for keeping an eye on things."

"Like Sally?" I asked.

"You'd better talk with Bill." My heart dropped into my stomach as he tilted his head and observed me. "Maybe Bill should hire you full-time. It would be simpler than trying to keep tabs on you too." He grinned.

What did that mean? Before I could offer a retort, Archibald turned up his collar and climbed into his Ford. I entered the Municipal Building and spied Lola at dispatch chatting with Edna.

"Hi, you two." I rubbed my hands together. "The chief in?"

"Yep. I told him you were here." Her headset crackled. "I think it's good news-bad news," she said with an arched eyebrow.

Lola and I leaned into the dispatch window. I was afraid to hear.

"The case is about to be closed, which is good for the theater. But it looks like Sally—"

"Edna!" Bill had entered the hallway.

"Yes, chief?" She slipped on her headset.

"Where's Ralph?" he asked.

"Anderson and Main. There's an 11-66 and he'll need to direct traffic," Edna said.

"Forget the defective signal. Have him call in to Suki for another assignment."

"Copy that, chief." Edna went to work.

Bill shifted his attention to us. "Come on back." He turned on his crutches and led the way.

Lola and I mentally crossed our fingers. We wordlessly followed him to his inner office, passing Suki at the computer in the outer office. She didn't look up. I was not having a good feeling.

Bill was courteous, juggling his crutches and adjusting a chair for Lola to sit on. I opted for the other guest chair that was wrapped in Bill's uniform jacket.

"Here, I'll take that," he said and removed his coat.

Bill settled himself behind the desk and then looked up at us, the intensity of his dazzling eyes distracting me for a second. "So you wanted to see me?"

Lola placed her hands in her lap. "Chief—"

"Bill, please."

"Bill...we..." She cut her eyes in my direction. "I'd like to talk to you about the theater. I know the investigation is still ongoing, but we're having a crisis. Not only is the show up in the air and that means no box office and that threatens our next production but—" Lola looked at me.

I smiled encouragingly.

"Now there is...talk...that ELT members are defecting to the Creston Players. That would ruin us. What would Etonville do without the ELT?"

Being the cultural center of our little burg.

I wondered if any of this was making a dent in Bill's police chief defense shield. He listened politely, and I waited for him to interrupt and explain patiently that as long as there was a dead body and no satisfactory solution to the murder, he could not honor her request, release the theater, and blah blah blah.

He held up a hand. "Mrs. Tripper, Lola..." He smiled.

I figured he was trying to let her down easy.

"I was going to call you later today to let you know that I am removing the crime scene tape. The CSI team has taken all necessary samples of materials pertinent to the case and scoured the area."

Lola clapped her hands, ecstatic. "I can't tell you how pleased that will make the ELT. And me personally. Thank you."

He accepted her gratitude graciously and they discussed the timing of the removal and the cleanup of the stage floor. Meanwhile, I was of two minds. I was happy for Lola but releasing the theater meant Bill had wrapped up the case, probably with Sally as the prime suspect.

Suddenly the room was silent, both Lola and Bill staring at me. "Good news for the theater. Bill, do you have a minute? Lola, I'll catch up with you later."

Bill nodded and Lola exited, but not before sending me ocular support and shutting the door quietly.

"Would you like some coffee? I can have Edna make a run to—"

"Do you have enough evidence to charge Sally Oldfield?" I asked softly. "I bumped into Archibald on my way in. He seemed awfully confident."

"Look, Dodie, I know you have faith in Sally, but her lack of an explanation for being with Gordon Weeks, his blood on her hands, the ME's description of the size of the attacker..." He paused. "This is confidential. Although it will come out eventually. Archibald has information from a doctor in Boston. According to him, Sally is unstable and has been under psychiatric care for the last six months since her mother died."

I swallowed hard. Who had Archibald spoken with? Andy was her therapist...at least most recently. Surely Andy would have let me know if he'd communicated with a private detective, right?

"Have you confirmed Archibald's conversation with the therapist?" I asked. The molecules in the room shifted.

Bill sat up straighter. "What's that supposed to mean?"

"I know he's your friend but getting a room in the same boarding house as Sally? I think he had it in for her from the beginning—"

"That doesn't mean anything," he said.

"And then making late-night calls at the theater and meeting with people on the sly—"

"What people? On the sly? Have you been following him?" Bill's ruddy face had turned a shade darker.

"Look, I happened on him a few times and it made me—"

"Happened on him?" Bill choked on the words. "That's enough. This is over. I don't know what you think you know about Archibald, but he is a crack detective and more importantly *I* trust him." He was an inch away from shouting. "He's investigating a murder and doesn't need to check in with me every time he visits the crime scene!" He exhaled loudly. "Anything more you have to say?"

I was surprised at the chill in the air. I guess I'd pushed Bill a little too far this time. "Only that I think it's a bizarre coincidence that Gordon Weeks was arrested for an attempted break-in at Sally's home in 1997." I stood up. "Maybe Archibald can explain that."

"What are you talking about?" Bill's voice followed me as I turned on my heel and flew out the door, leaving it open behind me. Suki looked up as I passed, but I kept my head down this time.

"What's today's special?" Edna called out from dispatch.

I shook my head and waved good-bye. At the entrance to the Municipal Building I stopped dead in my tracks. Sally was being escorted by Ralph, whose expression indicated he was thrilled to have abandoned crowd control for *real* police business.

"Sally?" My voice quivered. "I have your—"

Ralph hustled her into the building.

The winter air was bracing—I needed to clear my mind and make some decisions. I walked past Betty's Boutique, avoided Coffee Heaven, and even ignored texts from Lola; she was no doubt delighted that the ELT could get back on schedule and open *Eton Town*. I didn't blame her. In directing the show, she'd contributed a ton of sweat and tears to the production and deserved to see her hard work pay off. Happy as I was for her, I was distressed by the direction events were taking. A rush to judgment as far as Sally was concerned: She was the low-hanging fruit. And what to make of Carol overhearing Sally say she didn't care about the money? What was she hiding? I needed to find out if Archibald's report on Sally came from Andy. He'd never even hinted that Sally was unstable.

I kicked up slush on the sidewalk as I traipsed down Amber at a steady pace. At this rate, I would end up at home when I needed to be at the Windjammer in half an hour. I turned around abruptly and beat a hasty retreat to my Metro. The safest, quietest place right now. I tapped Andy's number on my cell and waited as it rang, then went to voicemail. I listened impatiently as he said he was not available but to leave a name and number and he would get back in touch.

"Andy. It's me." I paused. "Sally's been arrested as the prime suspect in the murder investigation. I need to talk." I ended the call and slumped down in my seat. I'd have given anything to climb back into bed.

* * *

The word was out on *Eton Town*. We'd barely opened the restaurant for lunch when a stream of Etonville's citizens clambered in the door, setting the place abuzz. The show was on and the excitement was palpable. Of course, a few folks were shocked that Sally had been arrested. But mostly, her fate had already been grist for the rumor mill that by now had ground to a halt.

"Dodie, have you heard? We can open the show!" exclaimed Mildred.

"I sure did. Great news." I tried to smile as I rang up their lunch check for barbecue pulled pork on Texas toast.

"Mixed feelings for me. Glad the thing is finally going to get on its feet, but I'm afraid that the town may give it two thumbs down," Vernon grumbled.

Mildred swatted him lightly on the arm. "Don't let Walter hear you say that."

"What?" Vernon asked.

"Turn up the sound!"

"Didn't bother putting them in this morning. Nothing worth hearing around here anyway." Vernon shuffled out the door, Mildred, shaking her head, close behind.

"Everybody else is roaring to go," said Benny as he drew sodas. "A shame about Sally though. Guess the evidence is pretty strong?" He stopped pouring and studied me.

Like everyone else in Etonville, Benny knew what part I'd played in solving previous murders and assumed I had the inside track on Bill's investigation. "I guess."

"You're being cagey," Benny said.

"Not cagey. Disappointed. Instincts, you know?"

Benny nodded sympathetically and placed the drinks on a tray for Gillian to deliver to a table. "Even good instincts need a break," he said softly.

"Right."

Lola scurried in the door, cheeks flushed, eyes bright. Clearly exhilarated. "I've been texting you for the last couple of hours. Things are crazy busy. I called the *Star-Ledger* reviewer and I'm pretty sure he can make it Saturday night. Penny is emailing the cast so we can schedule the *final* final dress rehearsal for tomorrow night. We're getting a clean-up crew in there today and Walter is trying not to panic so—"

"Sorry, Lola," I said. "I need to speak to Henry."

"But—" She raised a hand as I headed to the kitchen.

"I'll call you later, okay?" I said.

I could not bear to hear all the chipper good news when Sally was being arraigned in a court in Creston. I needed to hide.

In the kitchen, Henry was chopping onion and pepper chunks for chicken kabobs while Enrico was prepping the moussaka for our Greek night. Georgette had even agreed to drop off freshly made baklava.

Benny burst through the door. "We got trouble."

Henry jerked up from his cutting board, worry lines immediately creasing his forehead. He hated to hear bad news. "What?"

"Yeah, what?" I repeated.

"We've got a trickle of water coming down the front of the dining room."

"A trickle?" I asked.

"So far," Benny said.

"The roof is leaking?"

"Looks like it. I'll get a bucket." Benny disappeared through a door that led to the basement of the restaurant.

I walked leisurely into the dining room to avoid creating a stir. No luck. Patrons had already scooted tables away from the front wall. I smiled reassuringly.

"Dodie, there's water coming into the restaurant," said one of the Banger sisters.

"I'm on it," I answered and scanned the ceiling. A steady drip fell about three inches out from the wall. I had a flashback to last week when JC lectured Henry on the perils of ice dams in the gutter melting and refreezing and blocking a path for the runoff. Forcing ice and water to back up under the shingles resulting in leaks. After a few minutes I had tuned out JC's suggestions on creating a watertight seal under the roof. I wish I had paid more attention. I fervently hoped this wasn't going to cost an arm and a leg to repair since the Windjammer was finally on solid financial footing after a few years of up and down fiscal uncertainty.

"Here," Benny said as unobtrusively as he could—considering the Banger sisters had made a point of moving their chairs to the other side of their table and covering their heads—and handed me a red plastic bucket.

I placed it under the leak and listened to the *plop, plop, plop* as water landed in the pail. Each drop sounded like a mini-explosion.

"Like last fall in the theater," said Abby, from two booths away.

Customers looked up. Those who had been unaware of the commotion were now tuned in.

"Remember? We had that big leak during the storm and Walter had to put a bucket on stage," she continued.

I remembered. "I think it's a small drip. This should do it."

Famous last words. Within an hour, leaks had sprung up across the ceiling, forming a straight line from the front window to the center of the room. People were ducking, rearranging plates on their tables, covering their food with napkins. I ran from leak to leak, substituting kitchen pots for buckets until I'd wiped out Henry's cooking utensils. It was ridiculous.

Lunch was ending, partly because it was two thirty and partly because people were running out of dry places to eat.

"Henry," I yelled, slamming through the swinging doors into the kitchen.

He looked up from slicing chicken as though he hadn't noticed that Benny and I had been making container runs for the past hour. "What?"

"We can't serve dinner tonight. The dining room is an obstacle course, customers are having to cope with buckets and pans and—"

Benny burst in. "Maybe we should call JC? See if he can get someone here to work on the roof."

"Good idea." Benny ran back into the dining room and I paused. "Henry, we should close up for dinner. Get this thing fixed so we can reopen tomorrow. The ingredients for the kabobs and moussaka will keep overnight. I'll call Georgette and have her put a hold on the baklava."

Henry reluctantly nodded. Enrico nodded. I nodded.

Geez.

23

By four o'clock, JC had managed to round up a roofing guy who came into the restaurant and assessed the problem. "Yep," he said knowingly.

"I'll bet it's an ice dam," I suggested.

"Yep. Gotta be."

His immediate solution was to drill holes into the ceiling to release the water and stop its flow from moving any farther into the restaurant. I watched as the roofer climbed a metal ladder and inserted an electric drill bit into the ceiling, flirting with electrocution. I was fascinated by his nonchalant attitude as he defied death. Which of course made me think of Gordon Weeks and then Sally and then Bill...

Benny emptied buckets and pans, Carmen wiped down tables, and Gillian texted, no doubt making plans for the evening. It was a cinch the Windjammer was on lockdown until the water problem was fixed. I sat at the bar, nursing a glass of Chardonnay...after all, the restaurant was officially closed. My cell phone binged. Lola asking what I was doing. I texted back: *Watching the roofer drill holes in the ceiling.*

Her return text: *Heard about the leak.*

My cell rang. "Hey."

"How bad is it?" Lola asked.

"We're closing the Windjammer for the night."

"Oh, I was looking forward to Henry's Greek moussaka. I wanted to get my strength up to face the stage. A cleaning company was in the theater this afternoon, you know one of those companies that specializes in removing certain kinds of stains...like rust and mold and..."

"...blood," I finished for her.

"Yes. Blood." She sighed. "Do you think we all misjudged Sally?"

I had no idea. Earlier, while keeping one eye on the roofer, I'd doodled a list of questions about Gordon Weeks's murder that I'd been poring over for days: *Why did he attempt to rob Sally's home in Boston in 1997? Did Sally know him even though she said she wasn't sure who he was? Who was she speaking with on her cell at Snippets? And who was in the picture and why was the photo so important to her?*

"So what's up tonight?" I asked.

"Walter, Penny, Chrystal, and I are meeting to work out the final dress tomorrow night."

"Are you replacing Sally?" I asked.

"I don't think we can add anyone new to the cast at this point. Are you interested?" Lola laughed lightly. "Maybe it would be good for you. Take your mind off the murder."

"That's okay. I didn't care for the costume the first time around and all I had to do was stand in the lobby and sell early American cakes. Speaking of which, there's not much left of our intermission treats."

"I figured as much. You did your best, Dodie. We'll have to let the theme food go this time around," Lola said.

"I suppose. Good luck," I said.

"Thanks. I'm going to plunge in."

* * *

JC's roofer finished by six and promised to be on the job, literally on the roof, first thing in the morning. Henry was grouchy and complained about the Windjammer closing, the cost of the repairs, the loss of income, etc. etc. etc. I was glad to see him go out into the night. I loved Henry, but sometimes he was too much to handle. Today was one of those times. I stuffed some leftover barbecue pork from lunch into a bag for my dinner later, wondering where Sally was at this moment. Surely by now she had "lawyered up." I was still musing on her future when I turned out the lights and locked the front door. It was only seven o'clock, but Main Street was empty, the lights off in shop windows. Only the Etonville Little Theatre would be humming with life tonight and—

A firm object was thrust against my mouth, wrenching my head backwards. It took a second for me to realize it was a gloved hand. I dropped the shopping bag with my dinner and an arm clasped me around my waist roughly, pulling me into a body. I whipped my head to one side and my face scraped against the scratchy wool of a coat. I inhaled the odors of a man's cologne and stale cigarette smoke blended with the smell of cold air. My heart raced. Fear battled logic, while nausea crept from my stomach to my throat. I tried to speak. "Mmph," was all I could manage.

"Quiet down," a threatening voice growled.

A dark sedan with tinted windows pulled up in front of the Windjammer and I was thrust into the back seat, a cloth hood slipped over my head, my hands duct-taped behind my back. I was disoriented, dizzy. I sucked in air, my chest heaving. I felt a hard object stuck into my ribs. I was betting it was a gun!

"W-Who are you?" I tried for belligerent. "W-What do you want?"

"I said shut up." He plucked my bag off my shoulder and dug around in it. Obviously unsuccessful, he tossed the purse aside. The car careened around one corner and made two more turns before picking up speed. My inner GPS told me we were headed for State Route 53. After that it was anybody's guess: Creston, the Garden State Parkway, New York?

I exhaled slowly. Why would someone want to kidnap me? What kind of ransom would they get for a thirty-four-year-old restaurant manager and part-time amateur detective? The car rocketed to the left, then lurched to a stop, then moved a few yards, then stopped again. It could be the end of rush hour traffic on the highway.

Maybe I could force their hands. Get them to talk and reveal something. Anything. "Can you take that thing out of my ribs? I can't breathe." I coughed a few times.

The man next to me shifted his weight, the gun still against my side, but his partner must have signaled something because the guy eased up. Still no further talking. We weren't in the car more than fifteen minutes when it swerved to the right and rolled to a stop. Very little light seeped in under the hood and the sounds of the highway faded into the background. Were we in a parking lot somewhere? Why stop unless they had plans for me—

"Miss O'Dell, I want you to listen to me carefully," a second voice snapped out of the blackness.

Every hair on my neck stood up straight. Where had I heard that voice before? Polite and civil. Certainly nothing like the gravelly tone of the guy next to me.

"You know what we want," he continued.

So there was a ransom. But what was it? What did I have?

"I don't know what you're talking about," I said boldly. It was the truth.

Gentle laughter. "So that's how you want to play this?"

The gun was shoved back into my ribs. "Where is it?" the guy asked brusquely.

My brain was burning rubber, running through a catalogue of options. "Why don't you give me a hint?" Again, I was serious, not joking.

The man next to me wasn't having any of it. "I'm counting—"

The soothing voice. "I was hoping we could do this with no fuss."

"No fuss? You gotta be kidding! My head is covered, my hands are taped together, and there's a gun sticking in my ribs. I'd say we've passed the 'no fuss' stage." Silence for a moment. "Why don't you tell me exactly what you are looking for and maybe I can help you."

Help them? It was the first thing that popped into my head. I was gradually calming down. If they'd wanted to shoot me I'd already be dead. But they needed something from me. They needed me alive. "Can we open a window? It's really stuffy under here." After a beat, I heard the window lower and a swish of cold air circulate through the car. I tried to gulp the fresh air. My backseat companion breathed asthmatically, air whistling in and out of his mouth.

"Now. What do you want?" I asked, as composed as I was going to get with a firearm inches from my heart.

Again the cool one. "The photograph."

"What photo—?" Then my heart banged in my chest. The snapshot I found in the theater. The one Sally was desperate to have back.

"So you do have it," he said smoothly.

I had given myself away. The photo had to be valuable, somehow related to Gordon Weeks's death and Sally's destiny. Valuable enough to make two men kidnap me on Main Street in early evening. It was on my chest of drawers. I threw caution to the wind and lied. "I don't have it."

A pause. "Where is it?" The gentle voice had taken on an edge of impatience.

I hesitated. It would be easy enough for them to break into my bungalow and find the print. And with it might go the possibility of solving the murder. "I gave it...to the police." The mood in the sedan altered radically.

"When?" The words and the gun were shoved at me simultaneously.

I sensed uncertainty and pressed my advantage. "This morning."

The engine rumbled to life. "We'll check it out. If you've been lying, we'll be paying you another visit and this time it won't be as cordial."

Cordial? He threw the car into gear and we zoomed back onto the highway. The silence was broken only by the whining of the tires on concrete, slowing down when I assumed we'd arrived at the outskirts of Etonville where the driver probably was anxious to maintain the speed limit. The sedan pulled off the road.

My captor tugged on my arm, easing me out of the back seat and leaving me unceremoniously on the side of the road. Hood and duct tape still intact.

He leaned over me, spitting the words into the fabric covering my head. "Remember what he said."

How could I forget?

The menace hung in the night air as the car sped off. I was sitting on a layer of frozen slush, my hands still awkwardly bound behind my back. I had to get this hood off my head. I laid back, scooted against the surface of the road, rubbing the hood back and forth hoping to shake it off. A bright light split the pitch-black night and the growl of a motor grew louder. Could they be back? Had they regretted dumping me here and come back for me? I rolled onto my side and worked my way to a standing position. Somehow standing I felt less vulnerable. The vehicle lumbered to a stop, the engine idling.

"Hey, you okay?" shouted a masculine voice.

Relief poured through my veins. "Help!" I yelled as loudly as I could.

A door slammed, the crunch of footsteps came closer. "What the...?" Then two hands slipped the hood off me.

I took gasps of the chill air and faced my rescuer. It was Timothy of Timothy's Timely Service, owner of the used Hyundai that provided transport for a few days, in a pickup truck. His shop was down the road a bit.

"Dodie? What are you doing out here like this?" He was mystified.

It was a good question. "Could you...?" I turned around to reveal my taped wrists.

"Well, I'll be. Somebody taped your hands!" He withdrew a Swiss Army knife, slipped a blade between my wrists and expertly snipped. "Let's get you to the police station."

"No! I...uh...need to get my car first. Then I'll go," I said.

I had no desire to set off alarm signals throughout Etonville before I could talk with Sally and Andy and figure a few things out. "Could you drop me off at the Windjammer?" I peeled the duct tape off my hands.

Timothy stared at me uncertainly. "This seems pretty serious."

"I'm fine. A ride to the restaurant would be a big help," I said.

"Well, if you're sure..."

"I'd really appreciate it."

On the ride across town, Timothy peeked sideways a few times as we traveled in silence. I was tempted to rattle off some wild story about this all being a mistake, maybe a prank of some kind. But even my imagination was exhausted. For the first time in a long time, I was at a loss for words. So I closed my eyes, memorizing every detail of the kidnapping caper that I could remember.

"Here we go," Timothy said and pulled up in front of the restaurant. By the clock on his dashboard I could see that it was only eight thirty.

I opened the car door. "Thanks." I hesitated. What else to say? "Have a good night." I shut the door and waved.

Timothy waited until I was in my Metro with the engine running before he maneuvered his pickup back onto Main Street. The lobby of the ELT was lit up; Lola's meeting was still in progress. All else was quiet. I was tempted to stop in and share the evening's drama, but she had enough drama of her own to deal with and I was shaking from the cold, my pants wet where I'd scrunched back and forth on the roadway and the skin on my wrists sore. I needed a hot bath.

* * *

I'd buried the photograph—in a plastic baggie—under the carpet in my bedroom, after eliminating the freezer—too common—and drawers as too obvious hiding places. I double-checked all door and window locks. Then tried to relax into the lavender suds, resting my head against the lip of the tub. I touched my wrists tenderly where red marks were a reminder of my captivity only a few hours before. How long did I have until they realized the police didn't have the photo? But what could possibly be so important about a picture of two twenty-somethings? What was in the photo that made the two men so desperate? I'd had it with tranquility; I needed some oomph. I dripped on the bath mat, wrapping myself in my terry cloth robe, made myself a cup of coffee, and settled at the kitchen table with my laptop and cell phone. Logically, I should have called the Etonville PD and reported my kidnapping. But I couldn't risk Bill sharing this piece of information with Archibald. After all, the kidnapper implied that he had a contact in the police department with whom he could "check out" my claim about the photo.

I tapped on Andy's number, hoping he was available this time. The phone rang once, twice, three times. I'd mentally begun to compose my message when he picked up.

"Hi, sis. Was thinking of you. Got an email from Mom and she's already hinting about Easter in Florida. But with Amanda's work load—"

"Did you get my message?" I asked quickly.

"Haven't had time to check them all day. Been really hectic. And I finally got Cory to sleep. Why?"

"Sally Oldfield's been arrested," I said.

Andy exhaled loudly. "Damn. She's now the prime suspect?"

"She's the only suspect."

"You're not involved in all this, are you?" He warned more than asked.

"Don't worry. Following up on a few things." I dared not mention my kidnapping or Peeping Tom or my Metro break-in. "Bill has a private detective working the case, you know with his broken ankle and all."

"Yeah. How's he doing?" Andy asked.

"Fine. Did the private detective speak with you?" I was sure I already knew the answer.

"No. Why?"

"He claimed Sally's doctor in Boston said she was unstable. I think they want to use that against her," I said.

"What? She's not unstable. Sad about the recent death of her mother, yes, but understandable. She's human, like the rest of us," he said. "Has she called a lawyer? Does her father know?" he asked.

"I assume so." After all, Charles Oldfield had been in and out of Etonville ever since that Sunday we'd almost collided on Main Street. I tapped a pen against a legal pad where I'd made a few notes: Archibald in Boston, picture of a young couple, Gordon Weeks...

"Who do you think the detective spoke to about Sally's mental state? Someone else in your practice?" I asked.

"Definitely not. I'd know if someone did."

"What about Gordon Weeks?" I asked.

"Who?"

I realized Andy hadn't gotten the news from Etonville, New Jersey. "The victim in the stabbing. Did Sally ever mention him?"

"Gordon Weeks? Not that I recall. Look, Dodie, what are you trying to get at?" he asked.

"The truth. I feel there's more to Sally's story than she's telling the police. I think she knew the murdered man but won't admit it. Like maybe she's protecting herself. Or him."

"I don't know the details of the murder, but the Sara I know would not be capable of killing someone or lying about it," he said.

"Maybe the Sara you know is not the Sally who's been living in Etonville these last few weeks," I said.

Andy was silent.

"There's so many loose ends."

"Such as?" he asked.

Despite his admonition to stay out of the investigation, I shared my research on Gordon Weeks and the break-in at Sally's childhood home in 1997 and my feelings that it was too much of a coincidence to be easily dismissed. Andy reluctantly agreed but urged me to tell all to Bill. I heard crying in the background.

"Cory's awake. Gotta go. Sorry," he said.

"Thanks, Andy. Miss you," I said.

"Me too. Stay out of trouble."

We clicked off. What had I learned? Sally never mentioned Gordon Weeks in therapy, and no one had spoken with Andy about Sally's mental state. That only reinforced my suspicions about Archibald and his Boston contact. My little hairs kicked up their heels.

24

I shot up, startled. My cell phone binged in my ear. I'd been dozing at the kitchen table, arms crossed under my head, my phone two inches from my face. I read the text from Lola: *Are u up*? The clock on my wall said eleven p.m. I must have dropped off an hour ago. I texted back: *Yes.*

I wiped some drool from my mouth, threw some water in my face to wake up, and brewed another cup of coffee. I had the feeling it might be a long night. My cell rang.

"Hi, Lola," I said.

"Dodie O'Dell?" The voice was familiar.

"Yes?" My heart went from zero to sixty.

"You lied to us. The police department does not have the photograph in question."

My kidnapper. How did they find out so quickly? *Did* they have someone on the inside? Archibald? I inhaled slowly to keep my voice from quaking. "But I gave the photo—"

His speech was clipped with a hard edge. "I want the picture in my hands by noon tomorrow."

Noon? Between my inevitable meeting with Bill and the Windjammer opening, noon didn't give me much time. "I don't have it with me. And I can't get it by noon. Later in the evening. Say nine? I'll call you to confirm," I babbled.

Silence for a moment, then he said, "No. I'll call you to arrange the meeting." He clicked off.

Another call came in. My hands shook as I answered it.

"Dodie? How are you doing? I know it's been a rough day. Over here too. But we have a plan in place if the turntable stops working and Walter is trying to cut some of Act Two so—"

"Lola..." Despite my best efforts to hold it together, my voice gave me away. She paused. "Dodie, what's the matter?"

"I think I might be in over my head," I whispered.

"Is this about Sally and the murder?" she asked.

"And kidnapping and a threatening phone call and—"

"What? Stay put. I'm on my way," Lola said forcefully.

* * *

Half an hour later Lola sat at my table sharing some French onion soup—without the bread bowl—that I'd liberated from the Windjammer. I'd filled her in.

"So let me get this straight. Someone kidnapped you over that picture we found in the theater?"

"Seems so. They want it badly too. I'll bet that's why my car was broken into. They, whoever they are, thought I might have had it all along. Maybe they thought I was keeping it safe for Sally."

"And Andy hadn't spoken with any detective?"

"Right."

Lola sat back in her chair. "This is getting stranger and stranger. And more complicated," she said.

"See what I mean?"

"You have to tell Bill. This abduction is serious stuff."

"Tomorrow. With the picture and all of my evidence," I said.

Lola's brow puckered. "Is it safe to wait? Call him now!"

I should have, but I knew the second I turned everything over to Bill, and Archibald, I'd be locked out of the investigation and probably unable to assist Sally any more. I had to get a few more answers before I surrendered everything I had on the murder. It was clear Sally wasn't going to help me dig into her past; I'd have to figure this out on my own.

"How's the final dress rehearsal going to go tomorrow?" I asked.

I had very little skin in the *Eton Town* game at this point—aside from the remnants of the intermission desserts—and listened to Lola's updated rehearsal plans and Walter's script changes and Chrystal's worries over the cost of the new schedule of performances because her costumes were rented for a limited run. I nodded appropriately and reassured Lola that it would all go well. It usually did with the ELT. I stifled a yawn at midnight.

Lola wanted to spend the night or, better still, have me stay with her, but I declined the offer. I had work to do and I felt safe enough with the kidnappers on hold; if they had wanted to harm me, they'd have done so by now. Lola reluctantly left after making me promise to call Bill first thing in the morning.

I powered up my laptop, downed a couple of stale cookies and set to work. Charles Oldfield. I typed his name and Boston in the search bar. I clicked on one of several links and an article from the *Boston Globe* appeared. It described his marriage to socialite Olivia Holmes in September, 1994—a small affair with only family in attendance—and the birth of their daughter Sara Olivia Oldfield several months later. Was it a shotgun wedding? Interesting… There was a paragraph on his background: born in Boston into a family of social strivers, prep schools in New England, Emerson College, worked in the Holmes family ventures in various positions. A brief story on a business bankruptcy. Nothing that sent up a red flag.

The wind whistled around the eaves of my house, sending a draft of air into the cracks around the window frames in the kitchen. But it was more than the winter weather that sent a chill through me. I was generally good at thinking outside the box and making leaps of imagination. Bill had more than once scolded me for too much creativity where a homicide was concerned. But I was sure I had stumbled onto missing pieces of the Gordon Weeks puzzle. I couldn't articulate my thoughts yet, I just had the feeling that if I could fit the pieces together, the face that would emerge would be the killer's. And it wouldn't be Sally Oldfield's. I needed my wits about me tomorrow and that meant a few hours of sleep.

* * *

I woke up every hour, the last time at seven a.m., my body achy, my mind muddled. In the shower I let the hot water wash away the remnants of sleep as well as my mental cobwebs. I felt alert as I dried my hair and dressed for warmth and utility: a sweat suit and an extra hoodie. I wasn't sure what state the Windjammer would be in today, but I wanted to be prepared for all emergencies.

At eight a.m. I texted Pauli to see if he could do me a favor. I knew from past experience that he was usually awake early, doing homework or working on his computer. He was on board. I could see his brown eyes shining at the prospect of one of my Internet assignments. I texted him the picture of Gordon Weeks Sally had texted me and asked if he could run it through his facial recognition software and remove the beard. I wanted a better look at Weeks's face. Pauli said he'd have it back to me within the hour. Next I prepped for my meeting with Bill: the kidnapping; the photograph; no one interviewing Andy about Sally's emotional state. I would avoid any mention of Archibald if I could help it. My referring to his friend was like waving a red flag in front of a bull.

After last night's rolling around on the ground in the roadside muck, I surrendered my down jacket in favor of my wool coat. Topped off with a muffler and wool cap, I was ready to face the morning. And Bill. I tucked Sally's photograph carefully into my pants pocket, checked out the street in front of my house, and treaded carefully to my Metro. As if it knew we were not messing around this morning, the engine turned over quickly and purred as I drove down Ames and onto Fairfield. With the brilliant morning sun and cloudless blue sky, I had difficulty recreating last night's scary, distressing episode. I still hadn't fully scratched the itch that was the lead captor's voice.

I found a space in front of Coffee Heaven, locked the car, and dropped some money in the meter.

"Hi, Dodie!"

It was Edna darting out of Coffee Heaven with a takeout container of coffees. "Hey there. You're in a hurry. Busy morning?"

"As a one-legged grasshopper in a jumping contest."

I wondered if it had anything to do with the murder?

Edna leaned in, exhaling wisps of air. "Sally's out on bail. Archibald and the chief huddled together in his office at seven a.m. Until Archibald had to leave to go to court." She took a few steps. "Got to get these back before they freeze. Hey, will the Windjammer be open for lunch? Hate to miss Henry's special."

"I'm not sure. Depends on the state of the roof and the dining room. Call in about an hour or so and we should know one way or the other," I said.

I shivered as I opened the door to Coffee Heaven and heard the welcome bells tinkling. Jocelyn looked up from behind the counter and waved me over. "Dodie, I heard the Windjammer roof collapsed."

"No, nothing like that. The roof is fine. Some ice backed up under the shingles and then water—"

"You know, years ago a roof collapsed on a house in my neighborhood. Someone was almost killed. Good thing nobody died during lunch at the Windjammer yesterday," she said seriously.

I gave up. "Right."

"The regular?" Jocelyn asked.

"Black coffee." My cell binged. It was Pauli: *Talk?*

I moved to the end of the counter to get a scrap of privacy. Hard to do anywhere in Etonville, still it was relatively early and the town was just waking up. I tapped on Pauli's cell number.

"Uh, hi," Pauli said.

"Hey, were you able to work on the picture?"

"Like, yeah. I sent it. But like, is there anything else you want me to do with it?" He sounded awfully eager for nine a.m.

I had a sudden inspiration. "You know how the police can use a computer program to make a suspect or victim look older?"

"Age progressed sketches," he said knowingly.

"Could you make a person look younger? Age regressed?" I asked.

"Easy-peasy. But gotta bounce now to get to class," he said.

"No problem. Send it when you can."

"Can do it in homeroom in a couple of hours. Like, how far back do you want me to go?"

"To his twenties. Thanks, Pauli. Hey, how's the photography? Any more cinéma vérité?" I asked, smiling.

"Nah. I'm ditching reality. Now I'm like, doing some cool things with underexposed film," he said. "Totally rocks."

"Nice. Can't wait to see it."

"Later." He clicked off.

Jocelyn returned with my takeout container. "Now be careful. A collapsed roof is nothing to fool around with." She shook a finger in my face and I nodded.

I checked out Pauli's text and enlarged the photo of Gordon Weeks. Without the facial hair he was an attractive man with a high forehead and a square chin. Seeing him clean-shaven gave me a feeling for his character. But there was something else about his face…what was it?

I said good-bye to Jocelyn and left.

* * *

I sat in a chair in the outer office of the Etonville Police Department waiting for Bill to see me. Suki was out of the office—attending to an 11-25 according to Edna. A traffic hazard she told me. Someone had left a car in the middle of the road because there were no available parking spaces at the Shop N Go. I was grateful for the wayward automobile. It meant I could avoid Suki's questioning looks. I ran through my talking points again until I heard Bill's door open and a clunking sound I had become accustomed to since his accident.

"Come on in," he said, leaning on his crutches. His sandy-colored hair glinted in the morning light, his mouth boasted a hint of his crooked smile. Any vestiges of our argument yesterday had seemed to disappear.

"Thanks for seeing me. I know you're as busy as a one-legged grasshopper in a—"

"Edna?" Bill looked down the hallway toward dispatch.

"Edna."

I followed him to his inner office and took a seat, both of us silent.

"Look I'm sorry—" he started.

"About yesterday—" I jumped in.

We halted.

"You first," I said.

He shook his head. "No. You."

I inhaled slowly. "Where to start?"

Bill's face tightened into that "oh no" expression he assumed whenever I laid out my theories and referenced my instincts. He propped his chin on his interlaced fingers and sat forward. "From the top."

He already knew my opinion on Sally's innocence so I dove into my story, careful to build my case slowly, emphasizing my research and circumventing my impulses. I'd save the hazardous stuff for last. I reminded him that Gordon Weeks's 1997 crime had been an attempted break-in into Sally's childhood home in Boston. Which seemed more than a coincidence. Then I described my finding Sally's photograph in the theater.

"The theater was still a crime scene," he said reproachfully.

"I know. But I happened to be getting my clothes from a dressing room…" I left out Lola's name and ignored the fact that I had gotten my clothes earlier in the week.

"And using the emergency escape?" he asked skeptically.

"Sally seemed really frantic about the photo, so I tried to recreate her exit from the theater the night of the murder. She had disappeared from the stage so quickly I figured she must have slipped into the emergency hallway."

"And you just happened to find this photo there," he added.

"Right."

He studied the picture that I'd laid on his desk blotter. "A picture of a couple of young kids." He turned it over. "Date stamped on the back. May 1994."

That reminded me of Pauli and his time stamps. Was the date important?

"What am I not getting?" Bill asked.

"Gordon Weeks gave that picture to Sally before he died."

Bill sat forward. "What? How do you know that?"

"Sally told me. She said he had it in his hand and...then seconds later he was gone—"

"She told us he was dead when she found him." Bill's voice grew quieter. "And by the way her prints were on the murder weapon."

Oh no. More bad news. "Maybe she accidentally touched the knife when she discovered Gordon Weeks?"

Bill bypassed my speculation. "So what about this photograph?"

"It's way more important than it might seem."

"How do you know?" he asked.

My palms were damp. I was more nervous than I'd ever remembered being with Bill. "Last night I had a little incident." Incident?

Bill placed the photo on the desk, his forearms tense. "What happened?"

"Well, you know the Windjammer had a leaky roof yesterday so we had to close early and clean up and I was the last to leave—"

"Dodie!"

"Right. And then I locked up and suddenly there was this guy." I described my encounter with the kidnappers.

Bill's face turned red. "You were hooded and bound?" he asked aghast. "What did they want?"

"The photograph."

Bill's mouth formed an O. I waited for the realization to sink in. "That's how I know it's worth something."

I finished with the late-night phone call from my abductor and the demand for the photo today.

"You were kidnapped," he yelled. "When were you going to tell me?"

"Take it easy. I'm here now. He's supposed to call me later today to arrange a place for a meeting," I said.

Bill hit his intercom. "Edna, get Archibald ASAP."

"What are you going to do?" I asked.

"Catch your kidnappers," he said and stood.

I placed my hand gently on his. "Slow down. I have one more piece of information. Do you know who Sally's Boston therapist is? The one Archibald supposedly spoke to about Sally's mental state?"

Bill looked wary.

"My brother, Andy."

"Your brother...?" he choked out.

"Yeah. And he never spoke to Archibald or any detective about Sally. I'm sorry, Bill, but I think your friend has been deceiving you," I said as carefully as I could.

Bill ran his fingers through the spikes of his hair in a frantic gesture I now could diagnose as extreme frustration. Archibald was on his way in; no need to stoke this particular fire. "I've got to get to the Windjammer."

"Call me when you hear from them. Immediately! And stay put in the Windjammer today. It's the safest place to be," he said firmly. "I'll assign Suki to keep an eye on the restaurant."

"Right. By the way, who paid Sally's bail?" I asked.

"Charles Oldfield," Bill said.

"Where are they now?"

"Creston for a few days until the court grants permission for her to leave the state."

"Did you check her phone to see if Gordon Weeks—?"

Bill nodded patiently. "We dumped her cell when she was arrested. We found calls to folks in town and her father. And texts to you," he added wryly.

So she didn't communicate with Gordon Weeks by phone. I walked to the door. "Bill, I'm sorry about Archibald."

"Dodie, there's stuff you don't know about him..."

I understood. They had a relationship that went back years. "Someone wants that photo badly."

"I got it covered." He nodded grimly and I slipped out, moving quickly past Edna yakking on her headset.

25

I stood on the sidewalk outside the Windjammer next to Henry, who was so stressed he had neglected to put on his coat. He glowered, arms bare and head turning red. He made me colder just looking at him. I was bundled up against the wind, my face buried in my muffler. Both of us stared upward at the roofer who held up shingles to demonstrate his point.

"Yup. Need new ones here."

In an effort to get to the source of the leaks, the roofer had had to chip away at the ice that had formed along the gutter and remove chunks which pried up loose shingles—destroying some in the bargain. He insisted that a waterproof membrane needed to be laid down to prevent further leaks and the rotting of the building materials under the shingles. The roof was probably an accident waiting to happen; I'd noticed water stains on the Windjammer's ceiling. Meanwhile, the roofer cleared out gutters and downspouts and insisted a cure, as opposed to a temporary fix, included a combination of sealing, insulating, and venting the space under the roof. The Windjammer was an old building that dated from 1898. No wonder the winter weather had taken its toll.

I dragged Henry inside with me and put on a pot of coffee. Something warm would do the trick. Then I sent him to the kitchen to do some prep for tomorrow's menu. With new water still dripping and the buckets and pots still scattered around the floor, the dining room was not in any state to host customers today. We needed more time to clean up—again—and get the place ready. I consulted with Henry on changes to the menu and inventory orders. Some food would hold up until tomorrow; some things had to be cooked today.

I sat in my back booth and laid out the order forms for meats, vegetables, and dairy products. My cell phone pinged and I grabbed it eagerly. Maybe Pauli had finished his regressive computer sketch. I checked the caller ID and tapped on the message: *Bring the photo to parking lot of primrose diner rt. 53. 7:00.*

My mouth went dry. I texted Bill. *They made contact.* Within seconds, he called me back.

"When and where?" he asked, all police chief–like.

I filled him in.

"Damn. That place is too open. They'll see us coming from a distance," he said, worried.

"Bill, what do you think makes the picture so significant?" I asked.

"I have no idea. I studied the thing with a magnifying glass. All I can see is two young kids, dressed up, smiling in front of some steps."

"Yeah, that's what I saw. We have to speak with Sally. She's the one who has to know."

"Let me figure out this meeting with the kidnappers. Stay out of trouble. I'll take it from here."

My cell binged.

"Bill, can you hold on?"

Before he could answer I checked the text. This one was from Pauli. I opened it and gazed at the regression of the photo he had sent: Gordon Weeks in his twenties was the spitting image of the young man in the photograph. My little hairs were having a field day. Every instinct in my body told me the young woman was Sally's mother, and that Olivia Holmes Oldfield and Gordon Weeks had been a couple in May of 1994. Thoughts zipped hither and yon. I had to get back to Bill. My fingers were clumsy as I tapped my phone again, but the line was dead. Bill must have given up, or had some other business to attend to. My return call went to voicemail. I punched in the number of the station.

"Etonville Police Department," Edna called out cheerily.

"Edna? I need to speak with Bill," I said rapidly.

"Hi, Dodie. How's the roof coming along? I sure hope that you'll be open for dinner before the final dress rehearsal tonight—"

"It's an emergency!" That was one word Edna responded to instantly. "What's the problem?"

"Where's Bill?"

"He had a 11-79 down on the highway."

I figured it was an accident.

"Don't know if it's a 11-80 or 11-81 yet. Major or minor injuries. But they called an ambulance."

Now what?

"Want me to get him on the radio?"

"No. Don't interrupt him. I'll check in later."

"10-4."

* * *

I gripped a pen and doodled on an inventory sheet. I needed to get to Sally. I had to know what she knew about Gordon Weeks. But she was squirreled away in Creston with her father presumably. I texted her: *Need to talk...I know about Gordon Weeks.* That should get her attention.

Henry and Enrico were entrenched in the kitchen, concocting a variation on chicken vegetable soup for tomorrow's lunch using the ingredients previously planned for the chicken kabobs. The roofer was chipping away at the ice dam and, with the inventory sheets completed, I was left twiddling my thumbs. I re-mopped the floor, re-arranged a few tables that had been shoved to one side to make room for the roofer's ladder yesterday, collected the buckets and pots, and otherwise prepped the dining room for lunch tomorrow. Which the roofer had assured us would happen. Closing the restaurant for a day and a half would take a bite out of the Windjammer's income this week.

I also checked the wall clock every minute or so. Waiting to hear from Bill or Sally. Finally a text came in from Lola: *Can you sit through the run at 7...could use some BFF hand-holding.* I knew exactly what she meant—I could use a little bit of TLC myself. My confidence level had taken a hit since my meeting with the kidnappers. I texted back that I would come if I could and wished her good luck.

I poured another cup of coffee, sat back down in my booth, and drummed my fingers on the table top. It was five thirty. Had Bill figured out a plan of action?

My cell rang and I checked the caller ID. I didn't recognize the number. "Hello?" I said cautiously.

"Dodie?"

"Sally! Am I glad to hear from you. I'm not sure if you know what's going on but—"

"Thanks for getting my photo. Can you bring it to me?" she asked, her voice tremulous.

"Where are you?" I asked.

She gave me the name of a hotel in Creston.

"Are you alone?"

"My father left. He had an errand to run and I told him I had a headache and wanted to take a nap," she said. "The police took my cell phone and my father took my car keys. I'm like a prisoner."

"I can be there in half an hour." I clicked off.

"Henry, I'm going out for a while," I yelled into the kitchen. I pulled my coat and scarf off the coat tree and hurried to my Metro. Next door at the ELT, actors and crew were straggling in. It was still a couple of hours before the rehearsal began, but apparently everyone was super eager to get this theatrical show on the road.

I fired up the engine and backed out of my parking space, hoping Suki was not in the area keeping an "eye on me" as per Bill's instructions, preventing my trip to Creston. I put the address of the hotel into my GPS Genie, then I headed down Main, over Anderson, and took the on-ramp to State Route 53. Traffic was light for rush hour on a Friday afternoon in New Jersey. I figured the highway gods were on my side today which was good because I had the feeling Sally and I were going to need all the help we could get. Where was Bill and why hadn't he gotten back to me yet? I could have texted him to let him know I was on my way to pick up Sally, but he might send Archibald to intercept me. Not a good idea.

Fifteen minutes later I exited the highway, followed my Genie to Creston where cars were bumper-to-bumper crawling through town. I rapped on the steering wheel, even blew the horn—which I never did—to urge the car ahead of me to beat it through a yellow light. My GPS indicated a turn ahead. I put on the blinker and turned right, passing through the intersection, and continued for half a mile.

"Destination is ahead on the left," said Genie.

I pulled into the parking lot of a high-end chain hotel. I ran into the lobby, glancing around for the elevator. Sally had given me her room number on the third floor. The receptionist flicked her eyes in my direction. I smiled and moved on. No time to be friendly.

I knocked on 314, my heart in my throat, sweating beneath layers of clothing. The door cracked open an inch, the safety lock still in place. "Sally? It's me." The door opened wide and I stepped in. I hugged her spontaneously; the circumstances seemed to call for affection and support. "How are you?"

She looked as though she'd been crying, but her hair was shiny and clean and she wore a gold thigh-length cashmere sweater, black leggings, and ankle boots with spiked heels. "Thanks for coming." She didn't move. Sally wrapped her arms around her body. "The judge said I'm not supposed to leave the state until the court order comes through. But I have to get out of here. Can I have the picture?"

"Sally, I know who Gordon Weeks is. Was."

She turned her pale face up to meet mine. Her eyes glistened and her lip quivered. "My…"

Could she even say the words? "Your father," I whispered.

"I think so."

"And the photograph? That's him with your mother?" I asked.

She nodded. "Do you have it?"

I was now hazarding a guess. "Was it their wedding day?"

She whispered, "Yes."

"The police have the photo," I said slowly.

Sally was crestfallen, disappointment like a shroud around her body.

"I had no choice. Someone wants it badly and was willing to kidnap and threaten me. Do you know why?"

Her eyes grew wide. "I have no idea… Can you take me back to Etonville with you?"

Charles Oldfield would probably not be pleased to have Sally out and about. But what could it hurt? As long as she didn't leave the state. "Let's go," I said.

Sally slipped off the bed. "I'll be right back." She hurried into the bathroom.

I studied the room. Green-and-blue-striped wallpaper, patterned green carpeting, and the standard furnishings: two queen-sized beds, night stands, a flat screen television, a chest of drawers, and a desk. A stuffed chair and ottoman occupied one corner. Sally had a suitcase open on one bed and clothing spilled out of it. Slacks, blouses, underwear. On the desk she had a notebook open to her Facebook page. I leaned in and scanned the screen. It was Sara Oldfield's site.

"I use that page for my family," she said, watching me. "The other page is for me."

"Sally Oldfield, right?"

She smiled for the first time. "I told him you were smart."

"Who?" I asked, an eerie sensation creeping down my spine.

"My father. Stepfather," she corrected herself.

I shifted my focus back to the Facebook page and pointed to a picture of a middle-aged man, dressed in an overcoat, his body turned away from the camera, his face in profile. "Is that him?"

"Yeah. That's him."

Goose bumps rose on my shoulders and arms. "Do you mind if I…?" I gestured to the notebook.

She nodded. "Sure."

I held the device close to my face. I knew he was the stranger I nearly hit two weeks ago when I slid through an intersection on my way to the Windjammer's baking class. But something else gnawed at my memory.... and then my little hairs bopped. I found my cell and tapped on photos. The picture I took of Archibald and the man he met in the parking lot of the diner on Route 53 appeared. I held my photo next to the photo on Sally's Facebook page. Both shots were taken from the same angle with the man's face in profile. No wonder he seemed familiar. It was Sally's father. I felt like I'd been punched in my midsection. "Come on. We need to get out of here." I took Sally's arm and ushered her to the door. The hallway was clear and I insisted we take the stairs. I had no idea what connected Archibald and Charles Oldfield and no desire to collide with either of them in an elevator.

In minutes we were in the lobby, then out the door and into my Metro. I wasn't sure what was going on with Bill and the kidnappers. But I knew in my gut I had to get Sally to some place safe. Some place full of people, well-lit, where she would be protected by a crowd. Where people would provide a convenient cover. I could think of only one location.

"Did you know *Eton Town* is opening tomorrow night?" I asked brightly and cranked the engine. The Metro jumped to life.

Sally's face lit up. "It is? I'm so glad!" She clapped her hands like a little girl.

"How would you like to see the dress rehearsal?"

Halfway back to Etonville I had the distinct feeling that we were being followed. When I speeded up, a car two lengths back hustled closer. When I changed lanes, it followed suit. Call me paranoid, but I squinted into the rearview mirror to get a look at the license plate. The setting sun had cast slanting shadows across the highway and all I could see was a dark vehicle. Meanwhile, I kept up a steady patter with Sally. How was the arraignment, who was her lawyer, how had she been occupying herself?

After ten minutes, we grew silent. She cleared her throat. "How do you know about Gordon...my father?"

I tiptoed into my discoveries based on the facial recognition software and the age regression, comparing the shot she'd taken of Gordon Weeks in Boston and her photo I found in the theater.

Sally stared at me in admiration. "Awesome."

"When Gordon Weeks showed up at the rooming house, did he claim to be your father?"

Sally stared out the window. Lights were popping on in houses as the day darkened. She nodded. "Yes, but I didn't believe him. I was so freaked out...I couldn't believe my mother would have lied to me all those years. We told each other everything." She paused. "I didn't want to talk to him. But he insisted we meet again and that's when I told him to come to the theater. He said he would give me something that would prove he was my father." She seemed to shrink into the passenger seat, her voice weakened. "I guess it was the picture."

"Sally, why didn't you go to the police with the whole story?"

"Gordon Weeks made me swear to keep quiet. He said it would be dangerous for me if anyone knew we had met. I was scared and didn't know what to do," she said.

Dangerous for Gordon Weeks as well. "Did you tell your father about Gordon or the photo?"

"My *stepfather*?" she said, her face hard. "He'd be the last person I'd share this with. I tried to play it cool. I knew he was coming to Etonville for the play. I thought somehow I could keep him out of all of this." She crossed her arms. "Besides, Gordon, my real father, said there was something about my mother's will that I didn't know."

"And Charles did?"

She nodded.

"Do you have any idea what it was?"

"No. He said to remember that he was my biological father."

Now what did that mean?

"And you didn't tell any of this to the police?"

"No. Just that I'd seen Gordon Weeks on the street in Boston, that he came to the boarding house and wanted to meet with me, and when I went to the theater, I discovered he was dead. It was the truth. Except for that last part. He lived long enough to open his hand with the photo." She smiled sadly. "I didn't think they'd figure out who he was. He told me he'd been out of the country for over fifteen years and only came back six months ago when he found out my mother had passed away. He said he still loved her."

"So your parents married...and your mother got pregnant. Did Gordon tell you why they split up?" I asked.

"They were young and my grandparents disapproved of him and forced him to go away."

"And the photo? What's so important about it?"

Sally shrugged. "I don't know. It's their wedding picture. I lost it before I had a chance to really look at it."

I entered Etonville and the dark sedan retreated a dozen yards behind me. The dashboard clock read six fifty. Time for Bill to meet the kidnappers. I whizzed through yellow lights and steamed up Main Street, coming to an abrupt stop in front of the Etonville Little Theatre. I bounced the Metro into a curb and threw the car into Park. "Let's get you into the theater."

As I escorted Sally into the lobby, the dark sedan cruised past the ELT and continued on down Main.

26

Penny stood in the center of the lobby and blocked our progress. "So you came back to the scene of the crime?" she said to Sally and pushed her glasses up her nose while slapping her clipboard against her leg. "We had to replace you."

Technically she wasn't replaced; Lola had said her character was cut from the ensemble and the Banger sisters were picking up some of Sally's lines. God help us. "Penny, Sally wanted to see the run through."

Sally nodded. Penny eyed her up and down. "This is a closed rehearsal. Anyway, you disappeared after the first final dress rehearsal. Actors do not leave the theater before curtain call and notes," she said importantly. "Even O'Dell knows that."

Penny looked at me for reinforcement.

"I had to meet my...father," Sally murmured. "He was in town for the opening of the show."

Maybe Charles Oldfield was the person on the other end of Sally's phone call in Snippets overheard by Carol. "Where's Lola?" I asked.

"Inside arguing with Walter about his cuts for Act Two. He's having second thoughts and Lola threatened to cut the entire second act if he didn't shape up." She cackled. "This won't help his tri-polar manic-depression. But that's show—"

"Penny!" Lola stuck her head into the lobby and shouted. "What are you doing out here?" Then she saw me. And Sally. She gasped. "Sally...?"

"We've come to watch the rehearsal. Good for Sally to get out of the hotel for the evening," I said with my lips while my body language transmitted "she's in trouble." Good thing Lola read subtext.

"Of course. Why don't you find a seat in the house," Lola said to Sally. Then she confronted Penny. "Please get the cast onstage for Walter's warm-up."

Penny left with Sally in tow.

"What's going on?" Lola muttered.

"I think she's in danger."

"From whom?" Lola asked.

"I'm not sure, but she called me, wanting the photo. Bill's supposed to be meeting the kidnappers with the photo about now, and I think someone followed Sally and me from the hotel," I said.

"You think the theater is safe?" Lola asked, skeptical.

"Safer than the hotel. At least here there are people all around her. Look, I have to call Bill. Can you keep an eye on her until the run starts?"

"Sure. Mildred's rehearsing with the choir and then Walter's doing his warm-up."

Despite the gravity of the current situation, I had to laugh. "What's he have planned?"

"He says he has a new one." Lola rolled her eyes.

"Hang in there. You just have to make it the opening tomorrow. And the *Star-Ledger* reviewer."

Lola groaned and crossed her fingers.

I stepped outside and called Bill's cell this time. Maybe he hadn't seen or heard his texts. When the phone went to voice mail, I left a message: *Call me ASAP.*

I darted next door; Henry and Enrico were wrapping up the afternoon's cooking and confirmed that the roofer gave the go-ahead for lunch tomorrow. The dining room was all ready and the inventory set. I reassured Henry that I would get in touch with Benny and Gillian and come in early to double-check all of the leaks. There was nothing left to do so I said good night and reminded them to turn out the lights.

I headed back next door; if nothing else, I could keep Sally company and support Lola by watching some of the final dress rehearsal until I heard from Bill. The lobby was empty, the overhead security lights providing the only illumination.

Inside the theater, the cast was assembling on the stage and Penny was blasting her whistle, trying to maintain order. Chrystal handed out tricorn hats to the men and watched as they manipulated their wigs, sticking hat pins in their fake hair. Mildred's singers were gathered to one side of the stage working their way through "Blest Be the Tie That Binds"; Edna waved, getting a reprimand from Walter to "focus," which she cheerfully ignored, while Vernon searched his pockets and a backpack.

"Hi, Dodie," he said loudly.

"Lose something?" I asked. His hearing aids.

Penny bounced up the aisle. "Vernon, Lola has some notes for you. She wants to see you onstage."

"Huh?"

Penny took him by the arm. "Let's go." She mouthed, "Like a lamb to the slaughter."

Sally had taken a seat in the middle of a row at the back of the theater, her coat wrapped around her shoulders as if she had come incognito. I had no idea if any of the cast saw her. I eased into a seat next to her. "It's got to feel strange watching the show from out here," I said softly.

"It is," Sally said, wistful. "I wish I could have gone on with them."

Penny finally had the entire cast gathered onstage, several actors stepping around the spot where Gordon Weeks had died. Walter was demonstrating his latest pre-show warm-up: another trust exercise with one actor leading a second actor—blind—around the setting. He handed out blindfolds to half the cast, paired them off—one of the Bangers with Edna, one with Vernon, Romeo with Abby, until all cast members were accounted for. I could see Lola twisting a strand of hair, her go-to nervous tic whenever ELT rehearsals turned a little looney. I was worried someone was going to fall off the stage, but I suppose that was the point of the exercise: Your partner should keep you safe.

Sally was absorbed in the process and watched intently as the twosomes moved carefully around the stage, giggling, and occasionally bumping into a piece of furniture. I wondered whom she relied on now that her mother had passed away. Besides Andy.

"Trust! Trust!" Walter exclaimed as one of the Banger sisters slipped the blindfold off one eye. "Your partner will protect you."

I wasn't so sure about that. Her partner was Vernon so it might prove to be a case of the deaf leading the blind.

"Watch this," Penny chuckled at my back.

I jumped. "You have to stop doing that!"

She ignored my plea and tapped my shoulder. "Romeo's leading Abby into the green room!"

Penny was right; Walter was occupied, floating through the couples stage right while Romeo had propped open the exit from the stage and was leading Abby into the interior of the offstage actors' lounge.

"Aren't you supposed to be monitoring them or something? So nobody gets hurt?" I asked.

Penny nudged her glasses. "Nah. Unless somebody trips and lands on their backside."

"Penny," Lola hissed. She pointed to the set of stairs that led from the stage into the house. "Stay on duty there in case someone gets too close to the edge."

"Later, O'Dell," Penny said and bounded down an aisle.

A sudden screech from the green room stopped everyone in their tracks. Blindfolds were raised, Lola flew onstage, and Walter looked around bewildered. "Someone betrayed the trust!"

I had had personal experience with betraying the trust and I *did* land on my backside last spring. Penny sorted out the mishap—Romeo and Abby had had a set-to with a closed door and Abby threw a fit when she saw where Romeo was leading her. Once Abby had been pacified, Romeo reprimanded for unprofessional behavior, Vernon and a Banger sister rescued from the storage closet offstage where they'd gotten lost, Lola insisted on starting the run through. Costumes were adjusted and the lights dimmed.

Act One of *Eton Town* started uneventfully, not necessarily a good thing for a play, with Vernon's opening monologue, the appearance of the two Eton Town families, and the slow steady rotation of the turntable. So far so good. Sally was engrossed in the evolving drama, but I'd seen this part of the play before and it hadn't appeared as though Walter had cut anything from Act One. Unfortunately.

I was feeling restless. My cell phone binged and Penny looked over from her stage manager's box at the back of the theater. She plastered a finger on her lips and drew the other hand across her neck in the universal gesture for a "quick death."

I nodded and hurried to the lobby. I couldn't afford to turn my phone off since Bill should be calling any moment now. I checked the text. It wasn't a number I recognized, but the message was clear: *Is Sally with you? A.* Archibald.

I started to shake. Speaking of trust…I had no idea what Archibald knew. Still, he was looking for Sally. Did that mean both he and Bill were looking for her? Or Archibald alone…or with the kidnappers. If he knew that Sally was with me and the vehicle that followed us from Creston saw us enter the theater, we weren't safe here. My mind galloped: Where could we go until I heard from Bill?

Lights shone through the glass of the entrance doors. The same dark sedan cruised by the theater again. Archibald had keys to the theater.

Locked front doors would not deter him. I had to move fast. I heard the strains of the fiddle that accompanied the wedding scene at the end of Act One. I ran back into the house as the curtain closed and the house lights rose. I motioned to Sally to follow me and sprinted down the aisle to the front row where Lola had her head bent over her script.

"I need help," I said.

She looked up. "Dodie? What's wrong?"

"I think they're coming for Sally and I have to get her out of here. Now."

Lola jumped up. "What should I do?"

I spat out the words. "I need a distraction if they come into the theater."

Lola stood up, her forehead creased. "What kind of a distraction?"

I scanned the house.

"I hate to ask this but could you postpone the start of Act Two? Maybe get the actors out here, milling around, creating their normal chaos?" I said.

Penny blew her whistle and shouted, "Take ten."

"Penny!" Lola shrieked. "Use the headset. Performance conditions!"

"Sorry. The headset's not working. I can't communicate with backstage," she yelled.

"Lola?" I said, panicking.

Sally was standing behind me, completely baffled. Lola turned to me, then set her chin. "Okay. Penny, get all of the actors in the house."

Penny hauled herself up and out of her seat. "What for?"

"Do it!" Lola was taking no prisoners.

Penny shrugged and blasted two toots on her whistle.

Walter stuck his head out from between the curtains. "What's going on? It's performance conditions! Penny, you can't blow your whistle during performance conditions!"

Performance this, I thought.

"Thanks," I said and squeezed Lola's hand as actors trickled off the stage, looking confused, shrugging their shoulders.

Penny tramped over to us and slapped her clipboard. "Lola, I'm supposed to be running the show. You can't stop the show unless *I* say 'halt.'"

"Lola? What's going on?" Walter demanded.

I took advantage of the disorder to snatch Sally's arm and pull her through the crowd and onto the stage. ELT members did a few double takes as people began to realize who she was.

"Hey, Sally!" Edna called out as we hurried past each other. "Nice to see you. How are—"

"Edna, you didn't see Sally. You have no idea she was even here. Police business."

Edna narrowed her eyes. "Oh! Got it. 10-4."

She hitched up her period skirt and headed to the house. The door from the lobby opened. A figure bundled in a winter coat stood in the dim light. No one I knew.

Uh-oh.

27

I ushered Sally through the green room door into the hallway that ran between the scene shop and the wardrobe storage. I'd had previous experience with the backstage locales. The shop was open, flooded with the glare of fluorescent light—someone had left the space unlocked and vulnerable. But lucky for us. I slammed my hand against the light switch on the outer wall and the space went black. There was enough ambient light as we threaded our way around saws, a work table, a tool cage, equipment, and flats. I flipped the deadbolt on the back door. Sally and I stepped outside onto the loading dock, occupied by debris and trash cans. The chill air was a welcome shock to my frenzied system.

"Where are we going?" she asked, scared.

"Some place where you'll be safe." I fervently hoped that was the truth. With someone tailing us, ELT confusion would only provide a distraction for a limited period of time. I needed to stash Sally somewhere quickly. The closest possibility was the Windjammer. I also hoped that whoever was tracking us assumed that we'd escaped through the shop and took off.

I unlocked the back door of the restaurant that led into the kitchen and thrust Sally inside, soundlessly shutting it behind us. The musty restaurant smells were comforting for a moment, its dark interior lit only by the light of my cell phone.

"Now what?" Sally asked, panting.

I forced myself to think calmly. Where to go? The basement was an obvious choice, but we could become trapped down there. It offered a place to hide but no means for a getaway. There was always the pantry with shelving full of boxes, canned goods, and dark corners. But once the light was switched on, we'd be sitting ducks. I was stymied.

Then the particles in my brain rearranged themselves and an unexpected picture flashed on my mental screen. The roofer had told Henry that the attic space below the roof needed sealing, insulating, and venting and Henry had gone up to check it out. There was a short, dangling rope in a corner of the kitchen that was attached to a panel in the ceiling. Yanking on the rope revealed an aluminum, collapsible, pull-down ladder. Henry had had it installed several years ago when there had been another roof leak. *When the problems should have been fixed.* Never mind. The pull-down stairs might save our lives.

I directed my flashlight at the rope and gave it a tug. Nothing budged. I dragged a stool to the dangling rope, climbed up, and jerked it again. This time the panel dropped an inch. Sally joined me and we heaved it down together, the metal stairs descending with a creak. I gestured for Sally to go first. She hesitated, so I gave her a gentle poke and she scrambled up the steps. I replaced the stool, took a final glimpse of the kitchen, and followed Sally up the ladder. At its top, I lay down on the attic floor, stretched out—with Sally hanging onto my legs—and wrenched the stairs upward a few inches at a time. The panel snapped into place with a clap that sounded like a detonation, then all was quiet.

The attic space was small, impossible to stand up in, so we crawled to a spot a few feet away from the stair unit. If my sense of direction was accurate, we were over the bar area. I leaned against a wall and tilted my flashlight toward Sally. She looked pale, a streak of black smudged across one cheek, her eyes gigantic, staring at me.

"We should be safe here," I whispered.

I flicked off the light and texted Bill again, my fingers trembling, my eyes glued to the pull-down ladder: : *In windjammer attic. Help.* Bill had our location. Now we needed to hang on until he arrived. The attic was stuffy and warm. I slipped off my coat and Sally did the same. Then I pocketed my cell. No point in giving away our hiding place with even a narrow shaft of light leaking from the attic to the floor below. Anyway, I had to preserve the battery.

My eyelids drooped; how long had we been sitting in the dark? Minutes though it felt like hours. Sally was still, her eyes closed; I wondered what was going through her mind. I rubbed my tired eyes. Walter and his bizarre warm-ups. Blindfolding actors' eyes...the little hairs on my neck twitched. There was something about Gordon Weeks's eyes in Sally's photograph. What was it? Then it hit me. He had one brown eye and one hazel eye. Like Sally. Proof he was her father! That's what made the picture so important. Sally hadn't realized it because she hadn't had time to study the photo—

A clatter from below jolted me forward. My heart hurdled into my mouth. Someone had discovered our getaway route to the Windjammer and apparently had a run-in with Henry's pots and pans. I tapped Sally's leg, placing a finger on my lips. I doubted she could even see me in the pitch dark, but I gripped her arm reassuringly. Footsteps around the kitchen, growing softer as the trespasser moved from spot to spot—the dining room? The pantry? Silence for a moment as the heavy treads melted away. Probably a trip to the basement. *Bill...where are you?* I whipped out my cell and texted again: *SOS.*

The sound of the footsteps reappeared and once again seemed to move from area to area, increasing in volume until I could swear the intruder was in the attic with us. My hands were clammy as I clutched my cell phone. A creak and a scrape sent a surge of sound reverberating around the attic walls as the collapsible ladder dropped. Instinctively, I scooted farther into the dark of the attic, willing Sally and me to shrivel into tiny balls of humanity, out of the arc of the powerful flashlight that swept to and fro throwing light into our hiding place. There was a pause in the activity. A grunt, then the light diminished as the ladder ascended into the ceiling. The footfalls resumed in the kitchen below.

I exhaled and leaned back against the wall, both of us enveloped by the attic dusk once again. I clasped Sally's arm to say "we've dodged a bullet for the moment."

She must have felt equally relieved because she shifted her body and stretched out her legs, accidentally kicking a loose piece of lumber. We froze. Had Henry left it here? The thud echoed around us; I prayed it hadn't reached the ears of the intruder below. Dead silence. Was our stalker listening to us as carefully as we were to him? I counted to ten, the footsteps faded away. I exhaled in relief for the second time in five minutes. This night had to end soon. It was murder on my nervous system.

"Found anything?" A voice drifted upward.

Though slightly muffled, it was still distinct. I recognized the smooth-talking kidnapper.

Suddenly I could smell the fear leaching off Sally. She latched onto my arm, her fingers clawing my hoodie.

"Not sure...sound...attic..."

The second voice was in and out, but I'd heard enough to get the gist. The stalker had heard Sally's scuffle with the lumber and any minute would pop open the panel and lower the stairs. We were easy targets. But I wasn't about to surrender without a fight. Every second I stalled was one more second I gave Bill. I removed my boots and motioned to Sally to do the same. My heels were low and rubber. Sally's were spikes. Then I felt around the floor and my hand grasped the short two-by-four Sally had struck. I now had four missiles and a makeshift blunt object.

"Go ahead," the kidnapper said clearly. He must have been standing directly under the pull-down door.

Another creak and scrape and the stairs fell, followed by the same explosion of light as before. "Sally? It's your dad. I know you're up there. Come on down, honey, and let's talk."

My chest tightened. The polite, soothing voice of the kidnapper belonged to Charles Oldfield?

Sally was immobile, looking petrified.

Charles waited five seconds. "I'm done fooling around. Now get down here." This time sounding less patient, more demanding. "You might as well join her, Dodie. Sally, you're in my custody. The court will revoke your bail if I report your disappearance. They'll put out a warrant for your arrest."

I gripped the boots tightly in both hands, the hunk of wood under my arm. "Not when they find out who really killed Gordon Weeks. Sally's *real* father," I said with ten times the bravado I felt.

Was it my imagination or was there a change in the atmosphere?

"I'm not playing around any longer," Charles snarled, all trace of his Boston elitist pedigree dissolving.

"You're going to have to come up here and get us," I shouted, hoping that loudness communicated confidence.

There must have been some soundless discussion below, then someone grasped the sides of the ladder and took a step. I eased a few feet forward. I could see the top of a head, thinning brown hair, a bald spot dead center. I aimed for the bull's-eye and let fly one of my boots. It clipped him on the top of his head and, caught unawares, he looked up. Its mate smashed the side of his face. He howled and swore and stepped off the ladder. Charles pushed him out of the way. "That's it. Down here. Now."

I flung both of Sally's spiked boots at Charles and when a thin streak of red appeared on his chin, I knew I'd hit my mark. I had only my hunk of wood left. Sally was now alert, perched on her haunches, ready to follow me into the fray. I edged to the lip of the opening and saw Charles, head bent, wiping blood off his face, while his partner waved a gun.

"Let me take a shot, boss," he said. "A few holes in the ceiling and they'll come running down. Watch."

OMG. Holes in Henry's kitchen ceiling? That was going too far. I clenched my teeth, then tightened my grip on the lumber, ignoring splinters that had become wedged into my palm. I was about to hurl my last defensive weapon when, in the corner of the panel's frame, I saw a pair of cowboy boots and two jean-clad legs. I had a moment of exhilaration followed by a sinking sensation. So Archibald *was* in collusion with Charles Oldfield. Bill was wrong about his friend and I was right. Small consolation.

"Detective Alvarez," Charles Oldfield greeted Archibald smoothly. "Trying to get my daughter out of the attic. We need to return to Boston."

"Dodie? Sally? Come on down. It's all over—" Archibald's face appeared in the panel opening.

I couldn't help myself. "I was right about you! When Bill finds out—"

"What?" Archibald asked.

"I know about you and Charles in the diner," I started in. "I saw you together—"

Archibald looked quickly over his shoulder, then stepped onto the bottom rung of the ladder. "Dodie! I'll explain everything—"

I maneuvered myself as close to the opening as I dared and chucked the wooden projectile right at his head.

"Hey!" he shouted.

Then things happened in a blur: Charles Oldfield's sidekick fired a shot into the kitchen ceiling, Sally screamed, and I lurched forward, sliding down several steps of the collapsible stairs, my stockinged feet landing squarely in Archibald's midsection.

And Bill appeared, winded, on crutches, backed up by Suki, gun drawn and pointed straight at the shooter's chest. "Drop it," he said. The voice of authority.

Charles Oldfield's body slumped in defeat, the gun dropped to the floor, and Bill and Archibald exchanged looks: Well done, they seemed to be saying to each other.

Huh?

* * *

I stamped my boots—now back on my feet—on the cement sidewalk outside the Windjammer to keep warm. After a few days of rising temps, winter had come booming back tonight with below freezing wind chills. I flipped my hood over my head. I didn't care that my fingers were going numb because I'd dropped my gloves somewhere between Sally's hotel in Creston and our escapade in the ceiling of the Windjammer. This was a picture I had to witness: Charles Oldfield and his gun-toting underling hauled off in one of Etonville's black-and-white squad cars. Ralph was doing crowd control, which consisted mostly of the *Eton Town* cast who, when they'd gotten wind of the commotion on the street, dumped the curtain call and flew out the front door, despite Penny's whistle and Walter's protests.

Lola had given up and joined the crowd. Suki had Sally in hand, taking a statement and explaining the next steps in her legal odyssey. Apparently, Charles's lawyer was on the level and would be following up with Sally, offering confirmation that charges would be dropped.

"Whew, wind chill is fifteen degrees," Lola said and hugged her Canadian goose down coat around her.

"I thought you didn't believe in wind chills?"

She grinned. "I didn't believe in the turntable either, but I changed my mind on that too."

Apparently, the balky platform had surrendered to Walter's vision and was good as gold throughout the final dress rehearsal.

"How did everything else go?" I asked, the question coming out in a puff of chill air.

"Not bad. Little slow. Actors were squirrelly. Vernon went up on his lines. The usual," she said.

"You know what they say…terrible dress rehearsal means a great opening."

Lola smiled at me. "Yes, they do say that. This theater thing is becoming second nature to you, isn't it?"

I laughed and nodded.

We watched Suki and Sally.

"She owes you a lot," Lola said.

I shrugged. "She feels like the younger sister I never had."

Bill and Archibald stood off to one side talking. I had to admit that I was a little miffed at the sight of them together acting so chummy.

"Archibald was working undercover," I said.

"Oh my!" Lola gasped.

"For the FBI, according to Bill. Investigating Charles Oldfield for corporate fraud. Something about him stealing Sally's mother's fortune for years." I shuddered inside my coat. "Etonville will have a heyday with all of this tomorrow."

"I do feel sorry for Sally. She lost her biological father *and* her stepfather. She's going to need support," Lola said. "So the two of you were tied up in the attic of the Windjammer?"

"We weren't tied up—" I said.

"I heard they shot at you a bunch of times!" Lola said, astonished.

"It was only one time and…" It was starting already.

Lola shivered and put an arm around my shoulders. "I could use a drink."

"Let's go inside the Windjammer. I don't think I'll be getting much sleep tonight," I said.

"I have to run next door and speak with Walter but I'll come back." She gave me a hug and walked off.

Henry pulled up in his car and hopped out of the driver's seat. I was going to have to listen to him rant about the bullet hole—

"Are you okay?" he asked, clearly alarmed.

"Fine. Guess you heard about the ceiling?" I winced in anticipation of his tirade.

He waved his hand dismissively. "Not important." He stared at me. "Sure you're okay?"

Wow. I nodded, dazed. It was Henry 2.0, a new, improved version of the Windjammer chef. He scurried inside the restaurant and I turned to follow him.

"Next time you text me during a crisis, give me your location. I had to run around town…your place, Sally's room at the boarding house, the theater…"

I faced Bill. His mouth ticked up on one side in the familiar quirky grin. "What are you talking about?" I said a tad huffily. "I texted you while we were in the attic. Why didn't you text back?"

"I was a little busy chasing the bad guys. I figured you were hiding somewhere and I was afraid someone would hear an incoming text." Bill leaned on his crutches and pulled out his cell. "Anyway, I got your SOS, but did you see what else you'd written?"

"What do you mean?"

He held up his phone. "Fido on rink Jane. Help."

I glared at the jumbled words. Auto-correct. I'd been so nervous my thumbs were all thumbs. "Sorry," I said sheepishly.

Archibald glided past us, muttering, "Surrender and deputize her."

I could feel the heat rising from my neck onto my face. "You could have told me Archibald was working for the Feds."

Bill's eyes followed his colleague settling into the black Ford. "It was all very hush-hush. Once the will was read, leaving the bulk of Olivia Oldfield's millions to Sally and Sally's biological father, Charles panicked. He needed the money. That meant eliminating Weeks. So he lit out for Etonville—"

"—to eliminate his competition. Sally's lucky he didn't go after her too," I said.

"Charles probably thought he could control Sally…and her money. Gordon Weeks was another matter," Bill said.

"*He* came to Etonville to find his daughter, Sally."

Bill nodded. "And Archibald—"

"Followed Charles," I added.

"Just Archibald's luck that his quarry ended up in a small New Jersey town with a police chief he knew from his past. Who needed help solving a murder." Bill pulled his collar up around his ears. "Kind of a tightrope act for Archibald, getting Charles Oldfield's help with the murder investigation because his daughter was the prime suspect."

"And the photograph was—"

"Proof of paternity. Two different eye colors—"

"I knew it! Heterochromium iridium!" I crowed. "Like Sally's eyes!"

Bill grinned slowly. "Yeah."

"The time stamp proved the wedding was May 1994 and Sally was born six months later."

"In between, Sally's mother and Gordon Weeks divorced, and her family forced her to marry Charles Oldfield. It wasn't a happy union," he said ruefully.

"Poor Archibald. He thought he could come to Etonville, track Charles Oldfield, and get on with his investigation," I said.

"But he didn't count on Sally or Gordon Weeks. Or you," he said wryly. His tone shifted to admiration. "Your instincts were on target with Sally. Good job." He tucked some stray strands of hair into my hood. "I have to wrap this up down at the station. I'll call you later."

Later? As in tonight, tomorrow, next week…? "I'll be here."

"I know you will. I'm glad," he said and smiled.

Yowza.

28

If Einstein and my great-aunt Maureen were correct, coincidences were merely God's way of remaining anonymous. An unseen hand at work. I tended to agree with them. After all, who was I to dispute the opinions of a genius and my favorite aunt: Gordon Weeks setting the events in motion by confronting Charles Oldfield in Boston about the will and his photographic proof of paternity; Archibald, hired by the FBI, keeping an eye on Charles Oldfield, a suspect in a white-collar criminal investigation; Sally, needing a break from her life, deciding to decamp for Etonville; Bill, breaking an ankle bone; Bill and Archie, old police academy chums, uniting in an effort to solve a murder; and Gordon Weeks's determination to find the daughter he'd never met. Everybody following everybody else and all roads leading to Etonville. It was a perfect storm of freaky flukes.

A hard-packed ball of snow whacked me on the back.

"Gotcha!" Romeo called out and grinned, scooping up another hunk of the white stuff while trying to duck my return throw. Which smartly hit its mark. Yes!

I had to smile. A late spring snowstorm had coaxed much of Etonville outside into the crisp air and bright sun today, causing the town park to hum with life. Mildred and Vernon were cross-country skiing on the now-snowy softball diamond. Getting in shape for summer, Mildred said. Better exercise than treading the boards, according to Vernon. Benny whizzed by waving and pulling his six-year-old princess on a sled until they crashed into a snowbank, toppling daughter and father onto the ground. They immediately segued into making snow angels, both of them giggling gleefully. Nice that the Windjammer was closed on Sundays.

Which reminded me that I had to text Henry about next week's menus. We'd decided to end the winter season with a bang. Southern comfort foods that hinted at warmer weather and long, lazy days in the sun: shrimp and grits, fried chicken, biscuits and gravy, blackened catfish, and fried green tomatoes. Cholesterol be damned. Henry was in a better frame of mind these days. Despite the roof repairs. As a result of his success with the Chamber of Commerce dinner, the town mothers and fathers diplomatically planned to eat every other month at the Windjammer... an equal culinary opportunity. Not to mention the fact that the *Etonville Standard* had awarded the restaurant another half star.

Lola gestured from across the park and shouted, "Come help us."

Wonder of wonders, she'd gotten Walter out of his pajamas and into the fresh air. And even more amazing she'd gotten him to join some ELT folks making a giant snowman with the remnants of an *Eton Town* costume. Chrystal had no idea they'd filched an old wig, tricorn hat, and ratty period coat. Everyone was more relaxed these days now that the Creston Players were no longer a threat to the future of the Etonville Little Theatre—they'd cancelled their plans for a production of *Our Town*—thanks to the brave *Star-Ledger* reviewer who wrote that "he'd never seen anything like *Eton Town*" in his thirty-year career. That "he'd never laughed so hard in his life." Walter claimed that he'd meant it to be a comedy all along. He and Lola took out another full-page ad in the *Standard*, touting the show's success. Without pictures this time.

They had another reason to feel pretty good. Sally had graciously made a substantial donation to the theater, guaranteeing its next production, taking the burden off the box office. Though she could easily afford to be generous, it was an unexpected gesture that made the young woman from Boston an honorary member of the Etonville community, with all the rights and privileges pertaining thereto. *Eton Town* had brought the village together. Folks not only came out in droves to fill seats, but after word went out that the intermission refreshments had disappeared during the murder investigation, they brought potluck concession goodies to replace the colonial cakes and pies.

I scanned the park landscape and only one word came to mind. Home. It felt warm and fuzzy to be part of a community. This community in particular.

"Hey, ready for a little nip?" Bill crept up behind me, thermos in hand. "Irish coffee."

I checked out his new cast. "Should you be moving around on that?"

"It's a walking cast. Meant to be walked on. Doc says maybe two more weeks with this thing." His mouth ticked upward on one end. "Besides, I can't keep up with you on crutches."

I took the thermos and poured some coffee into the lid. "What does an English boy know about Irish coffee?" I took a sip.

"I'm only English on my father's side. I'm full Italian on my mother's." Bill took the lid out of my hand and drank, smiling at me over the rim of the cup.

"Really? With your blond hair?"

He shrugged. "Strong northern European genes."

I stared at him. Bill had a backstory that I knew little about. I'd gotten obsessed with the past these last weeks—*Eton Town* and the American Revolution, Sally's history—and now I was curious to know more about Bill's origins. "Hmmm. Explains your fixation on chianti."

He dipped his head awkwardly. "Well, that comes from my last... girlfriend. She was into Italian reds."

Italian men, too, apparently. He'd never mentioned a previous girlfriend. "Oh," I said. *Yikes*, I thought. "So we're getting personal here."

"Thought you should know some of my history...and vice versa."

I took the lid of the thermos, filled it to the brim, and chugged it down. "Okay. Let's see. Jackson and I had a five-year relationship before Hurricane Sandy destroyed his charter fishing boat and he moved to Iowa—"

Bill put up a hand. "Is this going to take long? I mean, will you finish before dark?"

The days were staying lighter longer, but still, by late in the afternoon, the sun was setting and dusk approaching. "Probably not."

He snapped his Buffalo Bills' ball cap against his thigh. "How about I fix a Thai stir-fry, crack open a *California* pinot noir." He stifled a grin. "And we check out Netflix."

I was hot under my thermal underwear and it wasn't just the down jacket and cashmere scarf. It was now or never. I was running out of time. "Only if you let me fix breakfast..."

Lingering light played around the planes of Bill's face, his smile meandering from one side of his mouth to the other. He leaned in and kissed me sweetly. Right there in the middle of the Etonville town park. *Yahoo!*

"I like my eggs over easy and my bacon crispy," he said.

OMG.

About the Author

Suzanne Trauth is a novelist, playwright, screenwriter, and a former university theater professor. She is a member of Mystery Writers of America, Sisters in Crime, and the Dramatists Guild. When she is not writing, Suzanne coaches actors and serves as a celebrant performing wedding ceremonies. She lives in Woodland Park, New Jersey. Readers can visit her website at www.suzannetrauth.com.

SHOW TIME

ETONVILLE

LITTLE THEATRE

ROMEO & JULIET

SUZANNE TRAUTH

ARSENIC
AND
OLD LACE

TIME OUT
SUZANNE TRAUTH